THE FIFTH CODEX

THE FIFTH CODEX

by

JOHN SCHERBER

SAN MIGUEL ALLENDE BOOKS

San Miguel Allende Books
San Miguel de Allende, Mexico

ACKNOWLEDGMENTS

Any book starts as an idea and by its completion becomes a joint effort.

Thanks to my readers: Patti Beaudry, Lou DeRonde, Bill Dorn, Bill Hammond, Donna Krueger, Marcia Loy, and Ivan Schuster.

Cover Design by Lander Rodriguez
Web Page Design by Julio Mendez

The Fifth Codex
A Mystery Set in San Miguel de Allende

ISBN 978-0-9832582-5-4

San Miguel Allende Books
San Miguel de Allende, Mexico
www.sanmiguelallendebooks.com

Also by John Scherber

NONFICTION
San Miguel de Allende: A Place in the Heart
Into the Heart of México
Living in San Miguel
A Writer's Notebook

FICTION
The Devil's Workshop
Eden Lost
The Amarna Heresy
Beyond Terrorism: Survival

(The Murder in México series)
Twenty Centavos
Brushwork
Daddy's Girl
Strike Zone
Vanishing Act
Jack and Jill
Identity Crisis
The Theft of the Virgin
The Book Doctor
The Predator
The Girl from Veracruz

AUTHOR'S NOTE

The Fifth Codex is the second of the Murder in México series of mysteries, set in the old colonial hill town of San Miguel de Allende.

Brushwork. When a disgraced former U.S. vice president retires to San Miguel and buys one of the most expensive houses in town, Zacher senses he's up to no good. But when the man is murdered with an artist's paint brush, Zacher finds himself suspect number one and it's a race against time to clear himself before he's arrested for the crime.

Daddy's Girl. A brutal, sexually posed murder of a former madam, once a Zacher painting model, pulls Paul into the thick of another plot, this one going back years in its origins. Tired of being shot at and kidnapped, Maya hits the wall and leaves, and Cody comes up with a completely different view of who the killer might be. Working alone, Paul stumbles across the woman who might be the answer to his dreams, or just another nightmare.

Strike Zone. The search for a solid gold human skull, cast from the last remaining jewelry of the Aztecs and once in the collection of Hermann Goering, pulls the Zacher Group down to Oaxaca. Here the artifact may or may not be in the possession an old alcoholic GI who was charged with guarding the salt mine in Austria where the collection was stored at the end of World War II. A teachers' strike erupts in lethal violence around them as Goering's illegitimate son and his Panamanian thugs track their movements in hopes of recovering the artifact.

Vanishing Act brings the Zacher Group north of the border to track the disappearance of Cody's nephew, whose pregnant wife has been murdered, and their house burned to the ground. Is the nephew a victim or the perpetrator? The search takes them to New Mexico and Colorado as they try to sort out identities that may not be at all what they seem, and in a way they could never imagine.

Jack and Jill. When the murder victim fails to die as planned, but instead turns the table on the killer, Paul Zacher is called in to save the murderer from being arrested for a murder he tried to, but could not commit. So why does everyone still hate him if he's innocent? Is it only his incompetence? Unintended consequences spiral further out of control as Paul finds out what a rare commodity innocence can be, and organized crime emerges as a player in what had looked like a fool's game, where the smarter folks have left the table long ago.

Identity Crisis. Paul and his friends are hired to establish the identity of a man who fears he may not exist. He is murdered before they can help, and they are drawn into a race against time to stop a sinister plot to assassinate the governor of the state, so that his successor can approve a mining permit that will lead to environmental disaster.

The Theft of the Virgin. At an exhibition of memorable forgeries of great paintings, Paul spots one that is unmistakably genuine. When he challenges the director, the painting is stolen from the exhibit and the Zacher Group finds itself on the trail of a conspiracy to steal Mexico's greatest national treasure.

The Book Doctor. When the International Mystery Writers' Conference picks San Miguel for its seventh meeting, no one is surprised that murder is on the agenda. What is startling is that its first speaker is murdered in mid-sentence. Justus Barlow, noted critic and editor, falls to the platform halfway through his speech on the Death of the Adverb.

Can the 200 mystery writer wannabes in attendance solve this case, or will it take the quirky insights of Paul Zacher and his friends? As a painter, Paul finds himself at sea in the world of publishing, as he digs deeper to reveal its murky and unsavory secrets.

See the author's website for more details on release dates and availability:
www.sanmiguelallendebooks.com

To Kristine

PROLOGUE
THE COLLECTOR

There are more than a few reasons to visit the Plaza San Jacinto in México City. Certainly one is   the Bazar Sabado, when local artists come to display their work. There are also several reasons not to. One of these would have to be Pepe Perez, who was as fast as any kid in the San Angel neighborhood. At fifteen, he was slender and attractive; his dark hair lapped his ears and the dimples in his cheeks made him popular with girls. But even better, he could spot a business opportunity from a kilometer away, or even no more than arm's length, at the tips of his nimble fingers.

As he walked beneath the sculptured trees, less than five minutes earlier the two ten-peso coins in the left hip pocket of his white painter's pants had been in the open purse of a young grandmother crossing the plaza toward the market, her attention focused on the vegetable stand on the corner. She'd felt nothing except a slight bump as he stepped into her path, seemingly oblivious as he yelled something to a friend across the street.

The cluster of grapes he was eating, as well as the two bananas in his jacket pocket, had been unwittingly donated by the fruit seller on the corner. He flipped one grape after another into the air and caught them in his mouth as he watched the thinning crowd. He had not seen the inside of a classroom in three years, but his education progressed daily.

What he also saw this evening was an opportunity unfolding half a block down one of the streets that radiated from the plaza. Without emergency lights, an ambulance was pulling up at an unhurried pace before an old house on Calle Madero.

He sauntered along the street and stopped opposite the townhouse to tie his shoe as two ambulance attendants in white uniforms removed a stretcher and, after a moment's pause, were buzzed into the house. One of them stopped to prop the door open with a wooden wedge and Pepe watched as they ascended the stairs inside. When they turned at the landing above, Pepe slipped through the door and darted along the corridor to the back of the house. The door to the kitchen was open but no lights were on. He heard no movement in this part of the house. He found an apple in the refrigerator and chewed on it as he explored the surrounding rooms.

He had seen the interior of houses like this one before, glancing in as the doors opened. The kitchen was large and must have been luxurious long ago, he thought. Now it seemed old fashioned, with scrubbed wooden counters and a gray soapstone sink. Next to the refrigerator was a small door in the wall that piqued his curiosity. He pulled it open. Filling the recess he found an openfronted empty box with two shelves. It was held at the top with a rope. Another rope hung at the side and when he pulled on it the box moved upward. Pepe had never seen a dumb waiter before. When it creaked he stopped pulling and closed the door without making a sound, looking behind him.

Adjoining the kitchen he found a large pantry with one wall of glass-fronted cabinets containing several sets of dishes and stemmed glassware. On the opposite wall, behind paneled wood doors the cabinets held pots and pans. A series of narrow drawers to the side were locked. Silverware, he guessed; something to check on later. Beyond the pantry on the back of the house was a series of small rooms, all poorly furnished. They reminded him of his mother's home when she was alive, only the ceilings here were much higher. In one of the bedrooms hung an unframed and faded paper print of Our Lady of Guadalupe, foxed and curling at the edges. Next to it was an empty plywood armoire where he could hide if he heard someone coming.

He returned to the kitchen to wait. After a few minutes noises on the stairs signaled the ambulance attendants descending. An old woman was speaking to them in a whining voice. One of the men responded politely. They passed through the street entry and onto the pavement outside. A moment later one of the men returned, and, after turning out the lights, pulled the door shut and locked it. Pepe stood behind the darkened door and watched them through a small window with an iron grill. As they drove off he invisibly waved goodbye, a grin on his face.

He waited in silence, not yet certain that the house was empty, but no one had come to the door to see the old woman off. Removing his shoes, he climbed the stairs. The marble was worn in shallow curves beneath his feet.

The ceiling was lit by street lights coming through the barred transom and the windows above, and for a moment he studied a painted oval, the center largely decorative, but at each end holding a circular inset portrait; one of an elegant young man with curling side whiskers and an elaborate wavy hair style. In the oval opposite was a young woman, the shoulders of a yellow brocade dress just visible, her black hair pulled back in a bun, a rigidly straight part coming down to her forehead. Her full lips formed the hint of a smile as she looked toward the young man across from her.

Pepe shook his head, staring at her aristocratic white skin. His own was much darker. He knew no one who looked like that, nor did he know anything of history; his life was framed by the opportunities of the coming day, and whatever they would bring.

Two high-ceiling formal rooms faced Calle Madero on the second level, both overlooking the street through tall mullioned windows that came to the floor. Pepe inventoried the silver in the dining room. There were six massive candlesticks. He lifted one and mentally weighed it. Nearly a dozen serving pieces were arranged in and on top of the sideboard. The paintings were typical ancestor portraits that he didn't think would bring much. If Pepe had ever planned to get a job, which he could no longer imagine, a good choice might have been as an appraiser.

He crossed the stair landing to the other side of the house and pushed open a pair of painted and carved doors that protested under the pressure of his hands. He lit no lamps; there was sufficient light coming from the street to examine the room. Tall pieces of furniture covered with dusty white muslin stood along the walls, a gallery of soft sculpture. Pepe lifted one of the covers to find yellow damask upholstery on a mahogany sofa frame, much like the dress of the woman in the oval portrait.

Between the windows stood a rectangular parlor grand piano with a Brazil rosewood case, long silenced under the muslin. If Pepe had examined it he would have seen that the veneer was cracked and buckled, but he dismissed it as too heavy to remove from the house. His business was not much concerned with furniture, it was the accessories that interested him. In the corner next to the piano stood a covered harp, taller than his head. Another bulky white elephant. The five portraits of stiff dusty grandees— descendants of the *conquistadores* who had crushed and enslaved his ancestors—he dismissed as pocket change. But Pepe wasn't thinking day of reckoning, he was thinking payday.

Two fine onyx and gilt bronze clocks rested on a fireplace mantle of carved Italian marble on the outside wall. Between them a formal mirror took in the room from within a fluted gold leaf frame. The crystal chandelier, draped in its own muslin bag, hovered like an inverted hot air balloon near the frescoed ceiling. In one outside front corner, a roof leak had loosened the fabric wall covering, where it drooped like baggy clothes against the plaster. Pepe turned and went back downstairs in search of another apple.

What Pepe did not know was that the tenure of seven generations of the de la Vega family had come to an end that night as Doña Catalina de la Vega, eighty-six years old and unable to manage any more even with her maid's help, was headed for a nursing home in another eighteenth century mansion just eight blocks away. The familiar high ceilings and massive mahogany doors would be some comfort to her there, even if the house now had an institutional feeling. At least there would be more staff. Doña de la Vega had sorrowfully dismissed

Maria Ramirez, her last remaining servant, earlier that evening. Occupied with the thought of finding another job, Maria had failed to clean out the refrigerator before she left.

For nearly a week Pepe was not to be seen in the Plaza San Jacinto, and neither the tourists nor the natives missed him. His initial walk-through had told him his new project was beyond his own capabilities, and with two of his friends he spent days sleeping in the decaying mansion, while at night they stacked booty in the front hallway. In the small hours before daylight they loaded borrowed carts and transferred all the portable possessions of Doña de la Vega to a deserted house on a side street not far away.

When they had removed everything of interest, Pepe and his friends held an invitation-only open house for the local fences at their new warehouse. At the end of the day they stuffed the proceeds in a fine old leather briefcase that bore the initials and family crest of Doña de la Vega's long dead husband, Don Eduardo. The jewelry had sold first, and although there was nothing of great value, there were many interesting pieces in the Art Deco style. Doña de la Vega had taken the better items with her. One of the last things to sell was a trunk full of ancient books that had caused some debate among the boys as to whether it was worth moving. Pepe's view prevailed and it took all three of them to load it on the cart.

The trunk was purchased by the same man who had bought most of the old silver. His brother was a respected antiques dealer with a shop in the hotel district near the Zocalo, the great square at the heart of México City. When he delivered the silver to his brother's shop he mentioned the trunk full of books with ribbed leather bindings.

"Perhaps it would be worthwhile to have them too," said the dealer. "You never know what a trunk like that might contain, and from what you describe it sounds like they might be eighteenth century."

The old trunk itself turned out to be of some interest, covered in green leather with a vaulted lid edged in battered wooden strips.

Most of the books inside were medical texts, a surprising number in French, and therefore of insufficient interest to excite the dealer, although they might bring something online. Near the bottom of the chest on one side was a slender volume wrapped in parchment, not bound, consisting of about a dozen leaves written on both sides in some ancient script, and illustrated with intensely colored scenes, attached accordion style. The dealer unfolded it carefully on the long table in his workroom. It was certainly old. The initial page was damaged and all the edges frayed and fragile. The writing might have been Mayan, but he didn't know much about the old languages. In the unfaded areas, in from the edges, the colors on both the hieroglyphics and the illustrations were still strong. It had to be an old copy of an Indian original, and if it were sixteenth century, it might have some value. Not many Spanish copies of these codices survived, since the Conquistadores had little interest in the native culture.

Under C in his Rolodex he found the number of a man who had bought odd things from him in the past, usually artifacts with a Mayan origin. Occasionally this man purchased larger pottery fragments, but most often they were jade carvings that came from the midnight excavation teams in the Yucatán and Chiapas. This customer insisted on strict anonymity, and so his number was simply listed under "Collector."

He dialed the Collector and described the colonial era document, making no case for it being other than a copy. Privately, he doubted that it was worth the fee required to have it examined by an expert. There was some haggling before they agreed on a price of 5,000 pesos. Four hundred and fifty dollars, and the Collector reserved the right to return it if he didn't think it was worth it. The next day the dealer packed it in bubble wrap and shipped it off to San Miguel de Allende, a colonial town in the State of Guanajuato, in the *bajío* area of the central Méxican highlands. A town that might be at least as old as the document itself; a town that had played an important role in the War of Independence in 1810, and where one more secret would not be noticed.

By the time the package arrived on the last day of June, cushioned in its stout cardboard box, Doña Catalina de la Vega had already joined her bristly ancestors in the ground. She had survived only three weeks in the nursing home, and their portraits had been fenced to a dealer in Guadalajara for a tenth of their value.

CHAPTER ONE

Barbara Watt looked at her image in the mirror I was holding up. "I've forgotten how I was," she said. "So much has happened since we did this. Was one knee higher than the other?"

My work on the large nude painting of her had been suddenly interrupted five months ago when her husband was killed. That's a lot of time between sittings; longer than I'd experienced before, and long enough to create some potential problems. The original paint was dry, of course, and blending wet into dry is not that easy. I also wasn't sure if I could match her skin tones again. Five months of widowhood was a big adjustment and it could have subtly changed her face, but as I looked at her now I couldn't see any difference. She seemed to be handling it well. Of course, the forty million dollars Barbara inherited at Perry's death might have eased her pain.

When I say Barbara's painting was large, I don't mean it was a mural. There's something disturbing about larger than life nudes; but this picture was less than life size at forty by fifty-six inches. However, Barbara can be larger than life herself at times, so gauging the scale is difficult. Physically, Barbara is model size. Twenty-eight years old, she stands five foot-eight without her shoes, but unlike a lot of models, she isn't gaunt. I suspect she knows how much flesh is just right.

Her face is something to dream about. She's a natural blonde with shoulder-length hair, and while I don't know if she ever was a model, she could certainly model anything. Right now, she was modeling her own skin, which was exquisite enough to make most men's fingers reach out toward it. I knew that without touching it, although I had been invited to a number of times.

She was standing by the day bed I had posed her on five months ago, arms folded, and looking at the upholstery as if for an answer.

"I can't remember; so much has happened since we did this last."

"I can. Come back behind the easel and take a look." I sat on both my hands as she stood next to me. I had reached the point where everything was located on the canvas in thin washes. Her face was finished, and I had a only bit more to do on her hair, and then I could move on to the rest of her body. Portions of her left thigh and knee were done too.

"I see it," she said. "An inviting smile, but not too inviting, no teeth showing."

"Exactly. Except that I'm finished with your face. I just need to have your hair the same way it was along your cheek. And take a good look at your body position. I need that to be just the same. Notice how your left leg is higher?"

"Right. Is this it?" She reclined on the sofa and raised her left leg so the lower curve of her thigh was just visible before it disappeared behind her right leg.

"Just about. You should be looking at my head. I

want to get the angle of your neck right."

In the background a CD of Chet Baker ballads provided a serene atmosphere for painting. It was a vocal from the early period when he still had his teeth and didn't sound like he was gargling on the high notes. Tranquility is the best medium for painting.

"That picture of yours I bought from the Mérida show arrived today," she said. "I'm so excited! I'm going to hang it in the same space over the piano where Maya was. Don't you think? And since there's that Yucatán god in the background behind the dancer, maybe I'll bring some of the ceramics down from Perry's study to arrange beneath it."

"That picture would work there, but a lot of people will miss Maya. I think having some of the ceramics there would be great too, but you'd keep them in the cases, right? Putting them out would be too much temptation to handle them." I never referred to the fact that the ceramics were fake, but we both knew it.

Four years back her husband, Perry, bought an early nude of my girlfriend Maya in a saucy pose. It had hung over the grand piano in their living room ever since. Before Perry's death they had entertained a great deal and I had gotten half a dozen commissions from it. I hated to see the advertising go, although I liked to move pictures around myself from time to time. Seeing them against different backgrounds makes them new again.

"I hope you'll hang Maya somewhere else." I was mixing pigments for Barbara's skin and hair.

"Of course, I just want the dust to settle a bit. It's funny; Perry always thought of that painting as your lil' brown gal."

"Those were practically his last words," I said. I was there when he died.

"I don't think I want to know that."

"Sorry, but you know that Maya has hardly any Indian blood."

"That's what I told Perry. He didn't care. He just liked the phrase. Anyway the new picture is up at the house, still crated. I couldn't get it open. I need a man to do that and I want to see it again. Do you think you're man enough to take care of it?" She gave me her best smile.

"I'll give it a shot."

Maya came into the studio and greeted Barbara. She was still not quite at ease with her. Maybe it was because Barbara was nude and Maya wasn't. More likely it was because Maya had killed Perry in February, just as he was about to shoot me. A thing like that can take a while to work itself out.

Maya walked behind the easel and put a proprietary hand on my shoulder, looking at the picture and then back at Barbara. I had the feeling she was staring at Barbara's pubic hair. Maya never could get used to the fact that some people were blond all over. It's a Méxican thing, I guess. Some day I'll tell her about redheads. To a painter, it's all landscape, anyway.

"I know what you're thinking," Barbara said to her. "A few hills, a few valleys and here and there patches of bush." They both laughed uneasily. Models do have something in common. Maya had posed between thirty and forty times for me.

"I'm going to the market," Maya said. "Maybe we can have lunch together later." She went out.

"I'm going to do your breasts now," I said to Barbara, when Maya was gone. I started mixing some azo red and terre verde for the shadows.

"That sounds like fun. I haven't been having much lately."

"You'll find someone. It's only been five months. A lot of women wouldn't be looking yet."

"I'm not really looking, exactly. I've just been *thinking* about looking. I guess I'm used to having someone around, even if it's only to open crates and things. But now I have all this money to worry about. How will I know if someone truly cares for me? That sounds trite, but it was easier when Perry was still alive. I just wrote checks and I didn't have to worry about where it came from."

"Who wouldn't care for you? But I think you're going to find that some men won't want to approach you because of your money."

"Would that put you off?"

"No. I'd be all over you in a second if I didn't have Maya."

"I'll remember that. Can I take this choker off?

"I don't need it anymore," I said. She was wearing Maya's midnight blue choker, which made her seem even more naked, if that was possible. "Your breasts are coming together quite nicely."

"I do exercises."

I wondered how she did exercises to keep her breasts pert and pointing heavenward. They weren't exactly rippling with muscles.

I don't use much pink, but nipples are nipples, after all, and hers were not brown. If they had been I would have used pink anyway. Artistic license. We were quiet for a while. It's easier not to talk when you're painting. By one o'clock I was down to her hips. I'd leave the rest for another day. She picked up her Chinese robe from the back of a chair and pulled it over her head.

"Those robes aren't usually slit that high, are they?" It was open to her hip.

"I had it altered," she said. "It was too confining." We went downstairs.

Maya was unpacking groceries in the kitchen. It's an appealing place to work, with red and green tile from Puebla for the counters and back splash that went to the upper cabinets. I had done the tile work myself before Maya came to live with me five years ago. Above the sink, casement windows look out over our garden, framing one of our two fountains flanked by twenty-foot bamboo on the back wall.

Here in San Miguel de Allende, on the mountainous plateau of central México, the evenings cool off dependably because of the altitude, but the days are glorious and sunny and we can grow just about anything. Besides bamboo and cascades of bougainvillea, we have stands of hibiscus, ficus trees, oranges and limes, and half a dozen different kinds of bromeliad. Trumpet vine and jasmine compete on the pergola that reaches into the garden from the *loggia*. Three royal palm trees give one corner an oasis feeling, although tethering a camel there might be going too far.

The only downside to the climate is that there's a light frost about every second year or so.

I shredded chicken for the enchiladas, and while Maya was putting them together I opened a couple of beers and got a bottle of water out for Barbara. She believed, I think, that if she drank a beer, it would go directly onto her butt. You'd be able to see the outline of the bottle through her slacks.

We sat at the kitchen table. Barbara put her hand over mine. She had a way of touching people when she spoke and looking deeply into their eyes. I guess that was a thing with Southern girls—she was from Montgomery.

"I meant it when I said at your Mérida show opening that I was going to continue Perry's tradition of collecting. Remember that?"

"Were you ever a collector before Perry?"

"Boyfriends, mostly. But things are more serious now. I've been asking myself what Perry would want me to do with his money. You know that he saw himself as a collector."

"So you're thinking of carrying on for him?" asked Maya. When Barbara was present, Maya had a way taking poses that were more provocative than usual. Now, as she leaned against the counter, something was happening with her breasts that was not quite normal.

"In a way. Not that I'm knowledgeable like he was, but maybe there's a different direction I could get into, something he hadn't thought of or didn't know about at all. Does that make sense?"

I smiled. "I think so. Is it going to be only art from local painters, or antiques as well?" Perry's antiques collection had embraced everything from Mayan ceramics and seventeenth century colonial paintings to Navajo rugs, shipwreck coins, and jewelry.

"Both, I think. I've had a lot of time to look at and think about his collections over the past five months, and

I want to go beyond what Perry was doing. A lot of his things were just for atmosphere, like props, almost. I want to dig deeper and connect more to the culture here."

I had my own ideas about why she might want to do this. As a painter, I've known a number of beautiful women, mostly from behind the easel, and many of them were fairly sick of having their looks open doors for them. They wanted to be known for something weightier, possibly because they knew their looks weren't going to last forever. In Barbara's case she'd had Perry's example before her for years. It made sense to want to put her own spin on it.

"It's strange," she went on, "but something happened that relates to that, in a way. I had a call yesterday from a man trying to reach Perry."

"That'd be a long distance call," I said, "even if we had his number."

She let that pass, but Maya frowned at me.

"I told him Perry had died quite suddenly in February, and then he asked if I might still be interested in hearing about something he had for sale. I said of course. He didn't seem surprised when I told him about Perry. I wonder if he already knew."

"It wasn't a secret. What's he got? More ceramics?"

"No, a Mayan codex. I didn't even know what that was."

"It's an ancient Mayan form of book," said Maya—whose real name is Maria. "The leaves are attached at alternate edges and it would open like an accordion. There are only four of them still in existence."

"Well, that's pretty much what he told me, and all the others are in museums. He also said there's a sixteenth century copy of this book, let me think; it's called the Dominguez Codex, and it was made by a friar named Alvaro Dominguez. Damn, I wrote this all down, but I forgot to bring it along."

"Wait, I thought I heard that the Catholic Church had destroyed all the Mayan books?" I said, "Thousands of them. Work of the devil, that sort of thing."

"Apparently they tried," said Barbara, "but they missed a few. Nobody's perfect." She was dredging a bite size piece of enchilada through the green chile with her fork. She held the fork with a fine delicacy, as if it were an instrument of great precision.

"The early fathers were great cultural vandals," Maya said. Her face was somber. "They debated for years whether the Indians were even human."

She was no great friend of the Church, nor was her family, so it was odd that she still hid from them the fact that we lived together. I never thought it was because her father had continued to send her $1400 a month while she worked on her book about the early years of Ignacio Allende. He was the revolutionary hero who had been born in San Miguel, and who had posthumously given it his name after the War of Independence. When she finished the book the money stopped and Maya took a research job for an old professor of hers while she searched for a publisher. She was now researching the role of the various Méxican Indian groups in the War of Independence, contrasted with the Revolution of 1910.

"What did this guy sound like?" I said.

"An English speaker," Barbara said, "educated voice, hint of east coast accent, but not New York or New England, maybe mid-Atlantic, but not Southern. He didn't leave a number. Just said he'd get back to me."

"How much is he asking for it?" I asked.

"That's the hard part." She stopped eating and placed her hands on the edge of the island counter to steady herself. "One million dollars." She wrinkled her nose and her eyes got smaller. "I'd have to sell a few shares of Watt Industries." She paused a moment, sipping at her water, and pulled a wayward strand of hair back behind her ear. "Of course, it would be the jewel of any collection. Perry would be speechless. I think I'd be speechless too, if I actually spent that much."

"Sell a few shares? How many would be a few?" I asked.

"About 61,000."

"How many shares do you have?" I wouldn't have asked this but she had told me earlier in the year that her net worth was over forty million dollars, even after splitting the estate equally with Perry's two kids from his first marriage and allowing for the temporary dip in the stock's value after his death.

"I'd still have over 2,000,000 shares. Besides, it might be good to diversify; my investment guy in Houston is always saying that."

"Why not some great art?" I said. "There are lots of million dollar paintings around. That would be diversification."

"I prefer having pictures by someone I know. It makes it much more personal." She put her hand over mine again and softly rubbed the backs of my fingers, which made my toes curl. It also made the corners of Maya's mouth turn downward, but she didn't say anything.

"But how did your caller come to have this

codex?" I asked. "If the others are all in museums, this must be a spectacular thing to own."

"He said he found it in a ruined hacienda outside of a town called Valladolid, in the Yucatán."

"An ancient town, named for the one in Spain," said Maya, leaning forward on the counter with her chin on her hands. "It was once wealthy from the planters of sisal, so there are many ruined haciendas in that area. Some have been purchased by the gringos from Mérida and restored for small hotels. They are very pricey now."

"Do you believe that story?" I asked Barbara, leaning back on my stool. "I'm always skeptical when things of great value lie undiscovered for hundreds of years. They remind me of the urban legend thing, where a new Thunderbird is found with a week-old corpse in it. You can buy it for $400 but you have to replace the seats." They both shuddered. I got up and cleared the dishes.

"Well, I understand what you're saying," Barbara said, "and I'm not sure about the ruined hacienda part either. Maybe I'm not sure about any of it. Can you help me with some research? I'd be happy to pay you for your time and expenses."

"Another detective job?"

"Yes, but this time there's no reason for any violence, right? It's just research, and maybe some security when it changes hands. I thought too, with your background in history..." She turned and placed her hand over Maya's. Maya didn't pull it away.

"Maybe. Are you really thinking of buying it, assuming it could be proven genuine and not stolen?" Maya asked.

"I might. It fits so well with what I was talking

about. But surely it's not stolen, because its existence was not even known, right? Why couldn't an old codex have survived hidden in a ruined hacienda? Just the thought of the snakes in some of those places would make your skin crawl. No one would ever want to go there." She was looking into my eyes again. She wanted to believe it.

"What about getting Cody in on this too?" asked Maya. "It might be good to have some backup if you're thinking of meeting this guy."

Barbara was nodding. "I think we need to look at it, just to know what it is."

"I'm not sure we could tell what it is." I was beginning to develop a bad feeling about this, but I wanted to help her. Her fingers were on my pulse again and it was responding. Besides, she was my second best model. I hadn't started a new painting series yet after the Mérida show and I had no idea what came after the nude Barbara picture. Maybe Barbara in the Chinese robe.

I looked at Maya. "What do you think?" She nodded without enthusiasm. She was having too much of Barbara already.

"OK, we'll take a look at it. The place to start is to find someone who knows the other four books. And one other thing; did you get the name of the man who called you?"

"Arthur Brisbane."

At that time it meant nothing to any of us.

CHAPTER TWO

After lunch I borrowed Maya's laptop and spent some time on the Internet. Barbara had left her Chinese robe behind the folding screen in the studio and gone off wearing her street clothes. That was a good thing because that slit up the side would have caused widespread panic in San Miguel, perhaps revolution. We don't need any more of that, since much of the property here is owned by expatriates. Maya was parked at our dining table in the *loggia* sifting through her research notes on the different Indian groups who responded to the call for revolution in 1810. Periodically she ripped one of the three by five cards in half and tossed it aside. She could never reject anything without destroying it— something about sticking to a decision once she'd made it.

It had taken a while, but things had settled down again after Perry's death in February. The steady routine of painting and posing and research and writing were a tonic to her, and although she had agreed to take on this codex chore for Barbara's sake, I could sense her reluctance. I should have been grateful that she'd do anything at all for Barbara's sake. Maya had never quite trusted her, even though I'd never gone into detail about Barbara's interest in me. I'd never understood it myself; it was probably nothing more than the need to acquire things she didn't already have. I'd always gotten along well with women, but I didn't see what Barbara thought was special.

I started with Amazon.com looking for books on Mayan culture, particularly Mayan writing or codices. I knew the Mayans were the only Indian group in the western hemisphere to develop writing. The Aztec script, as exemplified by a fair number of surviving works, was all pictographs.

There was not a great deal of material available, but one book caught my eye. It was titled *Codex Maya: The Problem of Survival*. The author was Vincent Sandoval, Ph.D., and his books included three others covering the ancient cultures of Chiapas, the Yucatán, and Guatemala. In addition he offered an autobiography titled *My Life in Ruins*. I thought it had a nice ambiguity to the title. The cover showed a rather vain looking middle-aged man in a jungle shirt leaning on a shovel before a Mayan pyramid. He must've pulled on the shirt moments before he posed because there were no patches of sweat beneath his arms. He wore an Indiana Jones field hat and the shirt had more pockets than buttons. Directly behind him were the steep steps up to the sacrificial altar where the Mayans could toss the heads down to the crowd after they did open heart surgery. Nothing else on Amazon came this close to the mark. It seemed like the place to start.

I used that function on Amazon where you can look at individual pages of a book and discovered on the back cover that Sandoval taught at UNAM, the large university in Mexico City. Maybe this wasn't going to be that hard. Not surprisingly I was able to reach him in his office, because after all, how many big time professors spend much time in class?

I identified myself and said I had been told on good authority of the existence of a fifth Mayan codex, probably the original of the one known only from the copy made by and named for Friar Dominguez.

There was a startled pause, and then the sound of an indulgent chuckle, the kind that in a quiet moment might be heard all the way to the back wall of a lecture hall. It was as if he had just looked up from his shovel and was responding to a joke made by a colleague on the other end of the pyramid.

"Mr. Zacher—that was your name? I hope you won't think me impolite, but I fear you're being naive. I have worked in this field for more than thirty-five years. If there were a fifth original codex in existence, I would surely know about it. Is it possible someone is playing a practical joke on you?"

"I don't think so, although I don't know the man who has it personally. Is it that unlikely?"

"Well, the so-called 'copy' of the fifth codex, termed the Dominguez Codex, is a pious fraud. I've examined it and it appears to be mid-sixteenth century; that part I accept. But Friar Dominguez was an early scholar of the Mayan language, working for the interests of his Church. The copy he made purports to be a historical calendar of the Mayan people, going back to mythical times. And it continues into what would then have been the future, showing the Mayans docilely accepting the new religion of the friars. It was a tool meant to inspire submission, nothing more. In my view, the Mayan codex it was said to be based on never existed. Anyone who claims to offer the original for sale is trying to perpetrate an unspeakable fraud. What an idea!"

OK, a little skepticism is healthy. He wasn't interested in hearing any more about it so I thanked Dr. Sandoval for his time and hung up. I dialed Barbara.

"I just talked to a professor in México City who, from what I can find out, is the ranking expert on Mayan writings. He basically says your man Brisbane should be taken out and shot."

"That's only one opinion, Paul," she said. "I think you should keep digging."

Next I called Cody Williams, my retired detective friend from Peoria who had settled here in San Miguel five years ago.

"We've got another job," I said, "and this time it pays." Last time I played detective I had come away with forty centavos (just under four cents American) and a fake Yucatán ceramic figure. Cody and Maya got nothing. It seemed like a nearly equal payoff.

"What's the story?" He sounded like he was eating.

"Well, the client is Barbara Watt."

"The patron of the arts." It was not a question.

"The same, who is again being immortalized on canvas in this very studio."

"Give me the details."

"You can see it when it's done. I don't like to show half finished pictures."

"I can live with that, but I meant the details of the case. I knew you'd started that picture before Perry died."

Neither of us ever said, "before Maya killed him." It was always as if he'd been cut off in his prime by an accident. I told him everything I had gotten from Barbara, plus the conversation with Dr. Sandoval. "I wonder if your friends in the Chicago Police Department can get us the scoop on Arthur Brisbane, assuming there is anything to know?"

"They can if it's a real name and he ever did anything worse than getting a parking ticket in the States. I'll give it a shot." He hung up and I went out and found Maya dozing in the hammock under the bougainvillea. She put her hand out to me as I approached.

"So now we are involved with Barbara again, yes?"

I thought she had already signed off on this. "It's not like we're not already involved with her in the studio. At least with this codex thing she'll have her clothes on."

"Sometimes God is merciful," she said. This was a lot coming from an atheist. "I want to say something more, but you are going to think I'm insecure."

"I'll try not too. But we're all insecure about some things. I wouldn't worry about it."

"OK then. It makes me nervous to have you hanging around with her a lot. I think she is a hunter, and I thought that even before Perry died. It didn't matter to her then that she was married. She is always looking at men sexually, and she looks the hardest at you."

"You may be right. She is definitely a man's woman, not a woman's woman. My guess would be that she has very few women friends."

She looked into my face for a while, her hand rubbing my arm.

"This is a hard thing to say, and maybe it's nothing. But you and I are not the same. You are a gringo and many Méxicans are surprised to find me with you. I don't think about that much, but I am sure the same is true for you. Some of your old friends from Ohio might be saying, 'why did Paul Zacher pick a Méxican girl to be with?' Maybe there are times when you think it might be easier to be with someone more like yourself. And you look around, and there is the beautiful Barbara Watt, who wants you, and she is very rich. What more could you want?"

"There is something more than all that to want. It's you. I hear your argument, but I chose you because of who you are, not because I couldn't find an American girl. That's the only part of this that matters, although I think you're right about Barbara being a hunter."

I wasn't sure if that was all of it, but we left it there.

At 5:30 Cody called back. "This is interesting. I found your man Brisbane, but he's out of circulation. He's been on death row in California for eight years, going through the appeals process."

"What's he in for?"

"Kidnapping and two murders. He took a woman out of a shopping center parking lot in Daly City and a witness called the police. In the chase that followed he shot the woman and killed a cop when they boxed him in. He took two bullets himself but survived."

"I'll be surprised if he's now dealing antique Mayan codices from San Quentin," I said.

"My thought exactly. This one looks like a ringer. Maybe Barbara's caller just borrowed the name from the papers."

"At least we're off to a promising start. We have a document no one's ever heard of, which has no provenance, offered by a guy with a phony name who wants a million dollars. And we have a client who may be willing to pay it."

✠✠✠

The next morning I threw my tool kit in the artmobile, which is something like the Batmobile except it's an older white Chevy van and it has no armor. In the windshield is a bullet hole plugged with a chewed piece of Juicy Fruit gum. This occasionally pops out into my lap at speeds over fifty. Over the sliding door there are three pins to hold one end of a canvas tarp. The other end of the tarp has two grommets at the corners to fit the tops of support poles I plant in the ground to pro-vide a shaded area. I use it to paint landscapes by the side of the highway, hence the name.

I headed up the hill to Los Balcones, Barbara's neighborhood. Going up through Atascadero I passed on my right the ruins of an unfinished mansion with the carved square base of a tower. It was closely guarded by tall trees. Slender iron bars protruded from the top, awaiting the next level of concrete and stone. It looked like it had been sitting just this way for the last hundred years.

Atop the hill, on the rim of the basin that holds San Miguel, the sun was already high and it threw the sumptuous stonework on Casa Watt into sculptural relief. Los Balcones is an enclave of colonial-style mansions, usually in tropical fruit colors, all built during the last twenty-five years or so. Barbara's is the largest, brilliant in blood-red stucco and surrounded by ten-foot-high walls, topped by spikes. Both gates stood open—a mixed message. Walking in upright is OK, but you could get badly injured climbing over the wall. I drove through and parked on the manicured gravel of the horseshoe drive.

In the foyer Barbara hugged me and kissed my lips. A little forward, but that was Barbara. Protesting would be pointless. If Maya had been with me it would have been the same. Barbara's hair was fastened behind with a dark blue ribbon. She wore no jewelry with a white cotton tee shirt scooped deeply in front. It must have been her work mode. The way her jeans fit reminded me of Rebecca de Mornay in *Risky Business*. Any business with Barbara would be somewhat risky. When we came into the great room I saw that the enticing picture of Maya over the piano was gone. The space looked terribly bare.

The crate with the new picture leaned against the wall in a service area next to the kitchen. Barbara's name and address were on the front in black marker in big blocky letters. I set my tool kit on the floor and with a pry bar loosened the plywood front and pulled it away. Galería Mundo Maya had done a perfectly secure job of packing; the frame was protected all around with blocks of Styrofoam. Holding the picture up edge-wise to the light revealed an unblemished paint surface.

"I'm so happy to have this," she said. She moved back a few steps from it. "I love that tentative look the model has, as if she knows the god is just behind her, and she's not sure what he's going to do."

"It's that subtle arch in her eyebrow. I almost ran out of time that morning before I got it right. But it comes from not being sure what *I* was going to do. I had already asked her to pose nude and she'd turned me down. She had never posed before." I didn't tell Barbara that the body in the dancer's dress was Maya's, completed after I got back to San Miguel, because I had only time to paint the dancer's face that morning in the Plaza Hidalgo in Mérida. I had a feeling that any pictures Barbara bought from me in the future would be of herself. That was OK.

I changed the height of the wire on the back so I could use the hanger already on the wall. The standing nude of Maya had been a vertical picture, and the new one was square. I put it up and we stood back a few steps.

"Perfect," she said. "I could kiss you again."

"I'm sure you will."

"Tell me you don't like it."

"I love it."

"Then I will."

But she didn't.

We sat on the sofa that had the best view of the picture. I enjoy seeing where my paintings are hung, but I rarely get a chance. The green of the foliage and the gray eroded surface of the god were just right on the mottled pale gold wall. His gross features, the fat lips and thick hooked nose contrasted nicely with the model's delicate face. I hoped it would bring me as much business as the Maya nude. The frame borrowed tones of gray from the stony god. Galería Mundo Maya knew how to do framing.

"What should we do now?" she asked. "I could pose again."

"I forgot my easel. Without it between us I'd be helpless. It's my only defense against luscious models. But I want to ask you something seriously, OK?"

"Sure." She gave me all her attention, pulling one leg up on the sofa and turning toward me.

"Maya's a little concerned about starting a new case with this codex thing. We had a conversation about it last evening. She said an interesting thing."

"What was that?"

"That she thought you only related to men sexually. I hadn't thought about it that way."

"That's because you're a man." She leaned a little closer, but she didn't touch me.

"What do you mean?"

"That if a woman seems to find you attractive and you think she's attractive, you accept it as natural. Why question it, right?"

"I guess. But then she said you were a hunter. I thought that was harsh."

"I do too. I won't deny it, but I prefer a kinder word."

"What would that be?"

"I don't know. All my life men have wanted only one thing from me, ever since I was...well, I'd be embarrassed to tell you how young I was, but a long way from legal. I matured at an early age—girls often do in the South—so I've had plenty of time to get used to it. And I don't mind it. I have my own needs too, and it's been rather nice to have anybody I wanted, almost. I'd like to think that I turned the tables on all the men who hunted me before I was ready. That's how I got Perry. That worked out OK, up to a point."

She looked at me sweetly and put her palm in mine. I was picturing her as a young teen back in Montgomery, Alabama. Serious jailbait was the term that came to mind.

"But you're not serious about sleeping with me, right? I mean, this is just a game we play." I probably had a hopeful look on my face, although why I would be hoping this was true escapes me.

"Paul, dear, you've been spending altogether too much time behind the easel. You need to come up for air periodically."

"I see. How old were you when you first...did it? If you don't mind telling me." It was none of my business, but a painter does need to have some insight into his model.

"Fourteen. I had been saving myself for that special guy." A dreamy look came over her face.

"And was he special?"

"He was my father's lawyer." I wasn't sure whether that was special or not, but he must have been a high stakes gambler. Maybe it was worth it; I didn't want to go there, and I decided not to pursue it with her. She seemed lost in her own recollection.

"What does your father do?"

"He's an architect. He wanted me to be one too. There weren't many women architects in the South then. Maybe there still aren't. Anyway, I majored in Spanish. I never was good at fulfilling other people's expectations. I probably wouldn't have made a good architect."

The phone rang and Barbara took it in the kitchen. She was gone a while and I studied the picture, as I recalled Maya's comment about her. At the time I had dismissed it as the statement of a woman who thought she had something to lose. Barbara could probably make any woman want to put a moat around her assets, and rightly so. I'd had my share of daydreams about her. Then I noticed something about the picture.

If I were doing it again I might raise the angle of the girl's gaze to a higher point in the distance, and alter the position of her left hand, maybe lift her ring finger just clear of the others. I was second-guessing myself on a few other details when Barbara returned, slightly breathless.

"That was Arthur Brisbane. I said I was still interested in the codex, but I needed to see a copy of it. He said he would Xerox it and send it to me. He already knew the address, and repeated that I shouldn't mention this to anyone."

"How did he sound?"

"Businesslike. Calm. He said he understood that I would need to study it."

I got the promised long kiss in the entryway and as she pulled away from me, she said, "Tell Maya I'll keep a decent distance from you if she'll agree to help me with this, OK?"

That sounded good, but when would it start?

CHAPTER THREE

I passed the next three days without working. Barbara wanted to put our efforts on the painting on hold until she received the photocopy of the codex, while I wanted to push hard on it before the distraction arrived. Of course, she won. I had no argument; it was her picture and her body. As good as my visual recollection was, one wouldn't happen without the other.

I spent the time fiddling around in my studio. I swept and scrubbed the floor and washed the windows. In an art studio this can take some time. I went through my prop cabinet and threw a few things away. I set up some still life subjects that I found I had no interest in painting. Figure work was more captivating at this point and no one showed up to model. Maya was deep in her research downstairs, sorting through notes she had taken in the archive of the War of Independence in Dolores Hidalgo. The gallery in Mérida sent me a big check; they waited a month or so after a show in case any of the pictures came back. It gave buyers a chance to reconsider their purchase. On Wednesday afternoon Barbara called and said she wanted to bring over the photocopy of the codex. At last I would get to see what was about to upend the world of Mayan scholarship. I called Cody and asked him if he wanted to see it.

"I do," he said and hung up. Mr. Chatty. Ten minutes later he and Barbara were both at the door.

We spread the document copy out on the refectory table in the dining room, taping the pages together in a long strip. The postmark on the manila envelope read Querétaro, a big city about an hour from San Miguel, and it bore no return address. "It might not mean Brisbane really lives there," said Maya. I would have bet he didn't.

None of us had a clue about the Mayan language and the copy was in black and white on both sides, so we had no hint of the colors either. Fully assembled, it was about nine feet long. The first page showed a crumbled edge on all sides and it was not clear how many pages might be missing.

"This could be half the original," Cody said. "We'll never know." He leaned over with his ham-like hands braced on the table and his reading glasses halfway down his nose.

"It's beautiful, though," said Barbara. "Look at the calligraphy and the drawing. How different it is from all my colonial silver and religious paintings! I might need to have this. I've never seen anything like it." A million dollar price tag and she might need to have it. Like I might need to have a light bulb or a burrito, or a Havana cigar after selling a picture.

"If it's a fake he could have treated the leading edge with acid to make it look like that." I said. "It would make the paper brittle and it would crumble away in your fingers."

"I wonder if it's even made of paper," asked Cody.

"I have no idea what they wrote on," I said. "I suppose there are jungle plants that might work. Probably Brisbane would know that."

"Hold on a minute," said Maya. She disappeared upstairs into the bedroom and returned with a large magnifying glass.

"How are you going to be able to see the weave with that?" I asked. "It's just a copy." But she wasn't looking at the background.

"Look at this," she said. Her finger traced the edge of some of the calligraphy. "Look at the edges of the ink closely under the glass."

I leaned into the Xerox and saw that the edges of the figures, under magnification, were serrated in a way that gave a detailed profile of the weave.

"Well, there it is," I said. "We know it's not done on paper, anyway."

"In any case carbon fourteen testing would give the age, whatever it's made of," said Maya, passing Cody the glass.

"I can't see him letting us cut off a chunk for testing," said Barbara. "Maybe it's time we got back to that man you talked to in México City. What was his name?"

"Vincent Sandoval."

Cody went off to a place on Zacateros to make two more copies of the Xerox while I dialed Professor Sandoval.

"This is Paul Zacher again," I said. "I spoke with you a few days ago about the fifth Mayan codex."

"I remember it well. It's been the subject of more than a few jokes here in the department office. We don't get many inquiries like that. Are you calling to tell me you have it now, I hope?"

"I have a photocopy of it, but it's only black and white." There was a meaningful pause. I could sense the struggle between disdain and professional curiosity.

"Can you describe it?"

"With the individual sheets assembled it's about nine feet long and eleven or twelve inches high; the leading page is incomplete and crumbling, as are the top and bottom edges throughout. It's covered full length with hieroglyphs and drawings. Often the margins are nearly faded out or partly indistinct. It has ornate calligraphy, and the drawings are dynamic and lively. Interestingly, there are a few black-robed figures toward the end. Obviously, it wasn't made before the Conquest."

"Can you read any of it?"

"Not on my best day."

"Then I think I would like to see it. Can you send me a copy?"

"Of course." He gave me the address of his office.

"Mark it 'personal and confidential.'"

"I'll get it off to you today." I hung up.

"What now?" said Barbara, rubbing her palms together. "I'm getting excited."

"I'll send it off and we wait for a phone call with him laughing uproariously," I said. "End of story."

"Do you think? But maybe not," she said.

When Cody got back from the copy shop we all went out for lunch at Pegaso, stopping at the nearby post office on the way. Like Barbara, I too wanted to believe it, but it was such a great find, that if it were genuine, it was something like winning the lottery. My life to this point at age thirty-five had not been filled with deep disappointments, so I was not a confirmed skeptic, but even so my gut was telling me that this simply could not be the real deal. Whenever I saw a need to believe as strong as Barbara's, I was willing to give odds against it.

After lunch the others had gone and Maya was working on her notes when I came up behind her and put my hands on her shoulders. "What do you think? You're the resident historian."

She didn't have to ask me what I was referring to. She leaned back in her chair and looked up at me.

"I think it's interesting to have the black-robed bearded men being sacrificed in the last two pages."

"Yes. I couldn't make sense of that."

"It's not my period of specialty in history either. I mainly know the nineteenth century. But those men were meant to be friars of the early colonial period. If this were a fake, why put in something like that? I have seen reproductions of two of the other codices and they contain nothing like it."

"Could it have been that the ones you saw were all from an earlier period? Say, before the friars appeared."

She stuck her pencil back in her hair.

"Well, that's the obvious explanation, Paul. But if this is a fake, why put in something that has no precedent in the others? Wouldn't it be better to stay within the known parameters?"

I had copied paintings from several periods in the past, and the same thing applied; you didn't want to use anything, whether technique or choice of pigments, that wasn't used in the period you were working in.

"Chalk up one for the side of genuineness," I said. "Place that against the enormous odds against finding a fifth codex, offered for sale by a guy with a fake name. I think the balance is still tipped toward *no*."

✠✠✠

Two days later I was still waiting for Barbara to return while I repainted a wall in my studio—that was as close as I could get to real painting—when the phone rang.

"Dr. Vincent Sandoval here," he said. "Your copy arrived this morning and I've spent some time with it."

"Were there any more jokes in the office?" I asked.

"Perhaps when I see the original, but not at this point, because I haven't shared this with anyone. Based on this copy, here's what I can tell you." His voice had a cautionary tone. "The calligraphy is better than on the Dominguez Codex, which is natural, because the Padre was not Mayan, and he made some subtle errors. The first two-thirds of the text are virtually identical however, to the Dominguez Codex, which was done on parchment, and it survives intact. So you will realize that we can supply the initial missing parts of your document that were lost by the damage on the first page. Interestingly, this one then *departs* from the other codex and instead of showing the gentle submission of the native brothers to the truth of the holy faith, it has them rising in revolt, renewing the old Mayan ways and obliterating the religious emissaries of the Conquistadores."

"Hence the brutal executions on the last pages," I said.

"Precisely."

"Have you formed an impression as to whether it's genuine?"

"Well, the calligraphy is correct as well as being stylistically quite wonderful. The format is just as it should be. Things like the composition of the paper, the colors, the actual feel and presence of the document must await an examination of the original. But there is nothing in what I can see from this copy that invalidates it. I didn't expect to be saying that. If this is a fake, I almost feel that it had to have been made by someone I know. There aren't that many people sophisticated enough in Mayan culture to have invented this."

"Any gut feeling?"

"None at this point. But here's another issue. Had you opened the mailing envelope and resealed it before you sent it?"

I felt a prickly sensation on my skin. "How was it resealed?"

"With clear tape."

"No. I used no tape, and I didn't open it after I closed it. I just licked the flap."

"I see," he said after a slight pause. We both saw.

"Your departmental secretary didn't open it by mistake?"

"No. I checked with her. And it did say, 'personal and confidential,' as I asked." We were both silent for a while.

Finally I said, "I'm not certain at this point how I can get hold of the original without money changing hands, and we don't want that until someone like you can examine it. I'll have to think about it."

"Here's something else to think about then, as well. If the codex is genuine, it's of incalculable value. The Méxican government would stop at nothing to obtain it and neither would many others. None of the four remaining original codices is now in México. This fact is an ongoing humiliation because it's such a blunt reminder of the exploitation in México's colonial past. One is in the Museum of the Americas in Madrid, two others are in state archives in Dresden and Paris, and the fourth, the Grolier Codex, exists as a fragment in a private collection somewhere in Europe. Its exact location is kept secret for security reasons, although it has been published. Have you been told an asking price?"

"One million dollars. Not pesos."

"Except for the fragment, which was sold privately in the 1930s, none of these codices has changed hands within the last 150 years, but it sounds like a bargain, given the rarity. Be careful. I don't know what resources you have..."

"We have some: a moth-eaten old cop with three or four bullet holes in him, and almost unlimited funds. The price is not an issue, if the authenticity isn't."

"Well, again, be careful. Keep me posted, Mr. Zacher. I will follow this with great interest. Publishing this codex, if it proves genuine and you allow me to, would be the pinnacle of an already illustrious career. There's one more thing. Have you been given a provenance for this so-called fifth codex?" he asked.

"We were told it was found in the ruins of a hacienda near Valladolid."

Again the chuckle. "Mr. Zacher, have you spent any time in the Yucatán Peninsula?"

"Just a few brief trips; I'm a painter and I show in a gallery in Mérida. And my girlfriend Maya and I did some climbing in the ruins in at Uxmal and Chichén Itza. I know it can be hot and sticky."

"Hot and sticky? Let me bring you up to speed. I've been on more than a few digs there. After a month the inside of your camera is filled with four varieties of mold and fungus. Now I bring only disposables and I have them developed right away. After two months your teeth feel too large for your mouth. Even though I'm a scientist, I can't explain why this happens. After three months your shoes rot and fall off your feet. Now when I'm there workingI wear only shoes constructed from man-made materials. I have to get them at a Kmart in Laredo. Imagine."

"I see."

"You will understand then that there is simply no way this codex could have survived hidden in a ruined hacienda. The four originals in Europe exist today only because they've been in a sane climate for hundreds of years. The one in Paris has been sealed under glass since the late nineteenth century. Of course, dozens more codices have been found in tombs and temples all over Central America, always in the same condition. I've discovered eight of them myself. When I find them they exist only as rectangular piles of powdered limestone, the residue of the coating the Mayans used to seal the pages. All of the organic material has long since disappeared."

"So," I said, "if the fifth codex is genuine it must have been stolen from a collection..."

"Where its existence has either never been revealed, or it was forgotten by its owner."

"How could anyone forget something like this?"

"It might have gone unrecognized for what it is. It happens. The Paris Codex was discovered in a trash bin, where it had been discarded by a curator in the National

Archive. This was 250 years ago. But in any case, the next step needs to be an examination of the actual document. See what you can do." I was dismissed.

I hung up and turned to notice Maya standing in the door of the studio watching me with her arms folded. I related the other side of the conversation to her.

"So if this is true," I continued, "the codex predicts an uprising of the Mayan people in the Yucatán. I can't believe that. I feel like I know them from the time we've spent in Mérida, and in climbing the pyramids; they could never be like the Indians of Chiapas." She looked at me as if I'd missed something important.

"Paul, painting cute young Mayan girls does not mean you know the Mayans." She was leaning against the doorframe shaking her head slowly. I should have expected this.

"You mean there's more to it? What else could there be? I know their music is good."

She came into the room and placed her hands on my shoulders. "Paul, darling, sometimes when you are busy seeing things differently because you are an artist, you miss other things altogether. Do you know where the ancient Mayan city of Palenque is?"

"In Guatemala, I think?"

"No, that's Tikal. Palenque is in the heart of the jungle, in the State of Chiapas. Those Zapatista Indians now led by Subcomandante Marcos in violent revolt in Chiapas are the Mayans."

"The same Mayans of the codex, dragging the friars by the hair to their executions?"

"Yes, but now they have rifles. And they have the

Subcommandante."

I considered this for a moment. "There's one more thing. It's rather odd. The envelope we sent to Doctor Sandoval had been opened and resealed. He says his secretary didn't do it."

"Opened and resealed." Her arms fell to her sides and her face went blank. Maybe this was why her English was so good; she listened well and accurately repeated all the key phrases. This phrase would prove to be more key than most of the others.

CHAPTER FOUR

I wasn't ready to phone him for a chat yet, but it was not difficult to find the Subcommandante's website on the Internet. Welcome to the twenty-first century, where the revolutionaries have their own web pages. Next he'd have his own **BLOG** and he'd be on Facebook and Twitter. I read most of it, particularly the detail about a reorganization plan that would protect the Zapatista movement in case some of the leaders were killed. There was no mention of the fifth or any other codex. But then, Marcos was in hiding in Chiapas. There was no reason he would know about it. And why would he care? Besides, according to what we now knew, only six people in the world knew about it.

On Sunday Maya and I went for lunch at the Villa Antigua Santa Mónica, a charming old hacienda on the edge of Parque Juarez. I doubt that any Mayan codices have ever been hidden in it. Now it was part boutique hotel and part restaurant, with the tables spread out under the arches around a courtyard with a murmuring antique fountain and two parrots in a tall cage. Because it was only one story and the courtyard was broad and airy, with jasmine and bougainvillea climbing over the arches, it had a feeling of the country, even though it stands at the edge of *centro*.

"This codex thing is not moving very fast. You need to get painting again," she said, as we started with chips and salsa. "You've been spending a lot of time looking over my shoulder when I write up my notes at the computer."

"I've been trying to look down your shirt," I said.

"I can help you with that later. But I have an idea now. Why not start a picture of me with some clothes on? We could maybe find a costume in the props. It could be a new series."

"We could call it Maya Dressed, but no one would recognize you. A lot of the time they're not looking at your face."

"Really, Paul, you're dying here. You need a life. This detective business isn't enough for you, especially with Barbara all fired up now about the codex and not wanting to pose, although sometimes that's a blessing."

"I know. But we've both seen these periods before. I go through a dry spell now and then, and it's not unusual that it follows a show. I get so pumped up pulling everything together before an art opening that there's always a dead space waiting for me afterward. It's like a rest period. I need to go dark, the way your laptop does to save the battery when you don't touch it for a while."

After lunch we walked back and saw a battered bus full of house tour people stopped on Recreo near the bullring. The weekly house tour was the main fundraiser supporting the expatriate community's many charities, especially the scholarship fund for local kids. The ancient blue and white bus looked like it had been through the last revolution and would probably be on hand for the next. As the tourists were unloading they stared at the decaying facade of a house as if they weren't sure they had come to the right place. It had last been painted a bright cerise, but the stucco had fallen away in places revealing the stone core. There were no windows on the main floor; the only break in the wall at street level was a weathered plank door framed in hammered iron. The two windows on the second floor were grilled with iron bars and shuttered within. This is typical San Miguel. House fronts tell you nothing. The interior might be magnificent, or it might be full of chunks of concrete and chickens wandering about on the collapsed roofs, waiting for a *gringo* restorer who's about to get in over his head.

We walked on, hand in hand, hearing the shouting and the music from the bullring.

"I saw Marisol in the market yesterday," she said as we turned up Quebrada.

"How's she doing now?" Marisol's husband Tobey had been murdered in January of this year. Investigating his death was how I got started in the amateur detective business. Maya had asked me to help Marisol.

"She's better. She still doesn't know what she's going to do next, but I think she'll stay in the house. I guess there's enough money."

"I never did understand their relationship. He seemed rather cold, and possibly controlling as well."

"That's part of her problem. When you are controlled all the time you lose initiative. You don't have the ability to make decisions for yourself anymore. Look at us. I don't control you and you don't control me, so we both are able to make decisions."

The thought of anyone controlling Maya was a stretch. "You sound like a psychologist."

"I have read the book of Dr. Hoyce Brothers." She shrugged and put on what she thought was a master psychologist look.

"It's Joyce."

"OK, Yoyce." Here a leading y is pronounced much like a j, like in joghurt.

"I think Cody might be interested in her; not Joyce, Marisol," I said. Maya stopped abruptly and her hands made a flat gesture of denial.

"Oh, no, it's much too soon. She's hardly ready."

"I ran into him this morning in the *jardín*. His wife is filing for divorce. He's not surprised. They haven't been together for five years; she never wanted to come down here."

"How is he feeling?"

"Scared, but not petrified. He's already been alone a long time and at some level, I suppose he knew this would happen eventually. That's why he's thinking about a girl friend, maybe someone like you."

"But there are many unattached *gringas* here, many more than men. Anyway, that's not quite accurate. What he wants is me, the real thing." She drew herself up and tossed her hair back.

"That's true, I suppose."

"He would like to jump my bones." Maya nodded firmly.

I stopped suddenly. She was still grinning.

"Another delicate euphemism. Where did you get that?"

"It's a good one, isn't it? I got it from a book I read."

"Must have been a bodice-ripper."

"What's that?"

"Well, supposing you're wearing a kind of form fitting top with good cleavage, and I take the neckline in both hands..."

"Like the one I'm wearing now?"

"Yes, but in the books it would usually lace up the front, and when I savagely rip it open to reveal your lush perky..."

We had stopped in front of our house as I reached for my key. The door was standing open a few inches. "Not again," I said. "How many times do we have to be broken into this year?"

CHAPTER 5

I pulled out my cell phone and dialed Cody; the bodice ripping was a good thought, but it would have to wait for a more secure venue. I grabbed Maya's hand and we both continued up Quebrada as if we weren't yet at our destination. In the doorway of a shop about a hundred feet away we stopped and ducked inside. Cody picked up.

"Williams." Cody had spent years in East Coast charm schools.

"We've got another break in," I said. "Can you get over here with one of your .38s? I don't know whether they're gone or not. We haven't been inside."

"Stay tight." At that moment I felt tight enough to implode. The last time we had been broken into I had tripped over a dead body coming in and fallen on my face. I put my arm around Maya until Cody's Ford Escort drove up. Since she wasn't screaming, I knew she was seriously outraged. Screaming was an earlier stage, one she'd skipped this time on her way to a higher level.

"What have we got?" he asked. I could see a bulge under his left armpit, barely concealed under a Tommy Bahama shirt in a size I didn't think they made.

"Just the door being open a couple of inches. No one has come out."

Cody came in low toward the door and pushed it quietly open from the hinge edge. With the gun in both hands he went in soundlessly and we waited, pressed against the wall of the next house. Five minutes later he came back out. "No one inside," he said. "But you've been tossed by the best."

"Tossed" is a euphemistic term meaning the process of searching a house in detail, but it does not begin to describe what we saw inside. Every drawer had been turned out, the armoires had been emptied, all the finished paintings in the studio had been pulled out and dumped on the floor. My prop cabinet was emptied and upended. In the kitchen the contents of all the food shelves had been swept to the floor and every large container dumped out. The green peppercorn mustard and the hot sauce were both intact; we caught a break there. The dishes and glassware were mostly OK. The three of us stood in silence for a while, trying to absorb it all.

"Now we can decide what we don't need anymore," said Maya. Tears streamed over her cheeks. I put my arms around her.

"No problem," I said. "We don't have anything anymore."

Cody picked up the hot sauce and mustard bottles. "I guess these weren't big enough to hold the fifth codex."

"Should we warn Sandoval?" I asked Maya.

"I think they know he doesn't have it," said Cody, "otherwise why would we be sending him a copy? But let's think about what comes next. They will follow both of you, so don't lead them to Barbara. If you need to call her, use a pay phone, not your cell phone, if you can remember. I don't know who we're dealing with, but they may be able to listen in on your cell."

"How would you like to be our house guest for a while?" asked Maya. She slipped one arm through his, while she blotted her face with a tissue. "We don't see nearly enough of you."

"Sure. I don't mind a slashed mattress and ripped upholstery. Let me just run home and get my pajamas. I'm going to take the artmobile, if that's all right. If they see my license plate it'll be too easy to find out who I am, if they're still around."

He returned in an hour as we were trying to bring some order back into the house. It was a lot like moving in again, but with less stuff.

"Couple of guys in a black on black Suburban pulled out after me. I took a leisurely route over to Juarez Park and went into the Santa Monica. They didn't come in. They'd have been wide open if they had. I went through the great room in back, over the wall behind it, and up the hill to my place. When I came back out I was just another guy coming out of a hotel with a suitcase. They followed me back here. Here's their license number."

"Any idea who they are?"

"None. Anybody with a few extra pesos down here wants a Suburban, particularly in black. It's practically the national car of México. Never mind the fact that you can hardly get them around the corner on some of these narrow streets."

Half an hour after I called the Judicial Police and reached Licenciado Rodriguez, he was at the door. He had abandoned his suit jacket in the car and wore a crisp blue shirt with no tie. Unlike his predecessor, Diego Delgado, he was slender and nearly six feet tall, moving with the abrupt grace of a athlete as he stepped carefully around a pile of coats and tennis racquets in the entry. He shook my hand and shook his head at the same time. A good man for multitasking.

"Is it possible that this was caused by you being once again a thorn of someone's side?" He waved a notebook around the room to indicate the disaster.

"We have had no opportunity to be a thorn in anyone's side. Recently we've even tried to be helpful to the police. I think you will remember that it was I who supplied the evidence that caused the release of Licenciado Delgado."

"This is true. Thank you. He now collects garbage in Dolores Hidalgo. He told me it is better than prison, even though it smells nearly the same." He shrugged.

"Exactly. You get my point."

"So, what have you found to be missing?"

"Nothing."

"This is much work to wreck a place and have nothing. Your paintings are all still here?"

"Yes, and none are damaged."

"Señorita Sanchez has much jewelry?"

"Some, mostly old silver and Huichol pieces. Nothing is missing."

"You had no drugs here?"

"We don't use them."

"Tell me how you found this."

"Maya and I had been out to lunch and returned to find the door open a few inches. I called my friend Señor Williams and we went in but no one was here."

"I will take some fingerprints from the door and from your belongings. I believe we already have the fingerprints of you and Señorita Sanchez to compare them to. But I will need those of Señor Williams as well."

"He is upstairs."

"At what time did you go to lunch?" He was writing rapidly in his notebook.

"We left at noon, and we walked to the Santa Monica. We stopped in the *jardín* for a while on the way."

"So early?" Rodriguez dusted the door handle and lock and then spent more time dusting some of the food canisters and pots in the kitchen. Afterward we went up to the studio. Maya had put the pictures back in storage and the props back in their drawers.

"Señor Williams, I believe we have met. I will need to have your fingerprints. *Buenas tardes*, Señorita Sanchez."

"Good afternoon," she said. "Thank you for coming."

"It is nothing. We of the police are very serious about break-ins. Señor Zacher says you have missed nothing from your jewelry?"

"No. It is of no great value anyway."

"So you have no idea what the thief was looking for?"

"No," I said, just now realizing I had noticed as I came in that our photocopy of the codex was still on the dining room table. The burglar had not touched it; apparently only the original would do—I didn't for a minute think this was unconnected.

Rodriguez took Cody's prints with a small kit from his briefcase so he'd know whose to exclude. "This is all I can do for now. We will search the fingerprints and maybe we will be lucky. I will make a report. When we know more I will get back to you."

I went downstairs with Rodriguez and at the door I gave him the paper with the license number we had gotten from Cody. "This is from a car that followed Cody Williams when he left here today, a black Suburban. Maybe it's the burglar." He looked at it and his thick eyebrows moved upward a notch.

"I will look into this and let you know." As I watched him get into his car I was struck by the thought that if GM stopped making Suburbans, México would probably go back to burros.

In the kitchen I grabbed a couple of bottles of Chilean red and three glasses and returned to the studio. Maya put her arm around Cody and led him to the roof. I think it was his gun she was feeling. I followed them up. It was only four o'clock, but it had been a long day, and I still had to explain the rest of that bodice-ripping thing to Maya. I'm a visual person, and some things are better explained by demonstration. There are times when words fail me.

CHAPTER SIX

I n México every life form, human or not, is instantly alert to opportunity and this prominently includes the insect community, which is far more numerous than any of the others. Every container big enough to contain the codex had been emptied on the floor: flour, sugar, coffee, pasta, rice. By the time our cleaning woman arrived, tiny work crews had been mustered at every pile and lines of bearers were stretched out under the kitchen door to the *loggia*, each carrying a grain or particle of something good for dinner. Rigoberta, uttering cries of outrage, set to work with a broom and then a mop.

Because the floors throughout the rest of the house were dust free from her frequent visits, we were able to pick up the clothes and reinstall them in the armoires; closets had not yet been invented when this house was built. I ordered two new mattresses to be delivered after dinner and an upholsterer was coming in the morning with his truck to pick up all the furniture and cushions that had been ripped open. By noon, the house would look pretty good, even if short of staples and lacking padded furniture.

The next morning, Ramon Rivera, who owned Galería Uno on Calle Jesus, called to say he had a reporter with him who was writing a series of articles for a México City paper on the art scene in several provincial cities. The reporter had seen my paintings at the gallery and wished to speak with me and one or two other local artists. I covered the receiver and told Maya.

"Good publicity," she said. "Let's ask him to dinner. We can grease him up."

"I think it's butter him up."

"OK."

I could see she was ready to celebrate the return of our house to sanity. I was too.

We were ready at seven when the bell rang. In one of the floor piles Maya had rediscovered a slinky green dress that she hadn't worn in a while, and it suited her hair and skin color perfectly. I began to think again about a clothed Maya series. Maybe her hair could be up and we could pick an orange hibiscus blossom from the garden. Cody had put on a pair of black slacks and a beige cashmere pullover from his overnight bag. I wore a new pair of chinos and a navy blue tee shirt that said STAFF on the back. My favorite. The kitchen was again in pristine condition and Maya had replaced all the dumped staples.

"Jason Schwartz," said the reporter at the door, and shook my hand with a grip that seemed a trifle too firm. "I appreciate your seeing me on such short notice. And I appreciate the dinner invitation. That doesn't usually come with an interview." He peered at me through glasses with colorless plastic frames. The lenses magnified his eyes, pale blue with pupils I thought were slightly too large, but it may have only been the magnification.

I mixed a round of margaritas and a rum punch

for Cody and we sat out under the *loggia*. The sun was still up over the edge of the garden wall but I lit the perimeter lights anyway. When the sun passes below the western hills here evening falls like a theater curtain.

Jason Schwartz looked to be around thirty-five, my age, and he wore a khaki field shirt with numerous pockets and a faded, but pressed, pair of jeans. His straight sandy hair came just over his ears and was cut off square at the back of his neck. He had that stubbly kind of beard that's popular in the States now. I wondered how women felt about that. I thought I knew how Maya would feel: sandpapered. I had tried growing a beard once, but after ten days she said it looked like pubic hair so I got rid of it.

"Wonderful house," said Schwartz, his gaze taking in the old beams and the decorative stenciling I had restored at the ceiling. "Any idea how old it might be?"

"Like anything else in San Miguel, it's hard to tell. When you remodel you can fill in all the stucco seamlessly and it looks just about like it should. It's easy to make changes that aren't obvious if they're consistent in style with the rest of the house. So it could be 300 years old or it could be three or four. No way to know and the deed doesn't say," I said. "This layout is traditional, and my guess would be that some of it is probably seventeenth century."

"I've got a condo up the hill behind Parque Juarez," said Cody. "It's only four years old. You can go both ways in this town. Some folks prefer modern."

"Tell us about your article," said Maya.

"It's a Sunday feature series. I'll spotlight two or three painters here and then go on to Querétaro and

Guanajuato and then up to Zacatecas and down to Mérida in the Yucatán. Not every painter I talk to will get into the piece. I hope to get four or five articles before I'm finished. I plan to stress the difference in styles from one region to the next."

"I've got some things in Mérida now," I told him. "It's not as good a venue as San Miguel for some painters, but I've always had good sales there. Look in on Galería Mundo Maya when you're there. It's just off the main plaza. They've got three or four other good artists on view and a couple of them are local. But I'm not altogether certain that the differences in style you'll find are due to geography. The art scene has gotten so quirky in the last twenty years. I used to think that there were no rules in painting anymore, but after a while I found that was wrong. Everyone has to have a set of rules. It's just that they can't be the same as anyone else's."

Schwartz smiled blandly, as if he already knew this.

Cody jiggled his empty glass and I made another round. I guess he wasn't on duty.

"I looked at seven or eight of your paintings at the gallery here and I would have to say that you seem to have a set of consistent rules in your work. Isn't that true?" Schwartz asked.

"Absolutely, and it's also true you'll find other *atelier* trained painters whose rules are not very different from mine. But we're throwbacks to an earlier era of representational painting. The *ateliers* exist to revive the old skills. They won't graduate anyone who can't actually paint. 'Conceptual art' is not welcome. Where I parted company with them was in the issue of what to paint. They tend not to discriminate. For example, one of my best painting teachers thought that Bouguereau was the finest painter who ever worked."

"Now you are losing me," said Maya. "Who is Bouguereau?"

"An extremely successful academic painter in France in the last half of the nineteenth century. Technically, he was the equal of anyone who's ever painted; he can't be faulted on that score. But, at the same time, he was a great sentimentalist. His pictures ooze cheap emotion. He and his peers tried successfully to have the Impressionists excluded from the Salon shows."

"So what's it like being a painter here and now?" asked Jason. "I've heard this is one of the hottest art scenes in México."

"It comes and goes. In the winter we get the snowbirds from up north. They're not big buyers but they make a few purchases. I get the feeling that in the Midwest they're looking for things to match their sofa and lampshades. They're not big on nudes, so most of those I send down to Mérida. The snowbirds are more comfortable with still lifes and landscapes. They like folksy things too, with little kids and burros. Old houses and flowers. Now and then a *mariachi* with a guitar. It's a bit of local color to take home. I don't mind much because I do them in my own style, without sentimentality. Then in the summer the Texans come and they're more adventurous. I ship a fair number of things to Austin and Dallas. They'll buy a nude now and then and hang it over the bar in their rec rooms. They don't seem averse to a little skin. Maya has probably been toasted a lot after a football game. Of course the local *gringo* community is large and they buy things too. Their tastes are more diverse and they'll commission a portrait from time to time."

"Good living?" He looked at me carefully.

"Fair is about as good as it gets. Sometimes it's more like thin."

"Ever have to do other things to make ends meet?"

Now Cody was studying Jason as he spoke, but he didn't seem to notice.

"Not for years. I'd rather be thin."

"Have you ever gotten into collecting?"

"My only collection is of paintings that didn't sell. Why do you ask?"

"I thought I saw two Diego Riveras hanging in the entry."

"I wish they were. When I first started painting I did a few copies of pictures I like. Those are from that period. You could never sell something like that."

"Do you write about art, mostly?" asked Cody.

"Anything that'll find a reader, really. I only do freelance. I like the independence and I don't mind the travel. It takes me around México a lot. Earlier this year I did a series on the Chiapas rebels. Next year it'll be the presidential election. Wherever the news is, I'm there."

"What do you think of Presidente Fox?" asked Maya.

"He hasn't done squat for the Indians; there's still no deal with the Zapatistas, even though they sit down to talk now and then. He also hasn't done anything for the migrant workers; they still end up as mostly illegal in the

States. I had hoped for more, especially with Bush in the White House, being from Texas. It seems like if they want to work in the U. S. and there are employers who want them to come, it ought to be possible to make a deal. It'd be good for both sides. But nothing changes."

"México doesn't change much," I said. "Although it is up to about 1950 now, in some parts of it. That's why I like it."

"Any problem finding nude models here?" he asked.

"Modesty is still a value here and there aren't many Méxican girls who will pose nude. The ones that will are mostly art students looking for a way to raise tuition money, as you might imagine. Fortunately, I have Maya, and she's about the best I've ever come across."

She smiled disarmingly at him. I could see the candlelight through her long lashes. There are times when I wish she didn't flirt with everybody. Goes with the territory, I suppose.

As we ate dinner under the *loggia* I fielded a series of what I thought were no more than generic questions; what was I going to do for my next show? (I wish I knew), is the Méxican market better than the US? (Never tried very hard in the U. S. because I left too soon when I was still completely unknown), were supplies hard to get here? (Could be more variety, especially in brushes, considering the two art schools and all the painters here.) Schwartz made some scattered notes in his spiral notebook. When he looked over at me Maya tried to see what he had written. I glanced at his fingernails; they were cut square across and dirty. After dessert we went upstairs to the studio and Jason made what I thought was a careful examination of it. Maybe he was more serious than I thought, but was it all that interesting? He did spend a little more time before the unfinished nude of Barbara than anything else.

"Why did you choose the Yucatán for your second gallery?" he asked.

"I like the Yucatán better than any other part of México. I love the ruins, and the people are second to none, but I couldn't live there because of the climate. I picked a Mayan theme for the pictures I last sent down there and they sold out."

"A Mayan theme?" asked Jason. It seemed like he'd heard the word before.

"For the show that just closed I used Maya herself and half a dozen folk dancers from Mérida posing in front of different Mayan gods in stone, with the jungle behind. It was called 'Gods and Goddesses.'" He made more notes in his book.

"Ever take the opportunity to pick up some Mayan antiques when you were down there?"

"Too pricey for me. I'm not much of a collector anyway."

"I'm fascinated by that stuff, myself," he said.

The conversation wandered on for a while and then Schwartz slid the notebook back into a canvas purse-like satchel that hung on his shoulder. We said goodnight at the door.

"I'd like to be able to call you if I think of any other angle; sometimes when I'm writing a story something else occurs to me," he said. "Thanks for everything." It was about ten o'clock. I didn't have a sense of whether the evening would generate any useful business or not. I've never known how to create effective publicity. I didn't shut the door immediately, but watched as he walked briskly down the narrow sidewalk and at the corner turned toward the *jardín*. There were several empty parking spaces on our block, but apparently he had walked. I saw no black Suburbans start up to follow him.

Later, Maya and I sat in the kitchen with a brandy while Cody washed the dishes. He wore a flowered apron that barely tied in back. "Did you notice his shoes?" she asked. "I always look at the shoes. They were high, and the tops were up under his jeans. There were many laces, like the bodices you were talking about. The funny thing was that they had wear on the top. Over the toes."

"On top?" I said.

"Yes, they are the shoes of someone who walks in brush or high grass. Maybe jungle."

"Jungle? Interesting. I never look at people's shoes unless I have to paint them," I said.

"Women look at shoes first, then the hands. I think I know what men look at," she said. I did too, but I felt like this was yet another thing I didn't know about women.

"So he doesn't seem like someone who spends much time in art galleries. And this is definitely not a guy who is about to win the Pulitzer Prize for art reporting," Cody said over his shoulder. "I didn't sense any real insight. Even an old cop who doesn't know much about art could ask better questions than that. He never asked what you were trying to do as a painter, what your goals were."

"His notes said almost nothing," said Maya. "And he didn't say which paper he was writing for, and no one will have him listed on the staff because he is freelance."

"He had strong feelings about the Indians," I said.

"I don't imagine your man over at Galería Uno would know anything more," said Cody.

"Ramon Rivera would kiss the feet of anyone who uttered the word 'publicity.' I suppose I would too, even if his shoes were worn on top."

"Schwartz sure was interested in your attachment to things Mayan, though. I wonder how much he really cares about art?"

"Maybe I should have said, 'Codex #5,' and then taken his pulse," I said.

CHAPTER SEVEN

By Tuesday morning, no one had tried to shoot us and everything was back in its place in the house. I was up at 7:30. Maya had shown me her new underwear before we went to bed. It worked fine. The new mattress was resilient. I took a four-minute shower—there is never enough water in San Miguel—and as I put together breakfast the doorbell rang and I looked at my watch. It was 8:15, too early for callers. From somewhere in the distance I heard roosters crowing, which set off a troop of street dogs over on Pila Seca, which set off another troop over on Umaran, etc., etc.

I opened the door to Licenciado Rodriguez and another man in a tan summer suit. The stranger had a businesslike manner and a bulge under his left arm that I guessed was not a tumor.

"Well," I said, "You have solved the break-in. I congratulate the police of San Miguel on another fine job." Neither of them smiled. "Please come in."

"I wish to introduce to you Señor Tomás Leon; he is of the federal police."

"Mucho gusto," I said. No one offered to shake hands. Leon was younger than Rodriguez, trimly built but shorter, with immaculate hair and a narrow mustache.

Now that I was a student of shoes, I observed that his were fairly new and polished. Glossy black, like the Suburban he almost certainly drove.

"Señor Zacher," said Leon, "Licenciado Rodriguez has been looking at your break-in but now we have more serious business before us. Two associates of mine in the federal police were found early this morning both shot in their car near the Gigante market, on the *libramiento*."

"I am very sorry to hear that," I said. "I hope they recover." Here we go again. At least they weren't found in my entry.

"Unfortunately, they are both dead."

"Again, I am sorry to hear it." This was upsetting; San Miguel did not often experience crime at this level. Surely, though, it could have nothing to do with the codex.

"The reason for our visit is that on the piece of paper you gave to me yesterday was written their license number," said Rodriguez. "When I looked into it I discovered that these two men who were following Señor Williams were federal police. At first I did not feel at liberty to tell you who they were, but now, as you see..." He made a gesture of helplessness, as if he'd been overtaken by events.

"Yes, I see. That explains the black Suburban we saw, the vehicle of choice for the *federales*. And now you wish to ask me if being followed makes me angry. My response is that while it is not my favorite thing, it does not make me want to kill someone, especially the *federales*." My magnanimity got no reaction from Leon. "Is it possible that they were the ones who searched my house?" Immediately I wished I hadn't said this. What I really wanted was to distance myself from the murders.

The sense of personal space is a little different in México; closer encounters are permitted without awkwardness, but nonetheless Leon leaned forward too close to my face and made a gesture of dismissal. "We are not permitted to discuss this," he said. "The business of the federal police is usually kept secret. In any case, all of the questions will come from us. May I ask where you were last night between the times of ten and twelve o'clock?"

"I was here. My friends will vouch for that."

"Of course."

Cody appeared behind them. He had obviously been taking this in. "I will confirm his statement," he said. "Señor Zacher did not leave here during the evening. I should tell you that I am a retired police detective myself."

"But not in México, I believe?" said Leon.

"No. Not in México. For thirty years, in Peoria, Illinois."

"I see. Did either of you have any conversation with these men in the black Suburban?"

"No," said Cody. "I simply observed them follow-ing me in the late afternoon and I took down the license number. I did not approach their car."

"So, again, you were all here last evening."

"Yes," I said, "and we a had a dinner guest. A reporter named Jason Schwartz. He is writing an article about the art scene in San Miguel." Leon looked at me for a moment. Not a muscle moved in his face other than his eyes, yet he seemed to be struggling with his next question.

"You have known Señor Schwartz a long time?"

"We met him last night for the first time," I said.

"He was referred to us by Ramon Rivera, who owns Galería Uno, which sells my pictures here."

"I see. At what time did he leave?"

"He left around ten o'clock." Leon made a few notes and he and Rodriguez looked at each other.

"You spoke about art during this time?"

"Yes, and for a while about Mayan antiques. I told him I wasn't a collector and that I didn't know much about them."

Leon folded his notes and got up abruptly. "I wish to thank you for your assistance," he said. "I am sure we will have more questions in the future. Please do not leave the town." Rodriguez followed him to the door and I let them out.

"Serious guy," said Cody, after I closed the door.

"I'm sure you were serious too when a couple of your fellow detectives were murdered."

"Count on it. I didn't have a chance to tell you before they came, but I was up a lot earlier than you were this morning. I called my friends in the Chicago Police and got an interesting line on Jason Schwartz. They're not busy at that hour."

Maya came into the room. She was freshly showered and her hair was tied back with a white ribbon. The way she smelled made me want to nibble her neck.

"Speak," I said to Cody. "Something larger than a traffic ticket?"

"A couple things." He pulled some notes from his pocket. "Jason Frederick Schwartz graduated in journalism from Berkeley in 1993. He had been arrested there three times in demonstrations against the Gulf War. His file says he was unrepentant and he professed to being an admirer of the civil disobedience of the sixties, the sit-ins and freedom rides and so on."

I didn't remember that the Gulf War had provoked that much street action, but in the volatile Berkeley of old even a parking ticket could provoke a demonstration.

"And they let him graduate?" asked Maya.

"Yes, because he never went to trial," said Cody. "At demonstrations in the States arrests are made mostly to clear the streets and restore order. It's hard to get convictions on demonstrating alone because of First Amendment considerations. You need something like assault on a police officer or malicious damage to property to go to court. Failing to disperse by itself rarely stands up at trial."

"So he was never charged," I said.

"No. He would typically have been held overnight and released the following morning. But the other function of these arrests is so the local cops can supply information to the FBI, which is then used to update membership lists in radical organizations. Our boy Jason was fairly high up in a group called Humans First, which had been involved in several Weatherman-style bombings in the early 90s. One of the bombings maimed a postal clerk. Although he was never directly linked to any bombings, Jason Schwartz was a first class campus radical. Career, you might say, given his background. The kind that would attach himself to any cause that looks disruptive."

"A real trouble maker," I said.

"He was on the receiving end of some too," Cody went on. "I came across a couple of news stories on the

Internet that mentioned a lawsuit he filed for police brutality. Apparently on one of his busts they worked him over pretty well. The authorities never released the settlement amounts in those days, but it had to have been a big one to make the papers."

"So he could have retired, or at least coasted for a while. Do you think he's working for someone else now?" asked Maya.

Cody spread his hands in a wide gesture. "Journalism has always been a great cover."

"I felt like Leon had heard of him before. Maybe Schwartz's name has hit a few lists down here," I said.

"So did I. But it was obviously new to Rodriguez," said Cody.

"I can't see Humans First operating in San Miguel, or even México City. We don't need to import *gringo* radicals," said Maya. "We are able to grow our own quite well."

"Even Frida Kahlo and Diego Rivera were communists," I said.

She nodded.

"Let's run a hypothesis," said Cody. "I think the two dead federal cops were here because of your return address on the package to Dr. Sandoval. Someone in the post office opened it for them and copied it, resealing it with the clear tape. From that return address the two *federales* showed up and started following you, then tossed your house hoping you still might have the codex, not knowing you never did. That also means they've been watching Sandoval's mail prior to this. We don't know why they chose him."

"He seemed straight arrow when I talked to him.

Arrogant, perhaps, and long-winded. Probably full of himself. I suppose you get like that when you're always lecturing and people have to pay to listen to you."

"So that's an open question. But let's go on. Jason Schwartz shows up to do an article on you and the art scene. Naturally you bite. But then he steers you into questions about arcane Mayan lore and cases the place. When he leaves the federal cops are there; maybe he didn't notice them when he came. Within the following two-hour time frame, they're both dead. Question one: did they already know young Jason? They would have seen him coming in and out of here. Question two: does Jason have a compelling reason to not wish the police tailing him? Is it possible they thought they had missed the codex when they searched your house and he had it with him? The satchel he was carrying could have held much more than a notebook. You could see from the weight of it that it wasn't empty, and it had to be more than just pencils and press passes. There could easily have been a gun as well as a codex."

"And here is question three," said Maya, "one it makes me sick to ask. I understand that the *federales* have sources within the post office, but how does Jason Schwartz know about us?"

"There can only be one way," said Cody, "and that's that Jason has a source within the Federal police in México City. After all, he is a journalist, and being a journalist is mainly about sources. At least it was back home."

"Good," said Maya, nodding. "Now we have the police on us and Jason Schwartz on us and whoever is this Arthur...Arthur..."

"Brisbane," I said, "and we still haven't seen the codex itself. I think we need to update Barbara, now that two people are dead. She may want to pull out of this. I'm going to go out and get in the car and drive around the block. Cody, why not wander out about tens seconds afterward and see if anyone is following me?"

"Right."

No one was. My bet was that everyone still alive was out looking for Jason.

I reached Barbara a few minutes later and she asked me to come over.

"I haven't heard much from you lately," she said at the door. "I hope you've been painting a lot."

"I wish," I said. She was wearing the briefest of cut-off jeans and a red halter top, an outfit I couldn't imagine her wearing in *centro*. Adults of either sex rarely wear shorts here. I brought her up to date on everything, and I included the trashing of our house and the death of the two federal officers. I gave her Cody's theories as well.

Her mouth opened and she blinked several times. "Come in here," she said, pulling at my shirt. She sat down heavily on the sofa and tears flooded her eyes. "I can't believe it! Two people are dead from this? What have we gotten into? I told you there would be no violence because of this." Both of her hands were gripping my left arm.

"A collector interest like yours is not the only reason to want the codex, if it's real. The Méxican government certainly wants it, and apparently others do too, although their motives aren't clear to me yet. I think it might be time to reconsider whether you want to continue with this, with the two *federales* dead now. That's almost as many as last time I got involved in this detective stuff."

"But we're not bitter?"

"Bitter, hell! I've been working overtime just to keep your name out of this." I put my hand on her shoulder. Normally I tried not to touch her because I never knew when it might start something. "They're already onto me and Maya. You're the one at the center of this now; how does it make you feel?" She looked at me as if I'd missed the main point.

"But you must also see that if people are being killed, the codex has to be genuine! I'm sorry about the men who died, but it doesn't change anything. Are you blaming me? All I did was ask if it was real. So now the Méxican government wants it, this Jason Schwartz wants it, and I *still* want it." I thought this was a cold way to validate the codex, but I didn't say so. She was employing us and I wasn't being paid for my opinions.

"When I want something I usually get it," she said calmly. Looking at her face, I saw no emotion. She was looking through the tall windows into the garden below.

"You've got more guts than I thought," I said.

"I married Perry, didn't I? Anyway, I want to use the codex as a springboard into serious collecting. I'm way beyond trinkets now. I've got more Roman coins and colonial crucifixes than I can ever use."

"If you're determined to pursue this, then the next step is to have Sandoval look at it, if he's willing. I suspect he might even be eager. That copy really got him going. He seemed surprised that the issue of authenticity was still alive after he'd seen it."

"OK. When Brisbane calls back I'll try to set it up. Let me know if Sandoval is willing."

She put her hands on my shoulders and looked

into my eyes. "And sweetheart, I will cover all your costs for the damage. Remember, I said I'd cover your expenses as well as your time? Let me get you a check right now." I didn't argue. Instead I found myself looking at her shorts as she bent over to write the check. A painter is always alert to new poses. When I returned home I dialed Sandoval, not expecting to find him in his office on a Saturday, and I didn't. I left a message on his service and an hour later he called me back.

"This is getting out of control fast," I said. "Do you know someone named Jason Schwartz?"

"I don't think I do. Is he in my field?" he asked blandly, the unshakable academic.

"He's a journalist. He came here for dinner last night on the pretext of interviewing me for an article on the art scene in San Miguel. We ended up talking about what my interest might be in Mayan antiques."

"Interesting, but I'm not sure it means anything."

"But listen to this. He left at ten o'clock. Between then and midnight two federal officers who've been staking out my house were murdered out on the edge of town. The local and federal police have already been here to talk to us about it."

"Interesting that they were staking out your house. Do they think it was Schwartz who killed them? I'm not sure what to make of this."

"I don't know, either. As you can imagine, they don't volunteer much, but the federal guy reacted to the name. My sources indicate Schwartz was a known radical in the States. Anyway, I just wanted to tell you to be extremely careful. The government wants the codex, and so does Schwartz. And none of us has even seen it, which raises the next issue. My collector friend is not put off and would like you to authenticate the codex. I realize there's some risk involved now, and she is offering $2,500 for your trouble."

There was a brief silence on the other end. Then Sandoval said, "I am not easily put off either by these things, and my career in the field has always entailed a certain amount of risk. I have a counter proposal. I will examine the codex and authenticate it if possible. In lieu of payment from the prospective buyer, she will grant me publishing rights if it's genuine and she buys it. If it's a fraud, she will owe me nothing. I will cover my own expenses. Naturally, she would not be identified in the process."

"I think that would be OK. We'll try to set up a meeting and I'll get back to you."

When I hung up Cody was standing behind me with a holstered .38 on his broad palm and a leather shoulder holster in his other hand.

"Happy birthday," he said.

"It's not until October 15th; more than three months off."

"I know that, but if you expect to be around to take me out to dinner that day you'd better take this. We're playing with the big boys this time around. This is not just Perry Watt taking revenge on someone. There are two *federales* in the ground already over this codex. I suspect they're not that easy to take down. Let's just be prepared."

He showed me how to adjust the straps.

Maya came into the kitchen, saw the gun, and

placed her hands on my shoulders. A grim look came over her face.

"So it's reached that point," she said, shaking her head. "Now we are between the sword and the wall. All because of Barbara Watt."

I knew the feeling; Barbara had had me between the sword and the wall for some time.

CHAPTER EIGHT

My cell phone chirped. "Darlin', it's Barbara." Darlin' could only be me. I hoped the line was clear of taps, but who could tell? At least I didn't think Rodriguez and Leon suspected me of murdering the two *federales*.

"Arthur Brisbane called back a little while ago. He's OK to show the codex but he will only see Sandoval alone, and we are to have him come in on Friday and stay at the Sierra Nevada del Parque. The meeting will be on Saturday and he will call the hotel Friday afternoon and leave a message about the time and location for their meeting. Do you think it will fly? It's such short notice— Sandoval would have to come in tomorrow. I'm getting nervous. I can't stop thinking about those two dead men."

"Don't worry. The Zacher Agency is all over this. Cody gave me one of his guns. If we can set this up, then I think the five of us should sit down to dinner on Friday and sort it out. We haven't met Sandoval and we need to size him up. We don't want to be dealing with a flake, and we also don't want him to try to make an end run around us with a higher bid from someone else."

"I didn't think of that. What if he is a flake? Like some ivory tower guy who's never been off campus? I've known a few of those; they all think business is evil. If you light a candle at a dinner party they start fretting about global warming."

"Then we thank him kindly, pay his hotel bill, and send him back to México City. But I don't think he's that green because he gets out now and then. I know he's spent a lot of time excavating in the Yucatán."

"I wish Perry were here."

"I don't. He'd probably start shooting up the place. Sorry. I'll call you back after I reach Sandoval."

When I got hold of the professor at his desk he was fine with the timing and said he would clear his schedule. He sounded excited, but in a collected sort of way, as if his reserve of skepticism were still intact. It would be another adventure in archaeology, but this time without the rotten shoes and moldy cameras and big teeth. I let Barbara know and asked her to be here for dinner at seven on Friday if she didn't already have a date.

The Sierra Nevada is a tastefully understated boutique hotel on the Parque Juarez just up the street from the Santa Monica, but off Baeza so it doesn't actually face the park. It's on a tiny side street called Santa Elena and doesn't have much of a sign, but I suspect the people who need to know it's there, do. It is favored by film stars and politicians looking to avoid the hubbub and fireworks of downtown, and possibly the press as well. They can dine intimately and play tennis or lounge by the pool and be seen only by those they wish to be seen by. The rooms are large and luxurious with huge tiled bathrooms and spread out around an immaculately tended garden of citrus and jacaranda and bougainvillea. Not that I've ever been in any of the rooms; I got all this from reading the brochure as I waited for Sandoval to come to the lobby. It was 6:45.

The lobby flowed seamlessly into the bar, which had its own fountain in the center of eight or nine round tables. Through the limestone arches the garden approached like a well trained pet, clipped and manicured, right to the edges of the outer chairs. A trio called *Los Romanticos* in embroidered pants and short jackets played old Méxican songs. I nearly sat down at a table and ordered a *piña colada*. Then I saw a man who could only be the professor coming along the arcade from the row of rooms above.

Professor Sandoval, if it was Sandoval, was a big barrel-chested man with iron gray hair. He wore a blue blazer with gray slacks and a white shirt open at the neck. His expensive-looking frameless glasses were the kind where the bows attach directly to the lenses. He appeared to have just shaved; even the jowls flanking his chin were perfect, however, the curly hairs in his eyebrows seemed bent on escape. I guessed he was in his late fifties, like Cody. His walk was a little odd, with one leg never quite catching up to the other as he moved. He noticed me observing his gait.

"Snake bite," he said as he approached. "Got it on an old dig at Tikal. The nerves in my leg never healed right." It seemed like he was trying to explain his only imperfection to me. "Vincent Sandoval. I guess you're Paul Zacher." He held out his hand.

"I'm glad you could come. We're really out to sea on this. My friend Barbara Watt would like to buy the codex, but we need an expert." Since he had come this far I'd decided to tell him Barbara's name. We walked out to the artmobile.

"There are only two others you might have talked

to, Walt Ransome and Pedro Gutierrez, and they don't know any more than I do. I tend to think less. If I do publish it, that'll widen the gap." He laughed, as if anticipating the triumph. "I love that Sierra Nevada. I stayed there before once, seven or eight years ago. It doesn't change. Of course, I suppose San Miguel doesn't change much either, just a few more *gringos* each year."

"That's about it. Are you at all concerned about the *federales* keeping an eye on you? If they're opening your mail, what else might they do?"

"Not at all." He waved away the idea as if it were absurd. "Comes with the territory. When you're an archaeologist you're always watched for trafficking in antiquities. They invariably have a man stationed on the digs. I'm sure that's why they opened the codex copy. They probably open anything bulky addressed to me. I know most of them by name; they mean well enough, but I wish they'd watch the *unofficial* digs a little better. That can be heartbreaking. I can't tell you how many once-promising sites I've come upon that are now looted piles of rubble."

We pulled up at the house on Quebrada and got out. Sandoval stepped back into the street and looked it over. A couple with children in tow passed on the narrow sidewalk. "Seventeenth century?" he asked. "I'm looking at the window and door trim."

"The facade probably and parts of the interior as well, I think. It's hard to tell what's been added, since the designs changed so little over time. Whenever I've added, I stayed with the oldest style."

"I've looked into it a bit and in my view this kind of floor plan, with the anonymous front and an interior courtyard with rooms opening onto it from all sides, is very old indeed, way beyond Spanish tradition, and even Roman, back at least to early Greek. It's an upper class plan, of course. The Romans had apartment houses for the poorer folk, just as we do."

Inside, Barbara and Cody and Maya were having a drink out on the *loggia*. I introduced Sandoval and he looked around the garden. "What a sweet spot. I've got a high-rise condo in México City so there's no chance of a garden. I've got room for only a deck chair and a single hibiscus on my balcony." He agreed to have a margarita. Cody, as usual, sucked on a rum punch. Sandoval was eyeing Barbara as I set down his drink. Attractive Méxican women like Maya are not hard to find here, although they're not usually as sophisticated as she is, but true blondes with a face and body capable of stopping traffic are not that common in México.

"What's the likelihood that you'll be able to make a definitive pronouncement on the codex when you see it?" said Cody, when we all sat down again. "I'm sure there's not going to be any chance of carbon dating or spectrographic analysis of the paint."

This did not make Sandoval uncomfortable. "Yes, I'm aware of that. To a large degree, if the format, the wear patterns, the look and feel of it are all correct, then I'll be able to say. Except for the one in Paris, which is sealed under glass, I've held all the others in my hands at various times. I'll know. One special point will be the weave of the pressed cambium of the ficus it was made from. That's not easily duplicated, and most people who might try to forge something like this wouldn't know about it. But even more than that, these documents have a certain indefinable presence that would impossible to fake."

"Yet you've been skeptical about this from the beginning. From what you're saying, it sounds like an unlikely thing to attempt," said Maya.

"I'm cautious. People will try anything."

"Has Arthur Brisbane contacted you yet?" asked Barbara, leaning forward. She placed her hand over his. Sandoval squirmed and blinked. I don't think he realized it, but she would be touching a toad in just this way if she were talking to it. It was only her manner; conversation was a contact sport. He cleared his throat.

"I spoke to him by phone earlier. It's set up for noon tomorrow. He asked me not to reveal the location."

I lit the charcoal. Tonight we were having pork and chicken shish kabob with grilled yellow bell peppers, onions, and mushrooms. It had stewed all afternoon in a marinade of olive oil, lemon juice, coarse-ground mustard and spices.

"Just so we're clear on the terms of this," he continued, as I was poking the barbecue, "if I deem the codex to be genuine I will photograph it here in San Miguel after you purchase it. I will have the rights to publication, and I will not reveal your name or the present location of it. If it should turn out to be a fraud, then our business is finished. In either case I'll bear the cost of my expenses."

"Agreed," said Barbara, giving him an irresistible smile.

"How did you get into this field?" asked Maya. "Paul said you've been doing this for thirty-five years."

"I grew up in Albuquerque. My father was a car dealer there and he had enough money to indulge his passion for collecting Indian artifacts, particularly the pottery of the different pueblos. He had between thirty and forty pieces of the best quality. He even had three Maria Martinez pots before she was widely recognized. That was the atmosphere of our household. I was raised bilingual, of course. I became fascinated by the artifacts myself and I got a degree in cultural anthropology at Albuquerque and then came down here for a Ph.D. in Mayan Civilization. It always seemed to me that the Mayans had the highest level of culture of all the Native Americans. As I'm sure you know, they're the only ones to develop a written language. I began publishing and I've spent my entire teaching career in México City. I wouldn't have done it any differently. I have to say, though, that when Paul first called me I was shocked. The idea that there might be a fifth surviving codex gave us all a laugh. It would be like someone calling to say he had discovered a map to Eldorado or the fountain of youth."

"I suppose if it proves to be real it might be up there with finding an intact Mayan royal burial," said Cody.

"Nearly as good, only without the gold and jade. As a cultural relic it would almost be better, particularly since it would place the Dominguez Codex in its proper context; Friar Dominguez would have had to work from this same document to concoct his fraud. Everything would then be tied up nicely. I've always been suspicious of his work, as well as of his motives."

I skewered the shish kabob and placed the vegetables in a grill basket and started cooking. Maya made another round of drinks. She touched my face and gave me a big smile. "You might get lucky later," she whispered. I turned on the garden lights. Just having her was lucky.

Cody was swirling his glass slowly between his

hands as if pondering how to phrase something. "There's another aspect of this we need to look at, I think. What if there was another offer on the codex? A larger one, for example."

Sandoval's turbulent eyebrows went up slightly. He placed his palms together and leaned back in his chair. I noticed a large collegiate ring on his left hand with a red stone that appeared to be a ruby but probably wasn't. "If you are suggesting that I might be the conduit for such an offer you can rest easy. I've been in this field for a long time and my reputation is unimpeachable. Besides, my role in helping you is not entirely disinterested. It is traditional for the scholar who first publishes a historic document to give it his name. This one would become known as the Sandoval Codex."

There was a moment of silence at the table. I think he was hearing trumpets in the background. For centuries scholars would be saying, "That Sandoval, what a guy!"

"I guess calling it the Watt Codex wouldn't carry the same weight, would it?" said Barbara. "Anyway, I think it's better that no one knows I have it." The look on her face was not happy.

"But Barbara," Sandoval turned toward her with a smile. "You would have possession of the artifact itself, one of the incontestable treasures of Mesoamerican art. I would simply be giving it a name; it's just one of the small conceits of academe."

"The Sandoval Codex," I said.

"And what do you do, Cody?" he said. "Are you a student of history like Maya?"

"A student of human behavior you could say; I'm

a retired detective."

"That's right. One of the assets Paul mentioned to me in our earlier conversations. You were called in with Paul to help secure the transaction."

"Well, initially we thought it was probably coun-terfeit, not realizing then how difficult it would be to fake."

"And that may yet prove to be the case," Sandoval said. It appeared he'd enjoy it either way.

"If you do publish this one, what will happen to the Dominguez Codex?" asked Maya.

"It will be relegated to the pious fraud shelves of history, by no means one of the smallest areas of the archive. This is where I myself have always thought it belonged. The level of acceptance of Christianity it depicts has still not been reached today in many areas of the Yucatán, nearly 500 years later. The Mayan religion is, after all, older than Christianity, and may yet outlive it."

"I would shed no tears," she said, always the anti-cleric.

"I've heard there's a revival of the old ways in Chiapas," I said, serving the shish kabob.

Sandoval didn't comment as I passed the condiments around.

"Perhaps dinner is not the best place to bring this up," said Cody, "but I'd like to remind you, Dr. Sandoval, that two people have already died in this business. There is another party besides the government who would like to own the codex, and I doubt they'll put your name on it if they get it."

"Call me Vincent, please. I know this well, and I considered it before coming here and taking this on. But you must realize too that in the digs, we're constantly surrounded by thieves, and many of them would be quite happy to slit our throats. The entire field of pre-Columbian archaeology is under siege by thugs, and some of them wear academic robes at times, I fear."

"Do you think we might be dealing with one of your colleagues?" I was pouring out glasses of the Chilean red now. "Is it possible that someone picked up some information when we first called you, or maybe got wind of the codex when it was opened by the post office?"

"I doubt that very much. I mentioned it to only two of my associates, both men I have worked with for more than twenty years. After I saw the copy you sent I said nothing more to them, and no one else saw it after it arrived. Superb shish kabob, by the way, and Maya, the saffron rice is the perfect complement."

Barbara was delicately eating her chicken, spearing one tiny piece at a time. "Do you think there is any way the government could force me to give it up, like if they found out I had it? Assuming this goes through, of course." She set her fork down and folded her hands at the edge of the table.

"Only if they could prove it was stolen," said Sandoval, "which I think it must be, but proving that, or finding the real owner, is quite another issue, since no bereaved collector has come forward at this point. I also checked the international register of stolen art and found no mention of it. I myself don't have a problem with you owning it under these circumstances because it takes the codex out of the hands of the underworld and places it with a serious collector who has the means to take proper care of it. Such things can get terribly degraded when they're passed from hand to hand with no thought of conservation. In this case the continued survival of the codex would trump any moral or legal argument, for me at least. My guess is that whoever had it does not know it's gone, and I think it likely they didn't know they had it to begin with. But to answer your question, the government could confiscate it if they caught you trying to take it out of the country, and they could force your estate to sell it to them at the market price, should something happen to you. I think none of these are worthy of consideration at this point."

"Arthur Brisbane must think it's genuine," I said.

"Not necessarily. He may rightly feel that authentication is his only chance to get that kind of price for it. No one would buy it without an expert opinion. He has nothing to lose. If I find it to be a fraud, then he'll approach another potential buyer. Maybe that person then ˈengages an expert with lesser qualifications. Of course, no one else has contacted me about this. I didn't ask Ransome or Gutierrez if anyone had approached them because I didn't want to tip them off." He rescued a grain of rice from the lapel of his jacket and set it on the rim of his plate.

"I'm not sure I would have the same comfort level about owning it, knowing it was probably stolen," said Cody. "But I can see why you'd take the conservator's point of view, that placing it with Barbara would at least insure its preservation."

"Exactly. Consider the Elgin marbles, now in the British Museum. The Greek government has been trying for years to get them back in order to remount them on the Parthenon. The British government has taken the perhaps self-serving view that doing this would expose them to intense air pollution. I suspect we'll see them go back to Athens eventually, but only after the Greeks prove their ability as conservators. That may take a while. I don't expect to live to see it."

I made coffee for the group. I am particular about coffee, and while I do use dark roasted Méxican coffee from the mountains in Chiapas, it's not normally available in México, since it's almost entirely exported. I buy it at a little shop down on Ancha de San Antonio which in turn buys it in the States and brings it back, along with things like corn flakes, peanut butter, and chocolate chips. It's a niche business.

"Perhaps you would like a studio tour," I said after we had finished.

"Delighted," said Sandoval, and we headed upstairs.

"You don't mind, do you Barbara?" I asked.

"Of course not."

I pulled out some paintings from the racks and stood them against the wall, but the others were gathered around the easel looking at the nude of Barbara. I joined them.

"Stunning," said Sandoval. "Wonderful quality of flesh." Barbara's smile lit the studio. She put a hand on his shoulder. "Do I detect an echo of Manet in the pose?" he said to me. Maya stood at the back of the pack with an unreadable look.

"Very much," I said. "He's one of the painters I admire most."

"Where do you sell these?"

"Barbara's buying this one, but normally I show here in San Miguel at Galería Uno and at Galería Mundo

Maya in Mérida. I just finished a show there. Maya is usually my model."

"I go through Mérida often. I think I know that gallery. Just off the *zocalo*, isn't it?"

I nodded and we returned to the *loggia* for a round of brandies.

"You must be excited about tomorrow's meeting," said Maya.

Sandoval turned his chair sideways at the table and stretched out his legs. "Actually, I'm quite relaxed. I've learned how to pace myself on more then a few archaeological digs. There was one where we excavated for two years and got nothing significant. If you work up a head of steam, you run out of gas. I guess that mixes the metaphor, but you take my point. Of course you rarely come away empty handed."

"So tomorrow will be like a very brief dig." I said.

"Exactly. The shovel goes in once. It's either genuine or it's not."

CHAPTER NINE
THE COLLECTOR

Jason Schwartz was not a high roller, although he still had some funds left from his police brutality settlement in the nineties. As he awaited developments in the matter of the fifth codex, he was staying out of view, posing as a photographer in the house of Juan Lopez in an area of smaller homes in the San Antonio neighborhood, only tentatively invaded by the *gringos*. Juan, an elementary schoolteacher whose children were grown and married, had two small extra bedrooms that he often rented to painters taking classes at either the nearby Instituto Allende or the Bellas Artes. When Schwartz appeared in response to Juan's posting at the Instituto, he was not averse to taking in a photographer. Here Schwartz settled into a bedroom furnished with a single iron bed, a small wooden desk with attached dresser and mirror, and a picture of the Sacred Heart of Jesus on the wall. He shared the only bathroom with the family and a foliage painter visiting from Key West.

On the Wednesday before the arrival of Dr. Sandoval, Schwartz received a call on his cell phone from his contact in the federal police in México City. He was told the details of Sandoval's visit, including his stay at the Sierra Nevada, which the federal police had gotten from the tap on the professor's phone. At two o'clock on Friday his contact called back to say the police had obtained a copy of a message left with the desk clerk at the Sierra Nevada confirming a meeting at four o'clock on Saturday at an address on Cuadrante. Allowing time for his arrival, at four on Friday Schwartz called Professor Sandoval at the Sierra Nevada.

"This is Arthur Brisbane. I'm calling about the codex," said Schwartz.

"Yes," said Sandoval, who had just pulled off his shoes and was unpacking. "I received your earlier message from the desk."

"I will need to change the time of our meeting," he said. "I would like to make it noon on Saturday instead of four, if that works for you." He knew the *federales* would certainly be waiting for the later meeting.

"That will not be a problem," said Sandoval, "in fact, earlier is better. I am most eager to see the document."

"And just to confirm the address on Cuadrante?"

"Thirteen A," said Sandoval.

"That is correct. I'll see you then."

Schwartz waited until dusk and then packed his satchel and headed off for *centro*. Cuadrante 13A greatly surprised him. It was not the typical anonymous walled house front like the one belonging to Paul Zacher and others he had seen all over San Miguel; instead it was an immaculately restored eighteenth century mansion that displayed the great wealth of its builder and the considerable resources and expertise of its restorer. He was impressed, but not intimidated. Anyone with the money and taste to do this had to be a neo-colonialist oppressor.

He grasped a ring in the mouth of one of the polished brass lion's head knockers and pounded three times. The light above the doors came on a moment later and one of them opened on a thickset *gringo* in his forties with a small clipped mustache. His face held an expression of surprise.

Schwartz pushed the door open quickly and stepped through, pressing his silenced gun against the man's chest directly over his heart. "I'm not Sandoval, but I do need to see the codex. Now."

The Collector, occasionally known to some as Arthur Brisbane, but more commonly to his few friends and to the police in three northeastern states of the U. S. as John Schleicher, turned silently and walked through the foyer and the great room into his study, where he stopped at his desk.

"Take it out slowly, I'll be watching your hands," said Schwartz. When Schleicher reached into the top drawer and began to pull out a long thick manila envelope, Schwartz struck him solidly on the base of his skull with the butt of his gun and Schleicher fell heavily across the surface of the desk and did not move. Schwartz reached into his satchel and removed a garrote that he fastened around the Collector's neck and tightened until the cord disappeared into the flesh. He waited seven minutes by his watch as he sat in the desk chair and then rose and loosened the garrote. This was not his normal weapon of choice, but today he needed silence and an absence of blood. The Collector's body slid to the floor. He had not uttered a sound. Schwartz went through his pockets, but found nothing of interest. There was no wallet. He searched the rest of the house, but found no one else. Back in the entry he located the key ring and slipped out of the house into

102

the street.

To the left of the house wrought iron gates secured with a padlock enclosed a long carriage drive. Jason Schwartz opened the gates and drove in, closing them after himself. As he moved along beside the house, he heard the sound of feet spinning on gravel and, in the lights from the windows along the drive, he saw a massive Doberman rushing up the cobblestones toward him. Just as the dog began barking he fired two nine millimeter bullets downward into his chest and the dog cartwheeled over into the front of his car and then did not move. The spitting sound of the silenced gun was easily muffled by the walls along the drive. He pulled the body of the late Collector out through the carriage entrance of the house and, with considerable effort, loaded it in the trunk of his car. The man's bladder had given way as he died and Schwartz hoped the odor would not remain in his trunk. After securing the gate again he drove out of town toward the village of Atotonilco. It was 8:45.

The Sanctuary of Atotonilco is dedicated to Jesus of Nazareth and ranks high on any list of Méxican pilgrimage sites. Before the coming of the Conquistadores it was sacred to the Indians because of its hot springs. Father Hidalgo stopped there in 1810 to pick up the standard of Our Lady of Guadalupe to lead his troops into battle, and before that Don Ignacio Allende, San Miguel's native son and the subject of Maya's unpublished book, was married there. Adjacent to the church, which is in a process of almost continual restoration, are scattered the ruins of a vast cloister. Tonight, it was these ruins that were the pilgrimage destination for Jason Schwartz.

Schwartz had never been a religious man. The appeal of Atotonilco for him was that it was seven miles distant from San Miguel and when the Collector's body was discovered it would lie within the jurisdiction of the town's single part time policeman. Murder would be a surprise for him; it would buy time for Schwartz to finish his business in San Miguel. The absence of any identification would slow things up for a while as well. As he drove slowly past the locked church and around to the rear of the ruins, his right hand rested on the envelope containing the codex.

The vaulted roof of the cloister had fallen in decades, or perhaps a century, before. All that stood now was a field of arches and vaulted walls filled with piles of carved stones and rubbish, deadly silent in the moonlight. There were no houses on this side of town, and at his back, as he hauled the corpse from the trunk, was a dozen yards of construction debris backed by a stony pasture. No headlights appeared as he dragged the Collector as far into the rubble as he could, and then covered him with brush. John Schleicher had come to rest on sacred ground, like generations of others in the complex before him. Jason Schwartz grinned as he got back into the car, cranked up the volume of his tape player and returned to his humble room in San Miguel.

On Saturday he left his rented room at eleven in the morning and walked the seven or eight blocks to Cuadrante 13A because he did not want his car in view. In his satchel was the manila envelope with the fifth codex, the nine-millimeter automatic pistol with the silencer still mounted, the garrote, a black ski mask, and a pair of white cotton gloves. This part of

Cuadrante does not generate much traffic, even on a Saturday morning, and it was not difficult to find an opportunity to slip into 13A when no one was in view.

The house was as he had left it. He checked the floor at the side of the desk for a puddle, but apparently the Collector's little accident had all been absorbed by his clothes.

Schwartz had dressed that morning in a pair of khakis and a light colored shirt. Now he searched the Collector's closet for a jacket and found one in a subtle tweed. Schwartz and the Collector wore about the same size, only the Collector had been thicker in front. Left unbuttoned, the jacket looked like a plausible fit. He was glad to have it. Schwartz was not much of an actor, but wearing his victim's clothes helped him get in character. He placed the codex in the same desk drawer and moved the Collector's Glock Nine to one lower down. Then he sat down in the leather chair to await Dr. Sandoval.

At precisely noon he heard the brass knocker sound twice. He smoothed his thick straight hair back with his hands and went to the door. There waited an imposing man in his fifties, a couple inches taller than Schwartz, wearing a double-breasted blue blazer and an old fashioned tie. He carried a briefcase at his side.

"Dr. Vincent Sandoval. Are you Arthur Brisbane?"

"I am. Very pleased to meet you, Dr. Sandoval. Please step in. I hope you had no trouble finding me? The streets can be confusing here, with name changes every couple of blocks."

"None at all. Magnificent house you have here. I believe I've seen it in one of the design magazines."

"That's certainly possible. It's been in several over the years. Please come into the library."

Yesterday Schwartz had not given much thought to how this meeting would go, being more involved with the elimination of John Schleicher. Now, as they approached the desk he considered how critical Sandoval's opinion was going to be. If the codex were a fraud, then he had killed three men and a dog for nothing. That in itself was not serious, but the authenticity of the codex was critical to the Cause. If Sandoval rejected it, he would be left with finding another expert, one less knowledgeable, and he would probably have to eliminate Sandoval next. The man looked like more than Schwartz could lift by himself.

He gestured to the seat across from him at the desk and the professor sat down. Schwartz opened the drawer and slid the manila envelope to the center of the desk between them. From his briefcase, Dr. Sandoval drew out a pair of latex gloves and put them on. He carefully removed the codex from the envelope as Schwartz watched his face. The professor took care to reveal nothing. He examined closely the first few pages, then pulled out a magnifying glass and scanned the paper construction. Still silent, Sandoval went to the window and held the codex edge-on to the light. Then he sniffed it and sat down again.

He took from his briefcase the copy of the codex sent to him by Paul Zacher and, putting on his reading glasses, compared it page by page to the original on the desk. There was no sound in the room other than the breathing of the two men. After about twenty minutes, Sandoval leaned back in his chair, replaced his reading glass in a pocket of his blazer, and the tension left his shoulders. He stared into the corner of the room, which held a tall display case of Mayan ceramics, then reached again into the briefcase and withdrew a semitransparent pleated envelope slightly larger than the manila one on the desk. There was an elaborate closure along one side.

"Mr. Brisbane," he said, "I would like to give you this archival container for the codex, because it is indeed genuine. Please don't put it in the manila envelope again. It's not acid-free. I congratulate you."

The grin that now spread over Jason Schwartz's face was genuine as well. He picked up the manila envelope, tore it in two, and dropped the two halves in the wastebasket. It was almost like a baptism, with the codex reborn free of the original sin of doubtful parentage.

The professor himself now opened the archival container and placed the codex in it. "There is a slot inside with my card in it, also acid free, by the way." He fastened the closure and handed it back to Jason Schwartz, leaning back in his chair. "Just one thing bothers me," he said, "surely this was not found in a ruined hacienda near Valladolid?"

Schwartz grinned again, modestly, as if he had been caught in a white lie. He had not heard this story before, but he could improvise, and he knew that simple improvisations were best. "Actually, professor, I found it here in this house."

Sandoval knew he was not shaking, although the world of Mayan scholarship soon would be, but he wasn't sure there was no trace of tears in his eyes as he said, "I thank you for this opportunity, Mr. Brisbane. I don't expect I will have another experience like this in my life. I will report back to the buyer with my findings."

They both stood. For two men who had never met before, it seemed like a strong emotional bond had formed between them.

At the door, Schwartz shook his hand. "Thank you, Professor Sandoval. I can't begin to express how relieved I am." Schwartz almost hugged him, since now he wouldn't have to kill him.

The professor went blindly down the steps of Cuadrante 13A. People gave him a wide berth as he walked over the cobblestones, but he didn't see them. Because he turned to his left rather than his right, he did not go past the carriage drive, and therefore did not smell the aura of decay which, in the unusually warm weather, was beginning to fill with hundreds of flies to form a cloud around the dead Doberman. He lost his way and had to ask directions twice on the way back to the Sierra Nevada. When he reached his room he threw off his shoes and stretched out full length on the bed, trying to catch his breath. Half an hour passed before he dialed Barbara Watt, and she did not immediately recognize his voice.

His reserve of skepticism had vanished.

CHAPTER TEN

Normally a simple trip for a drink at the Sierra Nevada with a respected expert in Mayan antiquities would not feel like a practice run for the Nascar 500, nor would the car be a silver Mercedes sedan carrying two passengers as well as the driver. As Barbara spun out of her horseshoe drive, where the pebbles were always raked like the surface of a Zen garden, a spray of gravel cut through the air behind her. She hit the street before her house on two wheels, narrowly missing the artmobile parked outside her wall, flashed over to Santo Domingo and swept down the hill toward *centro*, airborne over the speed bumps. Each time she hit pavement the shock absorbers made a sound like a baseball bat hitting a pillow. Oddly, she was wearing neither a crash helmet nor a fireproof coverall. Neither were available in the summer offerings from the fashion house of Carolina Herrera.

Careening around the corner onto Recreo, she sideswiped a lonely burro ambling along the street after selling its load of potting soil. Fortunately the average San Miguel burro is a soft-sided animal, and the pearly silver skin of the 600 Mercedes was probably not scraped, just further buffed.

It was about two-thirty on Saturday when we pulled up before the Sierra Nevada. Even traveling over the cobblestone streets at barely subsonic velocity the ride was whisper quiet, and the dove gray leather seats were nearly as soft and supple as the inside of Maya's thigh.

I looked at my watch as we got out. "Three minutes and twelve seconds," I said. "I believe the pole position is yours."

As we got out before the Sierra Nevada, Maya whispered something in my ear that I didn't entirely catch, but it involved the word "*loca*." Barbara flipped the keys to the valet, who was delighted to receive them, and we ran inside. Mopping my forehead, I marveled at how unruffled she was as we went in.

When Barbara had called earlier to invite us, she said that Sandoval had phoned her shortly after one o'clock. His voice was shaking as he told her the fifth codex was genuine. He desperately needed to celebrate with someone and could he stand us a round of drinks in the bar of the hotel? He didn't feel able to go out. No problem. Maya and I met her at Casa Watt and she called Cody on her cell as she locked the front door. He began making his way down the hill from his condo above the Santa Monica, always up for a celebration and there hadn't been much excuse for one lately. When the waiters saw Barbara come into the bar a fight began over who would have her table and there was a sigh of dismay when they saw us join Sandoval. He had lost a considerable amount of his professional poise. His hair was a mess and he had yanked off his tie so that one side of his collar was above the lapel of his blazer. His eyes were rimmed with red and his glasses had moved down his nose. He was apparently aware of none of this. Both hands gripped a drink that I suspected was not his first. Cody walked in a moment after we did.

The professor rose as we entered and hugged all of us. Barbara kissed his cheek and held his hand in both of hers. He flagged down the waiter with an imprecise but still authoritative gesture, and we ordered margaritas, except for Cody, who had a rum punch. The waiter picked up Sandoval's tie from the floor and looped it over an arm of his chair before he left.

"This day," began the professor, shaking his head, "this day..." But he started to choke up and could go no further. Barbara put one hand on his arm and stroked his neck with the other. He no longer seemed surprised to have her touching him; he seemed to like it.

"Slow down, darlin'," she said. "We've got all the time in the world. It's México." We certainly hadn't used up much of it getting there.

"Thank you," he gasped, gripping her hand, which had now disappeared between both of his, "thank you for calling me in on this. When I think that it could have been Ransome or Gutierrez! What a close thing it was. Sometimes it's only about chance." His eyebrows went up and he shook his head as he took a deep breath. I didn't remind him that it was me that called him in on this, and I had never heard of the other two.

"It was Paul's doing," she said. "He found your name on the Internet."

"Amazon.com," I said. The Zacher Agency was nothing if not cutting edge.

Cody was waiting while Sandoval looked deeply into Barbara's blue eyes. He seemed about to take her in his arms. I don't think she would have stopped him. The waiters were probably placing bets on what would happen next.

Finally Maya shook her head with impatience, and leaning across the table toward him, pulled on his sleeve. "Professor Sandoval," she said. "How do you know the codex is real? What is it like?"

After a time he turned his gaze away from Barbara and rubbed his hands over his face. I think we were all holding our breath. As he collected himself I had a sudden idea.

"What if it's one of the other four, recently stolen?"

He disregarded this as something only a non-academic would say.

"Where to start?" He leaned forward with his elbows on the table. "To begin with, if it is not the best of the five—imagine that, it's now the *five* codices—then it is surely the second best in terms of preservation. The fading around the edges that we all saw on the copy is less a problem on the original because the medium, the ficus 'paper' if you will, is darker than the other codices, so there was less contrast for the copier to read. But to the naked eye, the peripheral hieroglyphics and images are still easily discernible." He paused and caught his breath. "The only loss of text is in the crumbling on the initial page, and of course, that can be filled in from where it was copied into the Dominguez Codex. So, in every way that matters, it's intact. And it is *beautiful*." Pausing on an emotional note, he shook his head and leaned back in his chair, taking a long pull at his drink.

"Away from the edges the colors are stark and almost fresh, the blues and the reds particularly. The calligraphy and drawing are high style and most certainly all by the same hand. In this sense it is clearly the best of the five, just from an artistic point of view. When you see it, Paul, as a painter you'll know what I mean. Think of the uniqueness of the handwriting of Dürer or Leonardo. It was a master who made this."

"And the weave is correct?" asked Cody.

"Absolutely right. There is no question of its authenticity."

Maya smirked at me.

"The world of Mayan scholarship is about to be severely shaken," he continued. "Consider for a moment the question of style." He placed his hands flat on the table and leaned forward. "Could a forger have taken the art of Mayan calligraphy to a higher level, one almost unknown except in a handful of obscure fragments of stone carving? Not likely, or even doable. To be so inventive within the context of Mayan culture would not be possible within the last 500 years. We don't have that mindset today and it cannot be faked because it's so foreign to us." Recovering himself, he ran his fingers through his hair and began to look more like the Sandoval we had seen yesterday. He adjusted his glasses.

"How about to a Mayan who had an artistic temperament? Someone who grew up in the culture and perhaps felt himself to be an heir to the tradition?" I was thinking of a person like Ramon Xoc from Izamal, the Mayan potter who had beautifully faked the ceramics that got himself and the dealer Tobey Cross killed earlier this year.

"There is more than one problem with that." Sandoval finished his drink and again signaled to the waiter with a gesture that included all our glasses.

"Although fragments of the Mayan language survive in spoken form today in the Yucatán and Chiapas, as well as Guatemala, it is partial at best, and the written language has not been known among the Mayans for hundreds of years. The script in our codex is mid-sixteenth century, just before the onset of cultural deterioration, so the period exactly matches the content. There has never been a Mayan native enrolled in university level Mayan language studies. To produce such a text you would have to be knowledgeable at a level beyond anyone working today, or ever, except for the ancients themselves. And I include myself in that group."

"So you are saying even you would not be able to do it?" asked Maya.

"Yes. Precisely."

"Well, I guess that's out, then," said Barbara, smiling broadly.

"Vincent," I said, "you must have noticed the style thing when you first saw the photocopy."

"Yes, but I didn't want to get too enthusiastic about it until I could check everything else. So I think I may have mentioned it but I didn't dwell on it."

"Then you're ready to publish it once we get possession of it?" asked Barbara.

"I can quickly clear my schedule to get back here to photograph it. What could be more important?"

"How did you find Brisbane?" asked Cody thoughtfully. "I'd like to know who he really is."

"Younger, I guess, than I had imagined, for a serious collector. But friendly enough, cooperative, and of course more than pleased when I said it was genuine. I made him a present of one of the new

Nuprex archival sleeves to keep it in. It'll be absolutely secure against moisture, ultraviolet radiation, insects, anything."

"He didn't happen to elaborate on the ruined hacienda hiding place story, did he?" Cody went on.

Sandoval grinned. "I did raise the issue and he backed right off from that account. He said he had really found the codex there in the house. I could almost believe that. It might have been in the original family for generations. I don't think I've ever seen a more perfect eighteenth century restoration, even in México City. It certainly would make more sense than a ruined hacienda outside of Valladolid." He shook his head.

Cody and Maya both looked at me sharply; a perfect eighteenth century restoration? Sandoval didn't notice.

"Vincent, I know you told Brisbane that you wouldn't tell anyone where you saw the codex. But I wonder whether if I said an address you would do nothing more than shake your head if I was wrong? That wouldn't be telling, would it?" This from Cody. Probably not the first interrogation he'd had a part in.

Sandoval had downed enough margaritas to find the idea appealing. I suspected that if Cody had suggested we should all go skinny-dipping in the hotel pool that would have been OK too.

"Take your best shot," he said, raising one eyebrow. "But only one, now." He leaned back in his chair, folding his arms and smiling at Cody as if he were his most promising archaeology student.

"Cuadrante," said Cody, looking him calmly in the eye. "I believe the number would be 13A." Sandoval did not shake his head, nor did he move in any way, except that his smile vanished.

"You're damn good," he said.

Cody and Maya both looked at me, and both their mouths formed the words "John Schleicher." I nodded when Sandoval took another big swallow of his drink. Barbara was giving us a funny look, but she had the sense to say nothing.

Schleicher was an expatriate with a warrant from New Jersey and a nasty criminal record, who earlier in the year we had suspected in the murder of Tobey Cross. Cody and I had drugged his dog and broken into his house while Maya played lookout in an attempt to find the murder weapon. We found a Glock Nine in his desk, but it didn't match the gun used in the crime. Schleicher never came after us, although he must have known at the time who did it. I assumed then he left us alone because he wanted to keep a low profile and minimize any contacts with the police.

It was chilling to me that now we had crossed paths with him again, and I thought of the two dead *federales*. He was an odd combination; a corrupt and self-indulgent career criminal with independent family means, a sophisticated sense of design and superb taste in collectibles. The only flaw in his taste that I could pinpoint was that he had never bought a Paul Zacher original. He certainly could afford one. Most people could.

Some of us were starting to drift away on the margaritas, so we decided to order *comida*, the mid-afternoon main meal of Méxican custom. The musical trio came in and tuned up. I could smell jasmine in the air. A conversation was going on

among Cody, Barbara, and Sandoval about how to arrange the exchange of money for the codex. The
professor was talking about how to compare the original
closely with the photocopy to make sure there was no
substitution. I didn't follow it because my own view was
that Schleicher/Brisbane was in a position to dictate his
own terms. Maya was gazing off into the garden. I would
have bet twenty centavos she was seeing this whole venture
soon coming to an end. It would be no loss to her. She'd
probably volunteer to help me put my gun into storage.

I was also speculating whether Schleicher, now
that he knew the codex was genuine, would shop the market for a better price, or perhaps boost the asking price
to Barbara. Of course there was always the risk that any
further moves on his part would bring the scrutiny of the
police. I was trying to think like he did now, since I didn't
believe he knew the police were already in this and that
the coffins were piling up, unless he'd had a hand in it. I
decided that the odds favored him going through with the
deal as proposed. He would be out clean with his million
dollars, no one else would be involved, and Barbara was
not likely to do anything to attract attention.

We passed on dessert as Sandoval was trying to
remember the words to some Mixtec song he had once
heard in a cantina in Oaxaca in the seventies. It seemed
like a long shot. It would have been lost on us anyway; none of us spoke any Mixtec. He was in a deeply
sentimental phase at this point as Cody helped him
toward his room. Sandoval had a right to be. He had spent
his whole professional life searching for new insights into
the Mayan culture, and this one had fallen into his lap. He
had not even been wearing his artificial Kmart shoes; he

had done it all in his tasseled Cole Haan loafers.

Barbara picked up the tab. "I wish he hadn't wandered off like that. I wanted to hear more," she said.

"Maybe if we hadn't dawdled on the way?" Maya said.

Outside the valet was polishing the last speck of dust from the Mercedes. He handed me a couple of brown hairs he said were caught in the back door handle. They could have been burro. I opened the rear door for Maya and slid in next to her. Cody sat in front with Barbara.

"You can tell me now, since Vincent is gone," she said, not starting the engine. She had the key in her hand but her hands were in her lap. Her tone was that of someone who has held her tongue for half an hour and was now ready to be back in the loop.

"It's Brisbane," said Maya, leaning forward. "We know who he really is."

"Do I know him?"

Cody turned toward her in his seat. "You may. His name is John Schleicher, and he's local."

"I've heard that name. I think I was going to ask him to one of our parties, but Perry said to pass on him."

"What reason did he give?" I asked. There were many to choose from.

"I can't remember. Maybe Perry never did say exactly why. Sometimes he did that. He knew how to do a quiet blackball. Maybe it was just a wrinkle of his nose, something like that."

"Well, the address that I guessed for the codex meeting is the house of John Schleicher," said Cody. He didn't add how he knew. "I think we might take a drive past there on the way back."

"Why don't you switch with me then, Cody? I want to be a passenger again. Be kind of nice to have a big guy in the driver's seat. Perry could never quite do that part." She put her hand on his arm. Perry had been about five-foot-seven and 140 pounds.

Cody changed places with her, moved the seat back, and eased the car out of the drive. We moved around Juarez Park and down Calle Nueva toward Ancha de San Antonio. In the tall trees above, dozens of white egrets squawked as they aimed their droppings at the tourists. It was nearly 4:30. As with many cars in México, all the windows except the windshield were darkly tinted. From the Ancha, Cody turned right on Pila Seca, a street that two blocks later became Cuadrante. Schleicher's house was on the far corner on the passenger side. Cody slowed.

"Activity ahead," he said. "I count two *federales* cars and two local police pickups." The San Miguel uniform police were now using small pickups in their patrol duties. As we cruised past Cuadrante 13A two cops in olive uniforms emerged from the carriage gate carrying the bloated body of a dog between them. A cloud of angry flies followed. The dog's upper chest area was black with crusted blood. When they placed the body in the rear of one of the pickups the feet stood up stiffly above the side. None of the *federales* were in view. Barbara at first put her hands over her face, then pulled them away.

"Wait! Is this the house?" she asked. "Stop, stop, pull over. I need to know what's happened here."

"Sorry, Barbara," Cody said. "We can't afford to mix in this. You're looking at an organization that's full of leaks." The chauffeur had taken charge. He maintained the same casual pace past the house until we reached the corner, then placed his hand on Barbara's knee. "We need to stay away from them. Let's sort this out at your house. We have to keep you out of this. Remember the two dead *federales*." I don't think the police noticed us passing. There's more than one big Mercedes in San Miguel, although not many as fast.

As the car moved up the hill toward Los Balcones, we all must have been going through the same series of questions. Barbara made no protest at being overruled, which surprised me. I had always thought that, like Maya, she didn't take instruction well. No one else spoke either. When we got out of the car on Barbara's drive Maya whispered to me, "That is the dog you drugged before when you searched Schleicher's house in February, isn't it?"

I nodded. "It wasn't the dog's fault; just a bad choice of owners."

Although we were already too sober, Barbara made coffee and we sat around her great room. I tried to study my Yucátan picture over the grand piano but I was too distracted to see it.

"So John Schleicher is dead then?" asked Barbara when she sat down. She hadn't said anything while she made the coffee.

"That would be my best guess," I said. "That dog was his first line of defense."

"And if he's dead..."

"Right. The codex is gone," said Maya, not sounding at all sad. She looked at me and then lowered her eyes.

"What have we gotten ourselves into?" Barbara

was shaking her head. "All that man wanted to do was sell us the codex. I guess I won't be liquidating the 61,000 shares of Watt Industries now."

"Anyone else thinking what I'm thinking?" asked Cody.

I looked at his eyes, then I saw it. "Sandoval," I said, "but it's not. I don't buy it."

Maya was shaking her head. "It's not Sandoval," she said, "not even for a million dollars."

"No way," said Barbara. "No way."

"OK, just a thought," said Cody. "I was ticking off suspects in my mind."

The name of Jason Schwartz crossed my mind, but I didn't say it.

CHAPTER ELEVEN
JASON SCHWARTZ

E arlier that day, Jason Schwartz, following the authentication of the codex, had watched through the narrowly open slats of a window shutter as Professor Sandoval skipped down the front steps of the mansion, stumbled, recovered his balance and headed over the cobblestone sidewalk and around the corner out of sight. Schwartz waited until he thought the professor was a block down the side street, then he gathered up his satchel, slid the codex inside, and walked out the front door, locking it behind him. Whistling a Fleetwood Mac tune, he passed briskly down Cuadrante, continued as it changed to Pila Seca, and then turned left toward the San Antonio neighborhood and his room at the Lopez house.

At the first trash can on Ancha de San Antonio he paused briefly and dropped Schleicher's key ring inside. No sense being a litterbug. After all, he was a guest in México, and it was a country where manners counted. Turning right off the main street he pulled out his cell phone and hit the speed dial.

The man who answered said, "Security."

"It's Schwartz," he said. "I've got it and it's authenticated. I'll be leaving San Miguel in half an hour." He flipped the phone closed and slid it back in his pocket.

Back at the house of Juan Lopez he pulled together his few belongings and tucked them into a zippered black canvas bag. Looking around the room for anything he might have missed, he glanced at the mirror on the wall above the bed and realized he was still wearing Schleicher's tweed sport coat. Maybe he was a little rattled after all, but he was only a road trip away now. Once in the car he could chill a bit. He pulled off the jacket, searched all the pockets and came up with nothing. He turned it inside out and then stuffed it into a covered trash can behind the house.

Passing down the hallway toward the front door he ran into Señora Lopez. He explained that he was leaving and pressed the key into her palm.

"But Señor, you have paid me for two more days!" she said.

He thanked her for her hospitality and said he needed no refund, going through the formal gestures of politeness that lubricate social interaction in México. On Palma, the street in front of the house, he jumped into his three year old Nissan and threw the canvas bag into the back seat. The satchel he placed on the seat next to him. Back on Ancha de San Antonio he turned off on Codo and went around the park and up to Correo, then turned east and went up the hill through the arches to the *libramiento*. At the *glorieta* he picked up the Querétaro road, feeling like he was home free.

Leaving San Miguel behind, he reached into his glove compartment and pulled out a handful of tapes. He settled on Fleetwood Mac's *Rumors*, one of his inexhaustible favorites, and cranked up the volume on *Go Your Own Way*. He was. He had been ever since the days of Humans First in Berkeley. Mostly a bunch of damn naive saps, but a few of them had their hearts in the right place. Stevie Nicks was singing her heart out as he passed the spot where he had surprised the two federal officers and killed them. You do what it takes, he thought. No regrets. No one can keep you from going your own way except yourself.

After an hour he approached Querétaro. He had known he was low on gas when he left San Miguel, but he hadn't wanted to fill up before he left town and possibly be remembered by one of the attendants. He picked a Pemex at random and rolled up to the pump. His plan was to continue down Highway 57 until it branched off below Querétaro, and then take Highway 55. In this way he would go south toward Toluca and avoid the traffic nightmare of México City, ultimately passing through Cuernavaca and then Oaxaca on his way back to Chiapas.

Schwartz entered the station to buy bottled water, snacks, and gum for the trip. From the car at the next pump a teenage boy walked over and looked closely at the Nissan. He called his father over. They both knelt and looked at the peculiar splashy red stain across the bumper and grill. It was dry to the touch, but when the father leaned over and sniffed it he thought it clearly smelled like blood. Dog blood, of course, smells much like human blood, except to dogs. A moment later Jason Schwartz emerged from the Pemex store and entered the Nissan. The father and son were back in their car already and the father was on his cell phone calling the Highway Police.

Having achieved two of the essential road trip

conditions, a full tank and an empty bladder, Schwartz now pulled back onto the highway and went for two more. He reached into the glove compartment and pulled out an obscenely fat joint of his own cultivation from a small and obscure patch on a special hill up in the Chiapas highlands, and licked it all over. Just like a native girl, he thought. Maybe like that Maya chick. And hadn't she been flirting with him just a little? Maybe more than a little? He stuck one end in his mouth and lit the other with the car's cigarette lighter. He punched the play button of the sound system again as he blew out the most enormous drag he had had in days, since he didn't smoke when he worked. The Cause demanded discipline. The tune that came on was *Dreams*. Where was Stevie Nicks when he needed her? Of course, she was old enough to be his mother, but on these old cuts she was forever young. Schwartz was too young to remember the sixties, but he was a big fan. With Stevie singing he felt he had been there.

And yes, he had seen her in some of those recent concerts, even on Méxican TV, and yes, she was a little porky, OK? And frankly, Mick Fleetwood was more than a little old. But her voice was still there and Mick could still play. What the hell. Jason was home free. He stubbed out the extreme end of the joint between his fingers and swallowed it. Damn, he was good. He gave the gas pedal a little extra push. That collector had never said a word. Not that anything could have saved him; he was history the moment he opened the door.

Now he was below Querétaro on Highway 55, a two-lane highway with no median. Looking in the rear view mirror for the first time in a while he saw a Highway Police vehicle four cars back. Stevie Nicks was still reassuring him, so this was not at first an issue. It was only when the Fleetwood Mac tape reached the end of its influence and began to rewind that Jason Schwartz decided that it was time for action. He'd see how good the highway cop was, after all, fuzz was only fuzz whether in Berkeley or Querétero.

The speed limit on this stretch of road was 100 kilometers per hour and rarely observed, and now Schwartz, his pace slowed by the grass, realized he was going only eighty-five. He pulled away from the pack. The highway cruiser responded by moving from four cars back to three, and then to two.

Ahead, a pair of double-trailer trucks were moving significantly more slowly than he was, and a line of traffic was approaching from the opposite direction. He slammed the accelerator to the floor and pulled out around the two trucks ahead, just slipping back into his lane ahead of them as the approaching traffic arrived. Now, with the trucks between him and the Highway Police, he sped off into the hills, searching for an exit. In less than a mile he found an exit onto a smaller paved road and flew off Highway 55. He did not know whether the cop had seen him leave or not.

The road ran straight for a couple of kilometers, dividing plowed fields from scrubby pastureland. As he came over a slight rise he suddenly saw the highway cruiser top the hill behind him, gaining ground. Ahead the road rose again into a run of climbing turns. Schwartz sped up and disappeared around a bend. There he accelerated through another half dozen curves and the cruiser was long out of view. He saw a dirt road running off to the right, flanked by a stand of trees, and swerved sharply onto it, going faster than he should have, but his judgment was no longer quite perfect, and his reaction time might have lost something as well. He was reaching for another Fleetwood Mac tape when three gaunt cattle moved out of the trees and crossed single file in front of him. He skidded to the right, thinking to slip behind the last one, but his tires didn't hold on the gravel and he slid sideways through a curve and over a sharp drop of thirty feet, rolling over twice and landing upside down. It was probably the initial impact that broke his neck.

Less than two minutes later the highway cruiser passed the spot where Schwartz had left the road and his life. He continued past, noticing nothing of interest. By that time the small dust cloud raised by his skidding tires had mostly dispersed. Twenty minutes later the highway cruiser turned around and came back toward Highway 55, still finding no trace of the Nissan. Reluctantly, the cop gave up the chase. It may not have been the guy with blood on his grill. He had never seen the front of the car.

Two hours later a pair of *vaqueros* were working the area rounding up stray cattle, three of which had caused the death of Jason Schwartz. They did not find the culpable cows, which had fled in alarm as the Nissan slid past them on its way over the drop-off on the hillside, but they did encounter the inverted car. Schwartz had enjoyed the thrill that driving at speed without a seat belt brought, and he was now lying twisted in an unsurvivable contour on the headliner of the car. The *vaqueros* could tell without touching him that Jason would no longer be needing the contents of his wallet, nearly 4500 pesos, which they split evenly between them, nor would he miss those of his satchel. They pulled out the gun first, with two boxes of ammunition, then the codex in its sleek Nuprex archival container. The black ski mask, the garrote, the pair of white cotton gloves, and notebooks they left in the car. From the glove compartment they salvaged an impressive bag of marijuana and two books of papers. They missed his cell phone. It had flown out of his pocket and was now beneath his body, which they did not care to touch again. Searching the black canvas bag turned up nothing but clothes, shoes, and toiletries, which they took with them. Nothing goes to waste in México. Since the man's wallet was now empty and he was beyond help, they said nothing when they got back to the farmhouse after hiding the contents of the satchel in the tool shed. After dinner they went out in a field and each smoked a joint. The marijuana was better than they'd had in months; it had been a good day. They could always go back tomorrow and find the cows.

CHAPTER TWELVE

Cody sipped his coffee while Professor Sandoval was still sleeping off his jubilation in the sumptuous room at the Sierra Nevada. "It's got to be Schwartz," Long rays of late afternoon sun flooded the great room of Casa Watt. "The police wouldn't have had to kill the dog if they knew Schleicher had the codex. They'd have just gone in through the front door and taken it away from him. And did you see the dog's body?"

"What?" asked Maya. "All the blood on the chest?"

"Not just that. It was bloated and the legs were stiff. That dog's been dead at least twenty-four hours. Sandoval met someone he only thought was Arthur Brisbane at noon."

"Of course it fits that Brisbane was really that snake Schleicher. And if the dog's been dead for twenty-four hours?" I asked, but it was not a question.

"Exactly. Then Schleicher's most likely been dead just as long. It's a small loss for San Miguel," said Cody.

"But a very big one for me," said Barbara, staring into her cup as if it might suggest what to do next.

"So the professor met with Schwartz instead of Schleicher?" said Maya, putting the pieces together.

Cody turned to her. "He must have. Sandoval didn't know Schleicher. He had no expectations of what he might look like. I think Schwartz could have pulled it off. With those goggle-eyed glasses he could easily look like an academic, especially if he changed out of the lace-up boots. Now he has his authentication and the codex to boot."

"And a brand new Nuprex archival container for it," I said.

Barbara got up and went into the kitchen. In a moment she reappeared. "Sandoval doesn't answer in his room."

"Probably still dreaming of publication and glory," I said.

"And we're running about a step and a half behind," said Cody, biting his lower lip. "Not where I'd like to be."

"So how did Schwartz find out he was coming?" Barbara refilled the cups.

"The same way he got in on this to begin with. He's got a source in the federal police and they must have been tapping Sandoval's phone," I said. "Once they saw that photocopy we mailed him, they've been looking over his shoulder every step."

"But who is Schwartz, really?" She set the coffee carafe down on the tray and sat down again. "Why is he mixing in this?"

"Just an old campus radical. An unrepentant admirer of the sixties. He plays a lot of Jimi Hendrix and Janis Joplin, I would guess. Probably the Dead as well." Cody said.

"But not an academic, I think," said Maya. "Even though he might be able to pass for one. What use would he have for the codex? Could he sell it to finance some group here?"

"Then he might still be calling me!" said Barbara instantly. Her face brightened, as if she was still going to go to the prom after all and would get to wear her new dress. The dead were piling up but she was still dealing with this at the acquisition level.

"I don't think you'd want to deal with him, even if he knew you were involved, and I hope he doesn't," I said.

"Seems like the next move belongs to Jason Schwartz," said Cody, "but I don't have any idea what it's going to be."

We had come to a dead end. This was certainly not Barbara's first disappointment; I had given her a few myself. She was not taking it well. Grimly, she drove us back down the hill to Quebrada, and then dropped Cody at his car.

I had the desk at the Sierra Nevada ring Sandoval's room every hour or so. It was nearly eight o'clock when I finally connected.

"How are you feeling? I asked.

"Mentally wonderful, but physically I'm a little foggy. Has Brisbane called?"

"Not yet, but that's what I wanted to talk to you about. Could you describe him to me?"

"Of course. He was a youngish fellow, about your age, maybe five-ten, 180 pounds or so. Sandy colored hair, brushed straight back. Glasses. Nice tweed jacket, by the way."

"Mustache?"

"No, but he had one of those scruffy beards, you know, like they wear now."

"Vincent, the man you spoke with was not

Arthur Brisbane." With the condition Sandoval must be in I didn't feel like getting into the part about the real Brisbane being a murderer on death row in California. "You were in Brisbane's house but I think he may have been murdered earlier. The man you spoke with is the former campus radical I mentioned to you before, named Jason Schwartz. I don't know what his purpose is, but I do know he wants the codex badly and he has probably killed more people than just Brisbane trying to get it."

Silence. Then Sandoval said in a small voice, "Well, he's got it then. We didn't even have a chance to photograph it." His world had crashed into the same small pile of fragments as Barbara's.

"I don't know how much danger you or any of us may be in now that he has it, but I would take extreme care for a while. I'll keep you posted."

Maya was standing behind me when I hung up. "Surely this is all the killing now, right? They have the codex."

"Of course it is," I said, but I wasn't as certain as I tried to sound.

CHAPTER THIRTEEN

Barbara's voice was low and edgy with panic on the phone. It was the afternoon of the next day, Sunday, about 5:30. Maya and I had been talking about dinner without doing anything about it.

"Someone's been in here," Barbara was saying. "What should I do?"

"Get out of there right now," I said. "Get in the car and drive around until you hear from me. Leave the front door unlocked. Cody and I will be there in a couple of minutes. If it's Schwartz he may try to kill you just because you know about the codex." I couldn't think how he could know about her unless he'd forced Schleicher to tell him before he killed him.

I cut off her call and dialed Cody while Maya listened with her hands on her hips, then I ran for the artmobile. It took me longer than I wanted to get there, and parking outside Barbara's wall, I drew my gun and slipped into the driveway. There was no way to come up on the house invisibly, but hugging the hedge line helped as I approached the doorway. I saw no movement in any of the front windows.

When I turned the door handle and pushed it open a few inches there was no response. As I stepped inside a prickly sensation ran up and down my back. If it was Schwartz I would shoot first; I didn't relish killing anyone, but I knew he wouldn't give me a chance after what he'd done. I had gone a few steps inside the foyer and opened the door of the powder room when I heard a soft footstep behind me. I lunged to the left but before I could get out of range and turn a hand clamped into my shoulder.

"Let's stay together," Cody whispered, "take it room by room."

"Thanks a lot," I said. "I could have killed you."

"Right," he said. "I'll remember that next time."

The great room took up the largest part of the first floor, and it was clear that no one was there. On the left, a family room with a large flat-screen television also faced the garden. It had a more intimate scale, with a *boveda* ceiling. The drapes were drawn but there was still enough light to see it was empty.

On the other side of the great room the dining room also bordered the veranda, and then came the kitchen complex, with a break room and bathroom for staff, and a service staircase going to the second floor and down to the garden level below us. Again nothing. If Schwartz were searching for something, he would most likely be upstairs—but what did he want if he already had the codex?

Carpeting muffled the service stairway, so noise was not a problem going up, but the 200-year-old parquet flooring on the second floor was not going to allow us to pass without an audible protest. The doorway at the top of the staff staircase was partly open—not the way Barbara would have left it, had she not abandoned the house in a hurry. It was also not a staircase she would ever use herself.

Cody pushed the door open all the way. There

was no one in view, so we moved quickly into the study, which was the first door on the right. The powder room, with its door neatly concealed in the paneling, was empty. Cody checked the desk while I made the rounds of the display cases; nothing seemed to be disturbed. I pulled out the drawers of Barbara's rosewood case for small items. Each drawer was full.

Next to the study was a tiled full bath, also empty. Cody looked at me and we both shrugged.

The master bedroom was palatial in extent, paneled in cream-colored wood with elaborate plaster tracery on the ceiling. There were no dressers or armoires, which made me scratch my head for a moment. Two floor-length windows gave a view to the west of the garden below and the sloping hillside beyond with tiled rooftops cascading toward *centro*. Next to the master bathroom one of the panels protruded slightly from the wall and I pulled it outward. It concealed a large dressing room with a complete range of built-ins. Two drawers were open; one contained row upon row of panties, now in considerable disarray, and the smaller contained money. Right, Barbara kept a drawer full of cash, both Méxican and American, in her dressing room.

"Wouldn't you take this money if you broke in here?" I whispered to Cody.

"Not if you were Schwartz."

Schwartz would be too pure, I guess. I wondered about the panties, though. Nothing else seemed odd in the master bedroom, and we moved on to the string of bedrooms facing the hallway. We went through each one, with the attendant bathrooms. No one was on the second floor but us.

"One more thing," I said as we stood at the door of the last bedroom. "The servants' stairway goes down as well as up. If he were on the lower level he could have gotten out by now."

We flew down both flights to the lowest level. It held only a service area for the garden and pool, and occupied a small fraction of the footprint of the whole house. We passed through the stacks of hoses, water chemicals for the pool, garden implements and fertilizer bags and found no one. The door to the garden was locked.

I called Barbara and said we were finished and had found no one. We were at the front door when she pulled up five minutes later, wearing her lime green capris and a white halter top with tasteful cleavage. I don't think she went anywhere without cleavage. Her earrings were gold filigree jade droplets today, a color of jade that closely matched her capris, which laced up the front instead of zipping. A nice touch. I wondered if she had a bodice with the same feature, although if she had she would have already showed it to me.

She came running up the steps.

"You weren't tossed," said Cody.

"Tossed?" She looked confused.

"You didn't see my place after the *federales* visited me," I said.

"No, but I paid for it."

"If you didn't see it you didn't get your money's worth. This wasn't anything like it."

"It looked like the only thing that was disturbed was the underwear and the money," said Cody.

"That's all I saw too. What would anyone want with my panties? Come back in and we'll have a drink

while we talk about this. But you're sure no one was here?"
Now that she was stressed she had more of an Alabama
accent.

"No."

"But it could have been Schwartz, right?"

Cody and I looked at each other.

"Barbara, what made you think someone was
here? Did you hear someone?"

"No, it was just the two open drawers, I guess. I
never leave them like that."

"And you normally have a drawer full of money?"
I asked.

"Sure. I have to keep it somewhere, don't I?"

"Is any missing?"

"I don't know."

"You could count it."

"That wouldn't tell me anything. I never know
how much is in there. If it isn't full, or nearly full, I just
add some more." She set the drinks down.

"How about the panties?"

"Well, they were all messed up. I always keep
them in seven rows, all folded."

"One for each day of the week?" I asked.

"No, silly. That's just how many rows the drawer
holds. And they aren't embroidered with the weekdays
either, as I'm sure you noticed. How humiliating! I feel
like throwing them all away." She covered her face.

"Well, I saw a couple pair, at least, that you should
probably keep," I said. "They were hot." Cody put his
elbow in my ribs and shoved hard.

"Barbara," he said, "I've seen more than a few of
these things and this was not Jason Schwartz. This is what

we used to call an opportunity break in. Someone got in who was not looking for anything in particular, just looking. I wouldn't lose any sleep over it."

"Really? I've still been hoping Schwartz might contact me. Not this way, of course."

"I think it's more likely that we've seen the last of him," Cody said. "Maybe he's got a higher bidder for the codex, or maybe he never had any intention to sell it. It could be he's like the people who would steal a well-known picture that they could never resell or show to anyone else. It's for their own private enjoyment."

"With three people dead?" I said. "I think he's an ideologue. He's had more than twenty-four hours to contact Barbara. She's practically waiting by the phone with bags, or maybe drawers, full of money, and nothing happens. But he hasn't called, has he?"

"No. I would've let you know immediately. I'm not going to have any secrets about this."

"So I don't think he's going to call," I said. "And somehow I don't think a business proposition merits this kind of mayhem. This has more the mark of an idealist."

"The idealists will kill us all," said Cody.

"Great," said Barbara. She was starting to sound like Maya.

"I can't remember where I heard that, but Paul might be right," Cody went on. "In my experience money-based crimes don't generate as much bloodshed as crimes of passion or politics or religion. And it could be true that the bloodiest crimes come from the most intense idealism. Look at 9/11. No money involved. All pain, and no financial gain, only the glory of bringing down the World Trade Center. And 3,000 dead."

"We need to give him more time, though," said Barbara, "I mean, to call. It still could be just business and not ideology, couldn't it?"

"There's another aspect of this that we need to consider," said Cody. "Schwartz must have figured out by now that all we have to do is talk once to Sandoval and we'll know that Schwartz took Schleicher's place. That means we also know, or will soon discover, that Schleicher is dead, even though no body has appeared. So this is reason number two for Jason to come after us. But logically, he should have called Barbara right away. He had the authentication and so did she, so waiting would only increase the likelihood that she knew about Schleicher. The best plan would have been to call yesterday. I think Schwartz is gone, but for another day or so, let's act as if he weren't. Paul, you'll need to keep wearing the gun."

"I searched my wardrobe earlier for big shirts. I've got three I can wear over it." Today I was wearing a Tommy Bahama with silver and gray leaves over a yellow background, and a pair of well-worn jeans.

Cody turned to Barbara. "I'm assuming you have a security system?"

"The best; Perry only had the best of everything. You should have seen his funeral. When I contacted the mortuary in Houston I found out that he had it all planned. Even the music."

Cody didn't want to go there. "Are you sure you set it before you left?"

"I'm very careful. I didn't set it just now when I left to drive around, but I'm sure I set it when I went out earlier."

"Does that say anything to you?" I asked.

"What? Inside job? My cleaning woman and the gardener both know the code for it, but they've both been with me for years."

"Well, I think you should stay inside for another day," said Cody. "You'll want to be near the phone anyway. Is the Mercedes armor plated?"

"No," she said, looking surprised. "Perry didn't have any enemies."

I was at the point of saying, "None that lived," but I bit my tongue. Sometimes restraint is good.

"And Paul, if you and Maya can stay in tomorrow, maybe you should. If you have to go out, don't let Maya go alone. Stay armed. I'll be careful myself, but I don't think he knows where I live. Your Quebrada address he already had, of course, from the package we sent to Sandoval. Going to your gallery was just a ruse, aside from needing an introduction to you from Ramon."

"And after tomorrow?" I asked. "We can go back to just *living*? Or not?"

"We can't be sure, but my best guess is that he's gone if he hasn't contacted us by then. It would mean that he doesn't care whether we know he killed Schleicher, and he doesn't want the million dollars."

"My point exactly," I said. "Then we'll know he's an ideologue. Think of his background; his training was not as a Mafia runner or a street corner drug dealer or a carjacker; he was a campus radical. Like you said, the idealists will kill us all."

I knew Maya was sitting at home wishing this would be over soon. Effective risk management had been out of reach for her lately. We had three people dead; but that seemed about right for these things, judging from the last time I had played detective. We didn't have the resolution we wanted, but all of us were still alive. None of us had even been shot at. But at bottom, I wanted the same return to normalcy that Maya did.

"You know," I said, "I'm dying here. I've got to be painting again." I looked at Barbara. "Maybe we could finish your picture?" She smiled for the first time.

"How about Tuesday morning? We can be out and about then. What kind of makeup should I wear?"

"Anything. We're down to legs, feet, and background."

"Is the toe color all right?" She stretched her ankles out. Her toenails were coral.

"Perfect." I had already changed it anyway. Color design always trumps reality, which is not my favorite thing anyway, even in life.

Cody stopped me on the drive as I was getting into the artmobile. "I didn't want to spook her, but I think this was an inside job, probably one of the staff. I tend to agree that she didn't forget the alarm, it doesn't seem like her."

"But is she safe now?"

"This guy seems more sneaky than dangerous, but whoever he is, he's still around and it looks like he has the code to the security system."

"She could change the code easily enough, right?" I said.

"Sure, but if it's a staff problem, she's going to give it out to them again anyway."

CHAPTER 14

Monday passed without any disasters. Maya poked at her research notes, trying to recast them into a form closer to what Professor Wainwright could use in his book, or what she thought he should. Since she had finished her own book, she found herself more critical of the work of others. The phone did not ring. We had enough food on hand so that neither of us had to go out. Finally Barbara called just before 9 in the evening to say that she had not heard from Schwartz and to confirm her arrival at 8 the next morning. I hoped that meant it was over. At about eleven o'clock I came out of the bathroom to find Maya sitting on the bed, wearing her Liga Méxicana *fútbol* jersey. I had sensed that something was brewing all day. She had been hitting the keys too hard on her laptop as she worked, and she hadn't had much to say.

"I want to ask you a question," she said. "Why do you get involved in these things? And don't tell me it's because there's no other private detective in San Miguel. This town's gotten along without one for almost 500 years."

"Well, if you remember, it started in February because you asked me to help Marisol when Tobey was murdered. I'm not dodging your question, but I think you had something to do with it."

"OK, I can see that. But why this time? You realize that I walk around remembering that I ended up killing someone before, and I don't like it. I just wanted to be an academic. I was happy with that. Now three people are dead this time." She folded her arms over the number 16 on her chest.

"In the beginning it looked like a simple matter of getting the codex evaluated and helping Barbara with some security during the transaction. You know that."

"But what do *you* want? Isn't being a painter enough for you? You're good; a lot of people would like to paint like you do."

I sat down in a chair across from her, thinking about that.

"You might laugh at this, but maybe it's a little bit of public service. It could be that painting isn't enough."

"The only public service I can see in this is population control, and there are more subtle ways to do that. I don't like the way this is going. I sat around all day today, and yes, I was working, but knowing I couldn't go out irritated me. I want my freedom, the freedom to not be shot at. If you stay away from the border towns, México is not a dangerous place, in spite of what they say all the time on the American news."

"But isn't it interesting to be part of these cases? Think of all the dullards you could be with."

"It's interesting like a nightmare. It can be riveting, but I'm still glad when it's over, and I never look forward to the next one."

Maya slept that night with her back to me, and I never once put my hand on her bare butt. I hadn't been able to give her the answers she was looking for; I didn't have them myself. The public service idea translated as giving something back, but maybe what I was giving back wasn't wanted.

✠✠✠

In the morning I was already in the studio setting up when Maya let Barbara in. She had her Chinese robe with her and as she headed for the dressing screen at the end of the room, I said, "You can stay partly dressed if you want, I only need your legs bare."

"That's all right. I'd rather be naked. It would feel funny to be laying here in my underwear, like someone had walked in on me dressing or was looking up my skirt. Not quite decent, you know? Isn't naked more honest? Maybe it's just because of that break-in. Anyway, I don't want to be half dressed."

"Like it makes a statement? I'm glad you're telling me these things. I think a lot of men wouldn't have guessed that. But maybe you're right; there's something odd about it. Nude is more decent. At least it looks intentional."

She finished changing and then came over to the daybed and pulled off the robe.

I didn't try to analyze that any further, but kept busy mixing pigments. It's what I do best. Maybe I should stick to it. "Remember to lift your left leg a bit." The rest of her thighs and her calves were easy. Toes are a little harder, but less so than hands. I boosted the coral toenail polish into a more intense red and it worked fine.

When I was finished with her body I didn't need her anymore to do the background, but just having a model in the studio was reassuring after so much down time, and she was simply beautiful, even as landscape. "Is something wrong today?" she asked.

"You haven't tried to seduce me. I was getting used to it." I didn't want to get into the detective controversy with her, since she had pulled me into this.

"Maybe I've had too many lectures on art studio protocol. Or it could be I'm a little depressed. I just can't stand the thought of that bastard Schwartz running off with the codex. I was hoping I'd be raising funds for the purchase yesterday, so I'm not at my best. But I do still want you, darlin', in the worst way. Nothing has changed."

"I'm glad. It keeps me on my toes. Anyway, I'm wondering now how to title this picture. You didn't think to go back to your maiden name when Perry died?"

"Porter? Was that an option? I didn't think about it. Seems like widows usually keep their husband's name. Anyway, I think I prefer Watt."

I was glad her face was already finished; her present expression was not what I would have wanted. I worked until about one o'clock and Barbara left. There was more to do on the background, but I was happy with what I had and wanted to save some for tomorrow. After that I'd have to figure out what came next.

When Maya returned from the market later in the afternoon she had picked up a copy of Atención, our local bi-lingual paper.

She slapped it down on the table in front of me, as if it was something that made her point, and indicated an article at the bottom of page one. The strangled body of an American had been found in Atotonilco on Monday. It was identified as John

Schleicher, a wealthy *gringo* from San Miguel. The story didn't actually use the word *gringo*, although it was so commonly in use it no longer carried any negative overtones. Licenciado Rodriguez was investigating. I knew who would be pounding on my door next. This wasn't going to be over for me for a while. At least I was painting again.

The next morning I was again at work on the background of Barbara's picture. It was not one of the challenging parts, which was good since I was plagued by the thought in the back of my mind that I was about to be interrupted, always a distraction in painting. Cody and I had spoken the night before, and he was up to speed on the discovery of Schleicher. We both thought our risk had lowered as time passed, but it made sense to keep wearing the guns.

It must have been around ten, when the doorbell rang. With relief, Maya had gone to the archive in Dolores Hidalgo to work and I figured I might as well answer it. Otherwise they'd only come back at another inopportune time. I was right. It was Licenciado Rodriguez and Tomas Leon.

"Señores," I said, "please come in. I was expecting you." The Spanish word for expect or await also means hope for, so there was a delicate ambiguity in the phrase. It made it seem like I was more interested in talking to them than I really was, which was fine, since I couldn't turn them away.

"Thank you. I hope we do not interrupt your work," said Rodriguez. Leon was silent.

"I was just finishing up." I had one corner yet to do. "Please take a seat."

"You have heard about the misfortune of Señor

John Schleicher?" said Leon.

"Yes. I saw it in the newspaper yesterday. He was found in Atotonilco?"

"Yes. But it is thought he was not there to make a pilgrimage. Excuse me; I see you are wearing a gun today. May I look at it?" asked Rodriguez.

"Of course." I pulled it out and laid it on the table in front of him. He spun the chamber and then smelled the barrel. I knew it had been years since it had been fired, probably since Cody had last killed someone.

"I understood from the newspaper that Schleicher had been strangled," I said.

"This is true, but his dog was shot, we think on Friday, the same day that Señor Schleicher died."

"Was the dog shot with a .38 like this one?"

"No. It was a nine millimeter. But once again," said Leon, "we would like to be asking the questions. Did you know him well?"

"Not at all. I have heard he kept to himself."

"Kept to himself?" He looked blankly at Rodriguez. I was not sure I had used the correct Spanish idiom for this.

"Avoided other people. He did not go to the usual parties. He stayed away from the house tours and the English Library. We did not see him at Tio Lucas or the Santa Monica, for example. I never watched him try to pick up women at Harry's."

"But you would have known him if you saw him?"

"No, I guess not."

"So he may have been in those places without you knowing it?"

"I suppose." I felt we were going in circles. "You

might ask the waiters." Ever helpful.

"Possibly," said Rodriguez.

Leon leaned forward across the dining room table. "Last time we spoke you had recently had a visit from Señor Jason Schwartz. The night before, I believe. It was the same night two *federales* were killed on the *libramiento*."

"Yes, and since then I have been watching for him because I think you are correct in suspecting that he might have killed them. I'm wearing the gun for that reason. I have had trouble here before, as you know."

"Of course. This house is what we now call a 'hot spot,'" said Rodriguez. "It is marked with a colored pin on our city map." He looked pleased with himself for coming up with the English phrase. Leon glared at him.

"We feel you are somehow involved in this," said Leon. "But we do not know exactly how."

"I don't know how I can help you." I was still determined to keep Barbara out of this.

"You could perhaps begin by telling us why your name was on the return address of a certain parcel that was sent to Dr. Vincent Sandoval in México City. A parcel that was observed to contain a photocopy of a very valuable Mayan codex, should it prove to be genuine."

Observed by whom, I wondered. Of course, I should have seen this coming; it was only a matter of time. "The copy was sent to me by a man named Arthur Brisbane. He wanted me to help him discover if it was genuine, as you suggest." I hoped this would fly.

They exchanged blank glances. "Do you know this Arthur Brisbane?"

"No."

"Do you still have the envelope he used to send it to you?"

"No."

"Do you remember the return address?" Leon said. "For example, is he living here in San Miguel?"

"I don't recall. It could be there was no address. He called me to ask if I would help him authenticate it and said he would call back later. He didn't leave a number. I supposed he didn't want me to be able to find him because he thought the codex might be valuable. Wait, I think the envelope had a return address from Querétaro." I had not rehearsed these answers and felt I was getting in deeper now.

"Why would he send it to you?" continued Leon. "You are now an expert in documents of this kind? Or is it possible that Arthur Brisbane was only a name being used by John Schleicher?"

"As you know," I said calmly, careful with each word, "I have performed investigative tasks in the past. Perhaps Brisbane knew of this as well." This sounded lame, even to myself. "As for whether he was really John Schleicher, I guess it's possible. I wouldn't have recognized his voice and I had never heard of an Arthur Brisbane in the gringo community, but then, I don't know all of them."

"Would Jason Schwartz have known of this?"

"It appears so. When he came to dinner here he was very interested in what I might know about Mayan antiques. He asked if I was a collector."

"But you are not?"

"No. Painters cannot afford such things."

"I am now going to tell you something else that

has just come to our attention," said Leon. "The body of Señor Jason Schwartz was found last evening some distance south of Querétaro. He was killed from an automobile wreck and had been dead since several days. His possessions in the car contained no money, so we think someone else had discovered him first. There was no gun either, but there was a black ski mask and a garrote and a pair of white gloves. The garrote has traces of what appears to be blood and possibly human skin tissue. It is in our laboratory now."

It was now time for my eyebrows to go up and as they did a wave of relief came over me.

"There were other cars involved in the wreck?" I asked.

"No. He went off the road. So now there are four people dead in this matter, although we think there is no crime involved in this last event. Señor Schwartz was trying to escape the Highway Police when he crashed. A man at a gas station had reported him to have blood on his car and called the police. We have tested the blood and it was found to be dog blood, of a similar type to the dog found dead at the home of John Schleicher. We also think that it was this garrote that was used to kill Señor Schleicher. I only tell you this so that you may be more relaxed now."

"Thank you," I said. Leon smiled for the first time. It was not an icebreaker, but you have to start somewhere. I smiled too, but then I realized that the codex had now disappeared more completely than when Schwartz had it. It looked like a zero-sum game.

"So perhaps you can put away the gun, but there is more. Right now we can find no trace of the codex, but it was here in San Miguel somewhere, was it not?" Leon put on a hopeful look as he pretended to look around the room. "Because a Dr. Vincent Sandoval came to look at it. Yes, we know this too. We have his messages from the Sierra Nevada. He was to examine the codex on Saturday. This is also the day after we think John Schleicher died, as well as the dog, of course."

"I can tell you honestly that I've never seen the codex," I said. "But I know Professor Sandoval found the codex to be genuine because he told me so. You can ask him about it yourself. I think it's impossible, however, that he killed Schleicher. He's a highly respected archaeologist." Damn. Every time I opened my mouth I told them more. I'd be confessing to all the murders myself next. Maybe Cody could brief me on keeping my mouth shut in front of cops.

"And we will ask him in due course, but thank you for letting us know this. It is important that we find the codex now before others can find it. I do not wish to say too much, but this is not merely about possessing a document of great value, which of course, many would wish to do. It is a matter of national security at the highest level. I cannot say more than this."

The old national security argument. I wondered if Leon remembered Nixon and Watergate. Of course, he would have been a child at the time; he was not much older than I was. You never knew how much play these things got in México.

"I think there is more you could tell us, if you wished," he went on. "But you are not under suspicion for any of these crimes; I only hope you will change your mind and help us in the future. I have nothing else to add. Rodriguez?"

Rodriguez shook his head. "I only would advise you to remain watchful. We have no reason to think you have the codex; it may have been with Jason Schwartz. But soon I think there will be people looking for it again, possibly more dangerous than he was."

I put the gun back in the holster and followed them out the door. It wasn't over yet. As they pulled away in a black Chevrolet Suburban, Maya pulled into their parking spot in the artmobile.

"I thought you were going to spend the day buried in the archive in Dolores Hidalgo?" I said. Bad choice of words, but it was too late when I realized it.

"I gave up," she said. "My concentration is as nothing. Why are you still wearing the gun?" she aske with some alarm. I was eyeing the people on the street. They looked harmless. Who were we up against now? What would they look like?

"Rodriquez and Leon were just leaving when you came up. You took their space." We went inside and I told her the whole thing in detail.

She turned and faced away from me. "Look at my back now carefully."

"Very nice," I said. "A lean, firm look. Skin like a baby's bottom. Muscles still taut and smooth. Quite a fetching taper as it moves down toward your waist; no sign of any tortilla-induced muffin top. I'd say you could be model material."

"Do you see a target on it, a fairly big one? Three rings in addition to the bulls eye?"

"No." I knew what was coming.

"Well, I can feel one. I hoped it was over, even if Barbara didn't get the codex. Now we have national security."

"We're back in the soup, you mean."

"Back in the soup?"

"Found one you didn't know. It means we're in it again up to our eyeballs."

"OK. That one I know. I'll try to remember about the soup."

I should have told her how sorry I was that we spent so much time in the soup, but I was still working it out for myself. Instead I pulled her over and pressed her against me and kissed her neck. My fingers could find no target on her back, only the snap to her bra. It was the kind of distraction she welcomed. Much later I called Cody and filled him in on our visitors.

✠✠✠

On Thursday I finished the incomplete corner of the background of Barbara's picture and reviewed all the highlights, boosting a few here and there, and then signed it. After I cleaned up I set the picture against the wall opposite the sofa, pulled up the hassock, and sat down to look at it. It was the most interrupted project I had ever done, lasting from late January until mid July, but it hadn't suffered from the delays. The flesh tones were consistent and inviting, and I especially liked the hands, placed one over the other on her navel.

The look on her face was just right, suggesting the none-too-subtle availability of the sitter. If I were going to title it, which I wasn't, beyond the standard *Portrait of Barbara Watt*, I would have called it *What a Piece of Work I Am*. I think of this part of painting as my ownership phase; the time before a picture goes off to the gallery or to the buyer, and I get to sit and figure out what I've done and possibly why. If any changes are needed I can spot them now if I've missed them earlier. But mostly the picture belongs to me in a way that it never will again. My eyes flicker over the surface, scanning every point. If I'm going to learn something from it, this is when I learn it. Often the best time to come up with a new idea is during this ownership phase, and as I sat there an idea did come to me. Just then Maya came into the studio.

She sat down next to me and kissed my cheek, and then realized what I was doing.

"You know how desperate I've been," I said.

"Yes, and I think you will soon be more desperate if you don't stop looking at her. You will be sleeping in the guest room like when you have a cigar."

"It's only landscape."

"You always say that, but for you I think it is a landscape of the heart."

"No."

"I have seen you two. I have seen how she looks at you and touches you all the time." She folded her arms tightly across her chest. "I think she would like to screw your brains out."

"Nice phrase."

"Thank you. I can't remember where I read that. Maybe in your mind. But really Paul, something is passing in the air between you two. Méxican women may sometimes be short but they are not often blind."

"It all comes from her. I don't touch her. I wouldn't. Being a painter is a higher calling than being a philanderer."

"What is that?"

"Someone who just sleeps around. Like sportfucking. Anyway, I have you. I don't need anyone else."

She relaxed a little and tucked herself in against me. "It's a good picture. You have kidnapped her."

"I think you mean captured her."

"Yes."

"I was having an idea when you came in. You know how we were talking about you posing with clothes on?"

"Yes?"

"How would you like to pose as Frida Kahlo? We have that Tejuana outfit we bought in Cuernavaca two years ago. We could try that. We've never used it, except that one night."

"And that was very bad of you. You would not be thinking about Salma Hayek again from the movie?"

"No."

"But you do think about her?"

"Only that I would like to paint her."

"More landscape, right?"

"Of course."

"She does have nice hills."

"Very."

"I suppose an artist knows these things?" she said.

"Yes. Few things are certain, but this is one of them."

"And if she were available, you would have to think what to do?"

"Not likely to be available."

"So I should not lay awake at night wondering?"

"No, but let me know if she calls."

"But she is half Lebanese. She's not even a real Méxican woman."

"Close enough. She could have fooled me."

I went over to the prop drawers and pulled out the Tejuana costume from the deep one on the bottom. Nothing hit me in the back of the head as I went. I held it up to Maya. She slipped out of her jeans and top and put it on. The fit was still good.

"How about tomorrow morning? We can go through the art books to get the hair right from one of Frida's self portraits."

"How about her mustache?" she said.

CHAPTER FIFTEEN
NINJAS

O n Thursday, five days after the death of Jason
Schwartz, two men climbed a narrow path into
the hills above the village of Los Chorros, in
the State of Chiapas. It was a portion of the autonomous
zone, where the Méxican government had tacitly yielded
control to the Zapatistas. Neither man was above middle
height. Both carried rifles, which fired, although they did
not match, as well as light packs, one bearing the name
of a middle school twenty kilometers away. The older of
the two, and the more senior in rank, was named Luis
Rosas. He wore a camouflage jacket, and khaki pants tied
at the ankles with shoelaces. Tightly knotted on his head
was a black kerchief. The younger man went by the name
of Yolo. He wore painter's pants, which had once been
white, and a khaki shirt with many pockets, similar to that
of Jason Schwartz. Both wore boots, carried cartridge
belts around their waists, and dented canteens hung on
their belts.

To the northeast squatted the rounded peak of
Cerro Quérenton. The sun stood directly above it bathed
in the thinner mountain air. The path was clear enough
to follow if they kept their eyes on it, but it was not well
used. The track rose and fell, each rise winding higher.

Rounding the peak, Rosas and Yolo traversed a shallow valley and then climbed toward a long ridge. Half a kilometer along the ridge they stopped at a Mayan-style house invisible in the thick foliage; it had straight parallel sides with semicircular ends. The footprint was like that of a racetrack, but not more than seven meters long. The interior held a long table and two hammocks with mosquito netting. At the table sat another small man with an olive military cap. He was smoking a briar pipe. On the table before him lay a photocopy of the Mayan codex and a file of notes. Unlit Coleman lanterns stood at each end.

Rosas and Yolo took seats opposite him. They were members of the elite commando group of the Zapatistas, the Mayan rebels of Chiapas. Captain Gaspar spoke first.

"Subcomandante Marcos has received some deeply disturbing news from our friend within the federal police. Our agent in San Miguel de Allende, Jason Schwartz, had obtained a newly discovered Mayan codex and was on the way here to deliver it in person when he suffered an accident south of Querétaro and was killed. The codex was not found with him. It predicted the overthrow of the neo-liberal colonialist tyranny and had already been authenticated by an expert from México City, one not connected to the Cause."

"Captain, what do you wish us to do?" asked Rosas, patiently. He had no idea what a codex was. He was barely able to read Spanish on the street signs in town.

"You will go to San Miguel and recover it." He slid the file toward Yolo, who had finished sixth grade in San Cristobal de las Casas. He would be navigating on the trip. "Here you will find notes that were made of telephone reports from Señor Schwartz. They list the names and addresses of those in San Miguel who were involved with the codex. I have crossed off the name of John Schleicher, who has already been dealt with. The other name is that of Dr. Vincent Sandoval, the expert who lives in México City. He is being watched by others. The subcomandante wishes you to begin in San Miguel and watch these people carefully. It is our hope that the codex will find its way back to one of them. When it does, take whatever steps necessary to obtain it. The subcomandante depends on you, as does our Cause. Change your rifles for pistols at the armory in Los Chorros. A vehicle and travel funds have been prepared for you there as well." He pushed the codex copy toward them. "Take this with you so you will recognize the codex. The document itself is in color. Once you have it, handle it carefully. It is of immense value to us."

✠✠✠

On the Sunday following this meeting, Rosas and Yolo arrived in San Miguel in a battered Toyota pickup to take up their positions. At the same time, in the village of Escobedo on Highway 57 south of Querétaro, Padre Juan Nogal was removing his vestments after the last mass of the morning. As he kissed his surplice before folding it into a drawer, a man in the worn clothes of a farm worker entered the sacristy carrying a flat package.

"Excuse me, Father," he said.

"Yes, my friend, how can I help you?"

"I fear I have committed a sin against the dead." He stood at the doorway, his eyes downcast.

"How is that possible? The dead are with God.

They are beyond our transgressions. We must concern ourselves with the living."

"I took this from the wreck of a car. There was a dead man in it."

He passed the package to the priest. Padre Nogal undid the fastener and examined the codex. He was no more educated than most village priests, but he knew enough to recognize Mayan hieroglyphics. The look and feel of the document was older than anything he had ever touched before. The container was made from a material he did not recognize, and inside was a slot meant to carry a business card. He pulled it out and read, Prof. Vincent Sandoval, along with an address and telephone number in México City. It was clear to him that either the dead man had been Sandoval, or that the codex belonged to him if he were still alive.

Padre Nogal smiled. "This is a small matter," he said. "I will find out if this man whose name is on the card is still alive, and if he is I will return this to him. If he is not, I will send it to his heirs, if I can find them. In any case, your good deed has absolved you from any guilt. You have done the right thing. You have my blessing." He made the sign of the cross over the farm worker, who quickly departed.

CHAPTER SIXTEEN

The next morning we started work early. Maya posed in a Méxican Victorian-style arm chair, with burgundy brocade upholstery, that I brought up from the living room. Her back was ramrod straight as Frida's always was, and her hands were in her lap. With the aid of a box of bobby pins her hair was correct. I wanted to express the dignity of Frida as a painter, without the anguish of her disabilities or her tortured love life. Maya had studied Frida's self portraits and her expression bore the same look of serenity that some of them had. This might be a picture we would keep, maybe in the dining room over the mantle, which had never had the portrait it seemed to require. I located everything with washes and began on her face, as always.

I did not try to make her look like Frida Kahlo, I only wanted to express my thoughts about Frida through Maya. The ramrod pose, reflecting the apparatus Frida had needed to even stay upright at some periods of her life, was a strain on Maya's back and we broke for stretching every twenty minutes.

This picture was not likely to lead to a series or a gallery show, but it wouldn't hurt to add something to our own collection. Besides, in another week or so I'd have the $4,000 from Barbara. We only had to wait for the paint to dry enough to move it. In a year I'd take it back and varnish it. And we were still flush from the Mérida show. All we had to do now was avoid the next horde of Ninjas looking for the codex, whoever they were. Life is never simple, even for painters.

The face went well; it had that straight-on look toward the viewer that makes the eyes seem to follow you around the room. I saved the hair to work on at the same time as the background and moved on to the costume. I had always been good with fabric, even though I hadn't found much use for those skills lately. At about 12:30 we broke for lunch. Maya put on an apron while she ate to avoid spilling on the Tejuana outfit.

"You look very good in that," I said. "Most of these Méxican costumes are quite feminine and flattering. That was true of the folk dancers' costumes too from that last series."

"But you'd rather do nudes."

"Sometimes. It's a great tradition."

"Why don't you ever do nude men?"

"They don't sell. When you see them they're usually student work. I did nearly a dozen in art school, none since. Maybe I should paint Cody nude. Is that what you're thinking? The bullet scars could be interesting. They'd give the picture some texture you don't often see."

"I understand your point," she said.

Over the next two days we made great progress on the Frida painting. I talked to Barbara and arranged to deliver her picture on the following Wednesday. I offered to show it to her before it was dry, but she wanted to wait and see it in her house. She had heard nothing more regarding the codex and she had seen no Ninjas.

Late Sunday afternoon we got a call from Vincent Sandoval. He had picked up a message from his answering service at the university and returned the call. He was calling from a phone booth.

"I am only using phone booths from now on," he said. "I want to live to see the end of this." He didn't sound frightened, just sensible.

He went on to relate a call he had received from a Padre Juan Nogal in the town of Escobedo.

"I can't believe how lucky we got. The padre has the codex. He found my card in the pocket inside the Nuprex container and believes it belongs to me. I didn't contradict him. This has given me great ethical misgivings, but if it does not come back to us, then it goes to the police, and then to the federal government. Even worse, Schwartz could recover it. We've got to get control of it again; I'll sort out the ethical nuances later."

I told him about my conversation with Leon, including the death of Jason Schwartz and how Leon had invoked national security.

"I guess we won't miss Schwartz, although I can't see how it could be connected to national security," he said. "But I fear if the government gets it they'll destroy it, or at least bury it out of sight somewhere so that it can never be published. It would be an intolerable loss to Mayan scholarship. I couldn't allow it. I'm starting to wish I'd never seen the damn thing." This could have could been a line from Maya.

"I'm not sure I believe that. How did this Padre Nogal get it?"

"He says a farm worker presented it to him after mass this morning. The man said he found it in a wrecked car that contained a dead body. I should have realized it was Schwartz, but I didn't. I'm not surprised."

"What do you want to do?"

"Nogal said he would mail it to me, but remembering what happened the last time a copy of it came this way I said I would rather come down and pick it up myself. I wonder if you and Cody would like to join me? I'm feeling a bit vulnerable. Actually, very vulnerable, and you two are armed, I believe."

"True. I'm sure it can be arranged." I didn't hesitate to speak for Cody.

"How about tomorrow?"

"What time?"

"Shall we say one o'clock? Nogal said any time tomorrow would work. Monday's his light day. It's the church of San Ysidro, in Escobedo. He said it's two blocks off the plaza, on the south side."

"We'll see you there." I hung up. Maya was practically hopping at my side.

"So we're back in business," she said with a frown when I told her what we were going to do. "It's been so nice just posing and painting, hasn't it? Like before."

"I'll check your back again, if you want."

"That's OK, I know what's there."

"Do you want to go?"

"No. I think I'll go to Querétaro and check their archive at the museum. Now Professor Wainwright wants to include Indian activity during the overthrow of Emperor Maximilian. You know he was executed there in 1867."

"I didn't know that, but it can be a tough town for *gringos*," I said. Actually Querétaro is another sweet spot in México, with a beautiful string of squares in *centro* that flow from one to the other, perfect for an evening stroll. Years ago I had briefly considered settling there, but then decided that at nearly million people it was larger than I wanted.

"Only tough for Austrian *gringo* emperors who aren't wanted," she said.

"We'll take Cody's Escort, then. You take the artmobile."

I called Cody and told him the game was on again. He was neither disappointed nor surprised.

On Monday he appeared at eleven o'clock, shirt bulging under his left armpit. Mine was too. Maya was still pulling her papers together. "Be careful on the road," I said. "There's more to be done on the Frida picture."

She put her arms around me and pressed her face into my neck. "I hate to see that thing returning to us. It's like a traveling curse. I wonder why Barbara can't see that? Be careful. Come back to me." She hugged Cody briefly—not long enough, I could see from his face—and went out the door.

After she left we headed out of town up past the Gigante market near the *glorieta*. We passed the place where the two *federales* had died. Schwartz had not outlived them by much. "So the professor has a moral dilemma," Cody said. "Normally I guess it wouldn't be a bad thing for the codex to go to the government, but I find this claim of national security interests worrisome. That could be a cover for almost anything, as we've seen before. He might be right that they'll just bury it, but I'm not so certain the feds would destroy it, since it would be the only codex still in

México."

"He's being careful so he only uses phone booths now, and they're getting hard to find with all the cell phones."

"Once burned," said Cody. "What are you working on now?"

"Maya as Frida Kahlo."

"That would be dressed?"

"Strange, isn't it?" I thought of the one Frida had done where she's lying nude in bed giving birth to herself. It was not my favorite.

"No one will recognize her with her clothes on."

"I know. We'll probably keep it."

"How's the Barbara picture coming?"

"It's finished. I'll deliver it in two days."

"You must be sad."

"Not entirely. As long as I have the next one going, that's all I care about."

"Sometimes I think you wouldn't know who you are if you weren't painting."

"Don't start getting all psychological on me now."

"I guess you'll miss having Barbara around posing, though."

"It's just landscape, Cody. Hills and valleys. Get over it." We both pondered that for a while.

The hills and valleys around us flattened out gradually into shades of green. July is the midpoint of the rainy season, which means that every third or fourth day brings an afternoon shower for a couple of hours. Then the sun returns. An hour out we skirted Querétaro on the bypass and swung south on Highway 57.

"There's been an older Toyota pickup behind us since we left San Miguel," Cody said. "He's been back four or five cars and I wasn't sure what he was up to, but now he's followed us onto the bypass. I was hoping he might break off and go straight into Querétaro."

I looked around and located the truck about six cars back. The traffic was not dense, but there was more than I expected for a Monday at lunchtime. Of course, Méxicans usually did not eat lunch at noon. It was easy for the Toyota to hang back and not be obvious.

"What do you think?" I asked.

"Don't know for sure, but it looks like some new faces have joined the game."

"Are there more than one? I couldn't tell."

"There are two. Let's pull over at the next road stop and get a cup of coffee, stretch our legs."

I had assumed Cody planned to ditch them somehow, but instead we left the highway three kilometers later and entered the parking lot of a fairly large restaurant. It was one of those faceless eating places that look the same everywhere, with a lot of windows overlooking the parking lot under a long yellow sign that could be seen for a kilometer on both sides of the highway. It could have been along a roadside in the Yukon or the Mississippi Delta.

"Let's get inside fast," said Cody.

Standing at the host's station in a window by the entry, we saw the Toyota pull in and park in a corner of the lot, well away from Cody's Escort. Two Méxican men got out and headed toward the door. "Get us a table," he said. "I'm going to the men's room."

A waiter seated me and over the top of the menu I watched the two men come in and wait to be seated. They didn't look at me. Both were small and distinctly darker than most Méxicans from this area. One wore an olive tennis hat and the other was bareheaded. Cody had not returned yet and I ordered us both a cup of *café Americano*.

"Will that be all?" asked the waiter. "*Algo mas?*"

"That's only to begin with."

When he came with the coffee Cody emerged from the back and sat down.

"Are you all right?" I asked. "It seemed like a long time. You haven't been eating street vendor food again, have you?"

"Never, and I'm fine. I went out through the kitchen and slashed their tires. All four of them. I always carry my Boy Scout knife."

"Hell of a thing to do to a couple of poor Mexicans."

"Ain't it a shame. Let's get out to the car fast."

I threw some pesos on the table and we moved out the door and into the car. Our tires were squealing as we blew out of the parking lot. Glancing back, I could see the two men running out of the restaurant. This time they were looking at us.

Back on Highway 57 Cody looked over at me, and then in the rear view mirror. "Any ideas?" he asked.

"Could be the national security threat boys, but I can't see the angle. Besides, they're not driving a black Suburban, and they don't look like the type. They appear to know who we are, so I'm guessing that means they're connected to Schwartz, possibly as his replacements. They must be working from the same federal police contact he had. Only they don't look like reporters."

"I didn't see any notebooks when they came in the restaurant. I bet I know what their shoes look like, although I couldn't get a look at them."

"Most likely they don't know where we're going," I said.

"They probably know the general area, if it's near where Schwartz was killed, but I doubt they know anything more."

According to the road sign, it was another twenty kilometers to Escobedo, maybe twelve or fifteen minutes.

"How big is this town?" said Cody, glancing up at the rear-view mirror. He pulled the atlas out of his map pocket and shoved it at me. I found the right page.

"It's the smallest kind of hollow dot, but the circle around it is bold."

"Thanks. Check through the front of that damn thing and tell me what that means."

I fumbled around with it and finally found the legend. "It's 5,000 to 15,000 people."

"So, what do you think? Could be four to five churches?"

"Sandoval said two blocks from the southern edge of the square. It's *San*-something."

"Great."

A few kilometerss further we left Highway 57. Escobedo was spread out along the road, and the exit curved directly into the main street. It was like a lot of smaller dusty towns in México, the same butcher shops and pharmacies and tile stores, clusters of dogs sniffing hopefully at nothing and each other, and *topes*, speed bumps every fifty yards. An occasional chicken on the prowl. A row of new toilets faced the road, resting on gravel, and a small boy was peeing into the last one. Nothing goes to waste here.

We came up to the east side of the square, which did not appear to be older than a hundred years or so, although it can be hard to tell because architecture changes so little, but it was not a colonial town. Cody turned right and we circled to the south side where we found Iglesia San Ysidro almost immediately.

White adobe roughly surfaced the church walls, with an occasional crack running like thin black lightning down the sides. A single bell tower presided over a plain front with no fancy Baroque stone carving. The only decorative touch was an elaborately forged wrought iron lantern over the door. It must have been the proud gift of some local ironworker. I could sense the hard work and devotion that had gone into it. But nothing else on the exterior showed the same taste for embellishment. There was no landscaping. Rough square concrete pavers led to the door, flanked by bare dirt on both sides.

This unpretentious, businesslike church was not in the same league as its more prosperous neighbor on the square, and served the needs of a different class of people. Three cars up from where we parked was a late model Chevrolet Trail Blazer with Distrito Federal plates. It had to belong to Sandoval.

Inside, there was only a woman with a little girl beside her in the pews. The woman was kneeling and the girl was fidgeting with some pamphlets, rocking back and forth on the seat. She was quietly mouthing some song and the woman hushed her as we came up the aisle.

San Ysidro was too small to have any side altars and had only one glass display case near the entry with a bloody plaster Jesus in a diaper. A more impressive church would have had three or four. We walked to the front and turned left into what I hoped was the sacristy, passing a statue of Our Lady of Guadalupe that had to be eight feet tall. I guess San Ysidro, whoever he was, had to share the devotion of this congregation. We were about ten minutes late, mostly because of our coffee stop. Ten minutes is nothing in México. I realized we should have left our guns in the car, but then thought that I was not about to be in the presence of the codex without it.

Cody was ahead of me. As we approached the door to the sacristy he stopped and looked in quickly, his hand inside his shirt on his holster. It looked a little stagey to me, but why not be careful? Maybe the boys with the flattened Toyota tires weren't the only ones looking for us. Maybe Sandoval had been lured into something. I saw Cody's body relax and I followed him into the sacristy. Prof. Sandoval and a priest were there, leaning over a counter above a series of wide, flat drawers. The codex was spread open before them. They heard us come in. Sandoval turned quickly, and his expression changed to relief.

"Vincent," said Cody. Sandoval pulled off his gloves.

The padre stepped forward and put out his hand. "Juan Nogal," he said, "Welcome to San Ysidro. Dr. Sandoval has been explaining the contents of this codex to me. It is such a historic document, but hearing it translated I have become very worried for the future of the church. I hope you are here to reassure me." He was a young man; his smile was huge and his eyes flashed with humor. I had the feeling this was the most interesting thing to happen in his parish for a long time.

"Can we take a look at this?" I asked. They stood aside as Cody and I scanned the codex.

"I see we had the copy assembled wrong," said Cody.

"I wasn't fooled," said Sandoval, "but this is the correct sequence."

The first two pages were all hieroglyphics, with the edges of each character boldly outlined, reminiscent of the cartouche around the names of Egyptian pharaohs. The outlines were inhabited by smaller figures, some recognizable as trees or animals. Here and there I could make out the form of a Mayan house, identical with the ones being put up today in every corner of the Yucatán.

In the pages following, the hieroglyphics were dimmer because they were mostly confined to the edges, with a figure of a god or ruler prominent in the center. Little writing was used on the two final pages. The next to last page showed three black-robed friars on the ground in a row, each with the foot of a Mayan warrior on his throat. The last page held the image of a fourth friar, his arms held outward by two warriors, his robe peeled back, while a Mayan priest reached into the bleeding cavity of his chest and extracted the friar's heart with both hands.

"Mercy," said Cody, almost in a whisper, "with all the dead we've got now it kind of fits, doesn't it? Maybe mayhem follows this thing."

"On its final page the Dominguez Codex shows one of the same friars reading scripture to a Mayan village humbly assembled at his feet," said Sandoval, at my elbow. I was expecting him to snort, but it didn't come. Instead he glanced at his watch.

Away from the edges, the colors were strong, and all were naturally from vegetable or native mineral dyes. The red could have been blood; it had a brownish look and blood was certainly not in short supply when it was written. The blues were grayish, possibly from clay. I couldn't make a guess on the greens, which were in the olive range. There was no yellow, but several shades of tan. The black in the lettering would have been from charred wood. In spite of myself I felt in awe of the mere presence of the thing, and I thought again of the four people now dead because of it.

"I was telling the Padre how his intervention has benefitted science," said Sandoval, with a look that said *play along*.

"Perhaps you know the story of San Ysidro, our patron saint," said Nogal. "He was a poor farmer, as are many of my parishioners, but a devout man. He prayed and attended mass every day so that he neglected his farm labors. One morning his *patron*, Juan de Vargas, was coming to upbraid him when he saw angels plowing Ysidro's fields. After that, he left Ysidro alone. His corn was like that of no other farm. It is a legend many of our souls here like to invoke when they sleep late."

We both smiled, uncertain how to respond to this.

Finally Cody said, "I bet you've told that story before."

"Once or twice," he said, looking at Cody, "I see you are carrying a gun. It is sad that the possession of this magnificent document brings such risk."

"The sad truth is that there are other people searching for this codex whose motives we don't understand. Some of them were following us on the way here, but we caused them to have a car problem about twenty kilometers north of here."

"Perhaps they were not doing God's work."

"Bet on it, Padre," I said.

Sandoval was getting restless. "Perhaps it is best we go now," he said to Nogal. "Even to be in the same room with the codex is a danger for you. As I think I mentioned, four people have died because of it. This is why my friends are armed. I can never thank you enough for helping me recover it. Don't ever mention to anyone that you have seen it. Goodbye, Father."

We all climbed into Sandoval's car to decide what to do. He settled into a slumped position behind the wheel. "I've been wrestling with this since Padre Nogal first called me. I came to realize I can't possess the codex once I publish it, and I have no legitimate claim to it anyway. If I were to try to keep it I would be a continuous target for both the government and the Jason Schwartz group. But Barbara Watt would have the resources to protect it and keep it secret."

"What about the million dollars?" I asked.

"You know me, Paul. I couldn't profit financially from the codex. Academically is a different issue. I will give the codex to Barbara on the understanding that I will publish it, as we discussed before, and that she bequeath it to the National Anthropological Museum in Chapultepec at her death. She has enough years ahead of her that whatever political value this has will have dissipated by then—we should be able to trust the government. No money will change hands and no written agreement will be necessary."

"What would happen if some legitimate claimant

should appear?" asked Cody. "I'm still trying to get past the stolen goods aspect of this. I guess that comes from having been a cop."

"We would have to depend on Barbara to act in good faith. She would have no financial stake in it. We *do* acknowledge that at some point it must have been stolen."

"What now?" I asked.

"I'd like Cody to accompany me back to México City to provide security while I do the photography. Perhaps you could take his car back to San Miguel. Then he can return by plane or bus with the codex."

"That's fine by me," said Cody.

So we separated. I followed them for a while until they got out of town. There was no Toyota with fresh tires behind either car. I called Maya from my cell phone as I headed back toward Querétaro. She had not been bothered in the museum archive and thought she'd be back for dinner. I was feeling that I'd been neglecting her, even though this was something she didn't want much part of. The image that remained with me on the road back to San Miguel was that of Padre Nogal, glimpsed through my rear view mirror, motionlessly watching us leave from the side entry of San Isidro. Perhaps he was thinking of the black-robed friars having their hearts ripped out in the final pages of the codex. It must have seemed like a long way from Escobedo.

CHAPTER SEVENTEEN

That I was unable to paint the next morning should have been no surprise. I needed an open-ended time slot in order to work. The threat of impending events obliterated my concentration. Maya was still upset at the pending return of the codex and didn't feel like heading for Querétaro again until we had settled it in a safe place. At the same time I was sorry she didn't leave because I didn't want her anywhere near it, but I understood.

At 11:30 Cody called. He had arrived at the bus station on Canal and I went to pick him up.

"My teeth are furry," he said. "I wasn't expecting a sleep-over when we left. I guess it's not the first time, though. I had to take the bus because I couldn't fly with my gun and I wasn't about to leave it behind."

"Sandoval is all set?"

"He's good to go. He gave me this nifty tote bag to carry the codex in." He held it up. It had the college emblem on it. "No Ninjas yet?"

I checked the rear view mirror, but we were clear. "Nothing." We rumbled over the cobblestones. Shock absorbers last about a year here.

"I think we can probably use the cell phones, since these guys are clearly not connected to the government," said Cody.

"How about their inside man?"

"I don't think the government's watching us that closely any more. They're probably beating the bushes out in the *campo* around Escobedo looking for the codex. I doubt they're likely to find the connection to Padre Nogal. I can imagine what else the guys who brought it in found in Schwartz's car. They're not going to say a word."

"And if they did Nogal could plead secrecy of the confessional. If he trusted the police with it he would have called them first," I said.

"Not a great deal of confidence in the police here."

"Like Maya says, they are not well paid."

Back home Maya hugged Cody rather listlessly, I thought, and went upstairs to work. He watched her climb the stairs with a stumped expression on his face. She didn't want anything much to do with the process. When I asked her if she wanted to look at the codex, she just shrugged. It made me realize how much she wanted to distance herself from it.

I called Barbara and told her about the meeting with Nogal and the terms Sandoval had set for turning over the codex. I could practically hear her whooping on the other end.

"I agree absolutely," she said breathlessly. "In a heartbeat."

"And if someone can prove ownership you'll give it up?"

"Yes. Even that part."

"OK." I said. "I'm still concerned about security. Have you got a bank safe deposit box?"

Cody stuck a finger in my ribs. "They don't exist here. You must not have anything of value or you'd know that."

I shrugged. I keep any extra money in a pair of old shoes. It's never so much that I can't still wear them.

"There's a good safe in the house, but Perry had some clout with the manager and he also arranged to have his own box in the main vault at Banamex. I haven't given it up. It's big enough to hold the codex."

"Then I think that's the place because Schwartz's people tried to follow us down when we picked it up."

"But you lost them?"

"They experienced some car trouble and had to make a pit stop."

"You're so resourceful, Paul."

"Don't be getting sentimental on me. It was Cody who took care of them."

"That big burly guy."

"He is that. Anyway, you're agreed that the bank is the best place for it until we resolve the Ninja issue?"

"Is that some kind of turtle?"

"That's some kind of Méxican thugs who were associated with the late Jason Schwartz."

"Then the bank is the place for it. I don't want them trying to crack my safe. It's bad enough that someone got into my underwear and my money drawer. Can we do it now?"

"We'll pick you up in ten minutes."

"I'll pick you up."

Her silver Mercedes looked right at home outside the bank. So did Barbara. The cop on the corner gave her a deep bow as she got out. She tipped him a hundred pesos to ignore her illegal parking. As they say here, *no hay problema.*

"I'm going to be a moment," she said. "You know, I've never seen the original. I'll try to get the manager to give me an office where I can look at it before they take it into the vault. OK?"

I had forgotten that she'd agreed to pay a million dollars for the codex and had never seen it, only the photocopy. I didn't know whether that was impressively silly or impressively astute. Maybe a little of each, but it was impressive, nonetheless. Mostly I was more impressed that she was now getting it for nothing.

"Put these on when you handle it," said Cody. He pulled out a pair of latex gloves from his pocket. "They're not your size, but you can still get them on."

She slid them into her small alligator purse and went inside with the tote bag on her arm. We followed a few steps behind, watching the people moving past. The bank was under the arcade on one side of the *jardín*, and there was a fair amount of foot traffic. Barbara spoke to someone at a desk and he led her toward the vault at the rear of the bank. Unless the Ninjas were waiting inside, she was home free. Fifteen minutes later she was back.

"I can't believe how *colorful* it is," she said as we drove off. "Those Mayans were artists! You saw it, Paul. Don't you think it's high art? And the design, just the style of it! The person who made it had a great flair with calligraphy. But then how horrible at the end, with the old priests dying. One of them had white hair, and they were gripping it to pull him away."

"Just what Sandoval thought," said Cody. "He felt that of the five, this is the most artistic."

"It's like there's a heartbeat in it. I can feel these people's presence although I don't know what they're saying."

"Sandoval will fix that," said Cody, "when it's published."

Back at home I called Sandoval at his office to let him know Barbara had agreed to his terms and taken possession of the codex, ready to use the agreed upon code phrase "the eagle has landed," but he didn't answer. He was probably at the office of his publisher. Or he may have been in class. I left a message for him to call me back from a pay phone. Maya wanted to get back to her research so we had lunch and she left for Querétaro.

With the paint now dry, the next morning I loaded Barbara's picture in the artmobile and headed up the hill. The sky was crowded with choppy clouds, but it wasn't raining yet. Normally this time of year it holds off until late afternoon.

"It's beautiful, now I'll always look like that," she said, meeting me in her driveway. She gave me a close hug and kissed my cheek, then pulled back suddenly.

"You're still wearing the gun?"

"I thought you might try to seduce me now that you're in a better mood."

"The gun wouldn't stop me. You could leave it on, even. That would be interesting."

"I brought it because I don't think we're out of the woods yet."

"With the turtles?"

"Right. Maybe you want me to take this to the framer for you?"

"Not yet. I'd rather wait until I decide where to hang it." Inside she wrote me a check for the $4,000 picture price, plus $2,000 each for my and Cody's detective efforts. It would keep us in *fajitas* for a while.

We leaned the picture against the wall in various places throughout the house. She decided to put it over the mantel in Perry's study, in place of two of his " ancestor" paintings, as we called them, an old aristocrat with an elegant goatee and plenty of armor, hung next to a substantial woman in a stiff collar who might have been his wife rather than his mistress. One of the man's hands was on his sword hilt. I was glad we had chosen a bigger canvas for the nude, because the space required it.

"That pair was always too dour for me," Barbara said, "and besides, it's my study now. So what happens next?"

"I find some other delicious blonde to paint. That's all I know."

"Good luck. There are no close seconds. But I meant about the Ninjas."

"They're out there somewhere. I don't know how to smoke them out. I'll just try to be ready."

"Do you really think the picture is best here?"

"It certainly works in the space. My only quibble would be the other ancestors. All that skin might be too lively for their company."

"I saw some old bed linens here once, really old and fragile," she said. "In the middle was an embroidered hole."

I paused while this sank in--it took a while. "You mean they used to do it through a hole in the sheet? Not even three holes? Wow. So they never saw this much skin in their entire lives?"

"Just imagine. How much fun was that? But there would have been party girls who knew what to do. It was old México. There must have been a certain amount of fooling around. The men had different rules, just like now," she said. "The women didn't."

"I hope so," I said, "not about the rules, but the native girls. They probably didn't even have sheets."

"As you must know very well. Anyway, maybe you have some other things in your shelves I could put up? Not nudes necessarily, but what about still lifes? I've already got that one of yours with the tennis hats in the pool house. I think this room needs to take itself less seriously. It's too 'Perry.' Like maybe a few more modern rugs. Eclectic is good, right? You've got an eye for these things. Perry always thought a big price tag worked best with decorating."

"You'll have to take a look at the still lifes next time you're over. But I've always wanted to do you in that Chinese robe, too, ever since I first saw it on you."

"I knew you'd come around." She smiled sweetly, placing her hand on my shoulder.

"Paint you, I mean."

That's where we left it. It was good to have buyers with deep pockets. I cruised down the hill and went directly to the bank and deposited the checks.

At home there was no sign of Maya. I hadn't gone very far into the house when the small hairs on the back of my neck began to stand on end. The door had been locked; we never took a chance with that, but various visitors had gotten through that lock in the past and I never felt fully confident about it again, especially since we'd recently been tossed. Maybe the Ninjas were all locksmiths. I paused and pulled out the gun and slid the safety off. There seemed nothing out of place. I went upstairs silently. I heard nothing.

The bedrooms looked all right. The clothes in the armoires were as we had left them. In the studio the only oddity I could find was that one of the drawers in the tabouret was not shut all the way. When I worked I always closed them after I pulled out a tube of paint, but that was just a reflexive thing and I was not entirely sure. Maybe I'd been distracted.

Initially nothing in the kitchen seemed out of place. The cabinet doors and drawer fronts were all closed. On the counter next to the cook top was a newspaper I had been glancing at just before I left. There was a front-page story on delays in the repairs to the *jardín*. The paper was still in the same position relative to the burners, but the top of the first page was turned face down to the counter rather than up, as I had left it. The story did not extend to the lower half. Someone had apparently shaken out the paper and then set it down the wrong way. Maya had left for the archive before I'd gone to see Barbara. It could not have been her.

Nothing else looked odd in the dining room or the living room. No one flew out at me, lunging at my neck. I put the gun away and pulled out my cell phone and dialed Cody.

"Williams," he said. Always on duty.

"I just got back here from Barbara's. The Ninjas are back."

"Were you tossed?"

"Subtly. Just two things gave it away."

"Why don't I come for a sleep-over? Not much action over here. Give me ten minutes to throw some things together. Then why not leave and go for a ride? That way they'll follow you if they're still out there and they won't see me come in. I've still got your extra key from the last time."

I did a slow walk through the house again, but I didn't see anything else, and I think the garden was clean; I didn't count the oranges and limes. The banana tree had chosen sterility. Then I left. As I drove away I could see no Toyota pickups behind me, but maybe they had changed cars, or decided to stay behind and watch the house. If so, Cody would be ready. I called Maya and brought her up to date.

"So we'll be having company for dinner?" she said.

She always knew what to do, but I think she was discounting my belief that we'd had visitors again. She seemed positively cheerful. Or maybe she thought they wouldn't be back now that they knew we didn't have the codex. I wasn't so sure.

"No Ninjas behind me," I said to Cody in the kitchen when I got back. He had found the beer. I had gone up to Gigante market and picked up *fajita* fixings and three bottles of Chilean red wine, plus a bag of rice because I couldn't remember if we had enough. I also got brie and English crackers and some antipasto. Gigante market is a great place to shop, with a touch of serendipity; you can get caviar and tires in the same aisle.

Maybe it was the fact that Barbara had paid me $8,000 and expressed an interest in buying more pictures, or perhaps it was the fact that the codex was now in safe hands; whatever it was I didn't know, but I felt great. Maybe it was just Maya feeling good on the other end of the line in Querétaro. She had clearly moved out of her funk, although I wasn't sure why. Maybe she couldn't be down for very long and had her limit.

It was always great to have Barbara testing me, but it mainly made me feel virtuous. I'm not religious, and virtue is usually no more than OK, but in this case it was kind of exciting. In the end, coming home to Maya always felt best. When the known terrain is so great, why wander in the forest and possibly get lost?

Oddly enough, my recipe for *fajitas* is not Méxican. I have a cookbook called *The Food of Santa Fe*, and it's their recipe I use for *fajitas*. It's so good I've never looked for a more Méxican version. The problem tonight was that it should marinate for twelve to twenty-four hours. I had three, tops. Luckily, I had a forgiving group to dinner. I almost felt like inviting Barbara too, but that was too complicated. I flattened the chicken breasts, sliced them into strips; and this is the point where I would be thrown out of Santa Fe, and México as well, because I like them to marinate in their narrow state, rather than whole. Anyway, they were stewing in their brief marinade while I dialed Dr. Sandoval again, and once more, got no response. I left no message, thinking that the earlier one was adequate.

I guessed he was out having a couple more margaritas, maybe having a couple of his admiring students, but I doubted that. Sandoval's main potency seemed more academic, but he did deserve to be celebrating. I put five *Los Tres Ases* CDs on the player and fired it up. Just then Maya walked in. She dropped a folder of papers on the dining room table and carefully set her laptop down next to it.

I showed her the bank receipt for the $8,000. She pulled out her paycheck from Professor Wainwright for $2,000.

"You win," she said, "this time."

"And," I said, "I think Barbara is going to buy another picture. Maybe more than one." She wrinkled her nose.

"You mean she's going to be hanging around here naked again? How much can you stand? How much can I stand?"

"No, an existing picture. Now she wants to look at the still lifes. Maybe clean out the ancestor portraits from Perry's study and go more eclectic. If I paint her again it would be in that blue Chinese robe. She could put it out in her great room. Any problem with that?"

"No, as long as she's wearing something."

"Maya, skin is good. That's why you're so popular among the gringos here, remember?"

"True. But mainly among the men. I don't want to know the women who like me for the pictures."

"The men are about thirty-five percent of the population. That's not bad. Anyway, we're celebrating tonight. The codex is safe, even if we aren't." I waited for a reaction, but didn't get one.

"Is Cody here yet? I thought I saw his car."

"He's up in the guest bedroom putting his things away.

A moment later Cody came down and I made two margaritas and one rum punch. He was armed too. I lit the garden lights for atmosphere even though it was not yet dark. We sat in the *loggia* and sipped our drinks while the coals were starting.

"Why not draw them out?" Maya asked. "One of you could get them to follow you and the other could tail them. Maybe go down Piedras Chinas where there's room for only one car and then box them in?"

"What then?" Cody asked. "Have a big shootout and leave half a dozen bystanders bleeding on the sidewalk? Sounds like a good way to get our visas revoked, if we both survive. This is just me talking, but I'd rather not get shot again. I've just learned to walk normally again after last time."

"By the way," I said, "here's $2,000 from Barbara." I handed him a check. "There'll be more if it turns out we're still in the soup."

"I know that one now," said Maya. "In México we would say, 'between the sword and the wall.' But OK, so it's not a good idea. Even so, I'm tired of having this target on my back. It would be good to get rid of them."

"If we kill them, there'll just be more coming."

"So we eat, drink, and be merry," I said. "We'll deal with the Ninjas tomorrow."

"I think that's not how the saying goes," said Cody.

"I know we're supposed to be celebrating, but I don't think I can live like this," said Maya. "I'm a researcher and a writer, not a victim."

I was starting to get impatient with this. We were in it to the end, whatever it was, and I didn't see myself going to Barbara and saying that now, since we had our money, we were going to withdraw from the whole thing. But neither was I sure of my motives. Perhaps there was an element of wanting to stay close to Barbara, which would mean I was putting Maya through this for reasons that weren't quite honest. I was never good at analyzing these things. If I put a dab of paint on a canvas, it was never a question of why did I do that. The only question was did it work or not. This seemed to be mostly working now, aside from the dead.

"You're also a model," I said, trying to send her off in a different direction. "One of the best."

"*The* best, I think."

"I'll drink to that," said Cody, raising his glass. He didn't seem to be questioning anything. Maybe for him it was just matter of being on duty or not.

As Maya and I also raised our glasses there was a muffled pounding on the door, not quite like a knock.

"We're not expecting anyone else?" said Maya. "Barbara Watt maybe?"

"No." I went to the door and peered out through the viewer. No one was in sight, but it didn't offer much to the sides.

"Don't open it," said Cody, "come back out here out of view from the door. We don't know who's out there." Here they are, I thought. I knew this was coming.

He went to the door and pulled out his .38 and turned off the light. With his back against the wall he silently threw the bolt and pulled the door open, a little at first, then all the way. Nothing happened. We waited. Cody dropped to the floor and looked around the jamb. Then he moved out onto the sidewalk. "It's clear," he yelled back to us.

When we came out he was kneeling on the paving stones in front of the door. I looked over his shoulder. There was a hand on the sidewalk, the fingers curled inward as if trying to cling to life, or beckon to someone for help. Cody covered his own fingers with a handkerchief, picked it up and turned it over. It was bloody and under the fingernails were slivers of what looked like bamboo. He rubbed the cloth over the surface of a ring on the fourth finger and then peered at it closely. " UNAM," he said. "The Autonomous University of México, Sandoval's college, I believe. Poor guy. Now they know everything."

"Now they know everything," repeated Maya, leaning against the doorframe. The look on her face was unreadable.

CHAPTER EIGHTEEN

Cody turned to me as we went back inside. "I'm talking mainly about Barbara. We didn't think they knew about her part in this. But I'm sure Sandoval told them everything before he died. Let's get up to Casa Watt fast." He set the hand on the floor inside the door. What a thing to come home to. I couldn't get the whole picture out of my mind.

"You better come along," I said to Maya. "I don't want you here alone. If they're pounding on the door now they could be coming over the walls next." Probably the wrong thing to say, but why pretend otherwise? I grabbed the keys to the artmobile and we dashed up the hill.

"You know how I feel now?" I said to nobody in particular, narrowly threading my way through the arches on Santo Domingo, "I was the one who picked his name off the Internet and now he's dead. Tortured to death. He could have kept the codex, but he just gave it to Barbara." At the speed I was driving the tires were pounding on the cobblestones like a Cuban conga player.

"He was a principled man," said Cody, over the noise.

Maya didn't say anything. She just put her hand on my arm. We reached Barbara's street in Los Balcones and a moment later pulled into her drive. The house looked uninhabited. Cody got out and drew his gun.

"No one on the street," he said. No lights were showing in the windows, even though the sun was well below the hills across the basin of San Miguel. I got out of the car; he went to the windows, looking in, I went to the door. It was locked. I could hear nothing from inside. Of course the walls and front door were so thick you wouldn't hear a cannon firing inside. I was trying to decide whether we should break a window to get in when the silver Mercedes pulled through the gate and stopped behind the artmobile. Barbara got out gracefully and when I came up to her she smelled of martinis. Her hair was up and she was wearing a black suit with a sapphire pendant, and shoes with square black buckles. She had her key in her hand and a look of surprise on her face.

"What's...?" Cody came up behind her and swept her up with both hands under her legs so that his body was between hers and the gate and went up the front steps as fast as I had ever seen him move. I didn't know whether he was trying to shield her from a waiting assassin or he just wanted to put his arms around her. Either one would be understandable. We came up right behind them as he snatched the key from her hand and unlocked the door. She punched in her security code as he set her down.

"Wow," she said. "That's really the way to greet a girl." She reached up and put her hand on Cody's cheek. "Have the Ninjas arrived?"

"No, thank God," I said, as I pushed the door shut and leaned against it. "Not yet. I thought they'd gotten here before we did."

"I'm sure they did," said Maya.

"Well, I just went out for a drink with my neighbors down the hill on Cuesta de San Jose." She set her tiny purse down on the entry table.

"Timing is everything," said Cody.

I told her about the hand on the sidewalk. Her face turned chalk white and tears welled up in her eyes. She sat down hard on the sofa. "So Vincent is *dead*? Why is this happening? I liked him so much."

"Yes," Cody said, "we all did, but I'm afraid now that he told them everything before he died. The next logical move is that they kidnap one of us to force you to release the codex from the bank. I don't think we can afford to fool around with this anymore. We need some serious firepower in here. There's a local outfit called Segúridad Reyes that does this kind of thing. I know Pablo Reyes; he's a good man and he's careful enough to trust with this. What would you say about bringing him in? I'm thinking we need three men; one in back, one in front and one inside. Twenty-four hours a day. It'll cost a little but it'll pay in the end."

"Never mind the cost; I have that drawer full of money. I simply can't believe it about Vincent. I feel like I caused this whole thing." She was twisting the sapphire at her neck back and forth as if she were about to break the chain.

"It was John Schleicher who set it in motion," I said, but I was the one who had made the connection with Vincent. I felt like the Angel of Death. Maybe I should stick to painting; I was better at it and most people who posed for me were able to walk away at the end. Not a small consideration, now. Hadn't I gotten into this by just trying to help out Barbara? If I was so damn good at seeing things differently, maybe I should work at taking a longer view, because I hadn't seen any of this coming.

Cody got on his cell phone and called Segúridad Reyes. Half an hour later we were still waiting. Maya was pacing back and forth with her arms folded. She looked like she was ready to bite someone. It was not her best look, although she had good teeth. We had left the lights off in Barbara's great room and turned them all on outside, but there was a small sconce light still lit in the foyer and I could make out Maya's profile and enough of her expression to catch her mood. Barbara had fixed herself another martini and nearly finished it. She had offered us one, but the rest of us felt like we were still on duty.

"Two of these usually put me on my butt," she said, "but I'm feeling perfectly fine now. How odd."

Her voice had a lighthearted singsong quality to it, too optimistic for the circumstances, and each word too carefully formed. "Maybe I'll just go to sleep for a spell while you guys shoot people. Let me know how it all comes out." She was starting to sound more like Montgomery, Alabama every minute. There was a pointed snort from Maya, something she did well. I'd had quite a few of them pointed at me.

Just then headlights appeared in the drive. I looked through the peephole in the door. It was a Renault van without side windows, bearing the words "Segúridad Reyes." Three serious-looking guys in dark gray uniforms got out, hands at the guns on their hips. They looked around briefly and then came to the door. All of them were bigger than I was. Two of them were nearly as big as Cody.

"You're going to have to talk to them," I said to Barbara.

After a brief conversation, mostly in English, which I'm not sure she understood, Barbara signed some papers and then two of them left to take up positions on the grounds. The third man, whose nametag said, "Jurado," shuttered the windows and found a place in the kitchen, but kept the staff door open so he could see the great room.

I bent over Barbara on the sofa and took her hand. "Are you going to be all right? I'm worried about you."

She put her arms around me and kissed my cheek. "I'll be fine, darlin'. Call me in the morning, OK?" Maya didn't notice. I think she was busy adjusting her target. Then Barbara pulled me back down to her mouth. "Would you like to come up and tuck me in?"

I didn't respond. Maybe Jurado could do it. In a way I liked her style, though, but I wasn't sure why. She could mourn without breaking a sweat. Her tears, when they came at all, were discreet, and she rarely covered her face with her hands. I think what said it best was that her makeup never ran. Maybe it had come from living with Perry.

We went back down the hill in silence and on to the next unpleasant task. I called the police. I felt like I had badly fumbled this situation and was awaiting the punishment. But we weren't finished yet. I wanted to get rid of that hand.

Licenciado Rodriquez must have been at home because it took him more than a half hour to get to Quebrada.

"So it is still the hot spot," he said after the usual greetings. I smiled grimly. He hadn't bothered to suit up for this, wearing a pair of jeans with a carefully pressed blue shirt. He smelled like cigarettes.

"Don't take that pin off your hot spot map anytime soon. There it is." I pointed to the hand on the floor. "It was just outside the door when we found it."

"But why did you move it, if I may ask?"

"We had to go out suddenly and I didn't want to leave it there."

"You are very calm," he said. "You should be of the police."

"I think I have my hands full already, this being such a hot spot and all."

"And do you know the owner of the hand?" He hadn't looked at it closely yet. It looked to me like he didn't want to, although he wasn't holding his nose.

"From the ring, I assume it belonged to Professor Sandoval, the man who authenticated the codex."

"I see." He bent over the hand but did not touch it. "This is a bloody business. It seems that the professor was tortured, probably to supply information which you have not given us."

I didn't miss the implication, and I didn't like it. "I wasn't tortured."

"Perhaps we should change our tactics of interrogation?"

"Maybe, but the Inquisition is gone."

He regarded me for a moment before he answered. "So you simply came out of the door and there was the hand on the sidewalk?"

"Someone knocked on the door, almost like the police," I said. (This was not true, the police knock was distinctive, as I well knew.) "When we opened it there was no one there. Only the hand."

"Do you have a bag? A *bolsa plastica*?"

I got a Gigante bag from the kitchen and he gingerly lifted the hand into it. We went outside and I pointed out the spot on the sidewalk where Cody had found it. He looked at the pavement in the light of a flashlight I gave him, and then stood up again. I wrote down Sandoval's phone number and address in México City. "I'm sure you already have this," I said. I realized that I didn't know whether Sandoval was married or not.

"Señor Zacher, I am glad there are no more *gringos* in San Miguel like you. I fear we could not keep up."

"Artists are a unique group." I knew this went over his head, but he didn't look up.

Rodriguez was shaking his head sadly as he got in his car. I was left thinking of the new photos of the codex; ready for publication, but lacking the translation and notes that Sandoval's article would have supplied. They must have been either in his home or in his office at the university. I wondered whose hands they had fallen into now.

CHAPTER NINETEEN

O n Thursday morning we had finished breakfast and Cody was cleaning up when I called Barbara. She sounded like she had just gotten up.

"Did you have a good night's sleep?" I asked.

"Extremely. I think it was those martinis. The crew from Seguridad Reyes just changed over. They must be doing twelve hours on and twelve off. Pablo Reyes is here himself. They're probably shorthanded."

"Any activity?"

"I haven't seen a thing, but then that's why I have these nice guards here, isn't it? Pablo's very sweet. I made him coffee."

"I think he's married." I was just guessing.

"Is there any action over there?" she asked. "I feel miserable when I think about Vincent."

"I haven't seen any. We're going to have a war conference to try to figure out how to go on the offensive. I'll let you know if we come up with anything."

Cody hung up his apron behind the kitchen door and the three of us sat around the dining room table with a fresh pot of coffee. It almost felt like Churchill and Montgomery with the general staff in a bunker during the Blitz, except we lacked the uniforms and the charts. And Churchill. Maya took the role of Montgomery, a troublemaker who didn't originate a lot of plans on her own, but freely criticized the others.

"What I would like to do," began Cody, without a pointer, but opening a new spiral notebook, "is to bring in the police by putting them on the trail of the Ninjas. We could tell them that we believe they are behind the death of Sandoval, or at least, in the delivery of his hand. The two problems with this are that we have no evidence to support that claim and they probably won't move without more than our word; the second is that the Ninjas are most likely in place near Barbara's house, and we don't want the police to know she has the codex. I haven't been able to get around this. Any ideas?"

Maya shook her head. Her plan would probably have been to secretly move to Paraguay during the night, abandoning everything we owned, starting with my stuff.

"I don't have any," I said. "But I just realized something else. Assuming the Ninjas must be replacements for Schwartz, then the federal police informant has told them that Barbara put the codex in the bank. They would have had this from torturing Sandoval. Of course, the informant would not tell this to the local police, but if somehow they also know, perhaps from notes Sandoval may have made, then what's to stop them from recovering it from the bank on the basis that it's stolen?"

This brought on a grim silence. We had been thinking of the bank as utterly safe.

"Then we have to act as if they know; and it's got to come back out of the bank," said Maya, turning practical. "I know the police are able to get into bank vaults. Many people do not trust the banks for this reason. We have to hide it somewhere away from Barbara. Maybe Marisol could take it for a while?"

"We don't want any more targets on people's backs," I said. "If the Ninjas found out, we'd end up camped out inside her house."

"It's a nice house, though," said Maya, with plenty of art."

"There's plenty of art here," I said. "Too much."

"I think you're right," said Cody. "We have to assume the federal police know it's in Barbara's bank, and even if they don't know which bank that is, they can easily find out."

"We can get it out right away; but the problem then is where to put it. I think we can't place it in the care of anyone, it's too dangerous to that person."

"I think I know a ruined hacienda near Valladolid," said Maya brightly.

Looking at her, I was trying to think how to tactfully phrase what I was about to say. "I know a place for it, and I don't want you to know where it is," I said. "Because if you don't know, you can't be made to tell it. I just want to tell it to Cody because we are the ones with the guns. Are you with me on that?"

"I see," she said, calmly. "Then if I'm captured they can torture me and I won't be able to stop it by telling them anything. Somehow this makes sense to you, I can't think why. That's why I am going upstairs now and you two can figure it out." The look she gave me over her shoulder was acidic. Cody started to protest our good intentions, but there was no adequate response and she didn't acknowledge his argument. I thought she also looked conflicted, relief struggling with indignation at being out of the loop even as she was still at risk. Maybe we should get her a gun too. After she left, Cody and I leaned over the dining table toward each other.

"Here's what I'm thinking," I said. "We put it right back in Cuadrante 13A, Schleicher's house. The police have already been through every inch of it. They know Schwartz took the codex from Schleicher and they're both dead now. There's no path that would take them back to that house. There's also no reason to think the Ninjas know anything about Schleicher, other than that he's dead. They were called in after all that, and I'm thinking they don't even know where he lived. They wouldn't need to."

"That's perfect, Paul. The Cuadrante house is not going to be disturbed until the heirs have sorted all this out, and that will take a while. By the time anybody gets in there again it'll be over. I like it a lot; there's a twisted symmetry to it. Nobody's put at risk by it. Getting in there will be no problem; we've done it before. And there's no dog to mess with us this time, which is good, because I'm out of sleeping pills." Cody had drugged the dog the first time we broke in, back in February, on a different case.

Cody called Barbara and told her that we had to pull the codex out of the bank and why. I thought he handled it skillfully when he said he wouldn't tell her what we were going to do with it. I could imagine the look on her face. Maybe she could take guidance from someone as big as Cody. Then he asked to speak to Pablo Reyes to fill him in on the plan and to get a progress report. I guess surviving was progress enough. When he hung up we were set to go. Maya wanted to go up to Gigante to lay in some additional staples for Cody's extended sleepover.

He tended to go through food faster than we did.

"We'll take Cody's car," I said to her, "and we'll watch you pulling out. If anyone follows you we'll be all over them." She kissed me with what I thought was a special fervor and left. Effectively, she had signed off on our plan without knowing what it was.

Standing in the doorway as she pulled out, there were only two other cars on the street with a commercial van behind them, and I could see no Toyota going after her. I hoped the Ninjas were camped up at Barbara's, held at bay by the Seguridad Reyes crew. We followed Maya up the hill into Atascadero in Cody's Escort and then turned left toward Los Balcones while she went straight on toward the Gigante market. I felt like we were finally taking the offensive. It was time. When we pulled into Barbara's drive the Seguridad Reyes van pulled out the other end.

"There are two of them in the van," Cody said to me after he talked to the driver on his cell, "they're going to flush out the Ninjas and drive them off. If there's a confrontation it'll at least be even, but I don't think the Ninjas will opt for a shootout after Sandoval's murder. They've got to keep their heads down for a while. Meanwhile, as soon as they make contact, we'll collect Barbara and Pablo Reyes and head for the bank. Pablo will go in with her while we watch the street."

We waited inside to hear again from the van. After about five minutes they called to say they had spotted one man in a Chevy around the corner and when they approached on foot he drove off. They were somewhere north of *centro* in the Colonia Guadalupe now visibly following the Chevy but just keeping it in view and not trying to force it to stop. Barbara and Reyes were ready.

"Wouldn't we be more comfortable in the Mercedes?" she asked, wrinkling her nose at Cody's little white Escort.

"Of course we would, but let's take the Ford anyway," said Cody. "Maybe it'll remind you of your student days."

"Not even then," she said, pulling her hair back over her ears with attitude.

In five minutes we rolled up in front of the bank, and Reyes, in his impressive uniform, went in with her. We saw no one threatening on the sidewalk or the street as we waited. By the entry a white haired woman was selling walking tour tickets and two little girls in embroidered peasant outfits were selling flowers. I passed on all of them.

Barbara came out with the tote bag and Reyes emerged two steps behind her with his hand on his gun. Nothing but July morning sun. Young Méxican girls are trained from infancy to always smile on men with guns; it's part of their survival instinct, honed over many years of revolution. It's worked because it's been mainly the men who've died. The girls now looked up and smiled brilliantly at Reyes but he missed it as he scanned the sidewalk. Cody and I both had our shirts unbuttoned to the waist. The air was bristling with *machismo*. I wished I had more hair on my chest. When we got back up the hill Reyes dialed the others in the van.

"We're back," he said. "Keep him running until we get rid of it, maybe an hour or so. Then come back to the house."

We waited until Reyes was inside the house and stuck his head out and gave us an all clear sign. Barbara went in and we headed back through *centro* to Cuadrante 13A. I carefully watched the side mirror.

The great mansion was still immaculate. We parked on the side street next to the garden gate and got out. Cody fiddled with his picks for a while on the lock while I watched the street. I wondered who would own this place next and whether they would know anything about Schleicher. Probably the realtor would keep it quiet, confining herself to the General Santa Ana angle. Supposedly the Alamo hero (for México) had once owned it.

Inside, the garden was untended and the fountain held nothing except husk-like casings from bamboo and an assortment of dead bugs. At the back door Cody slipped through the lock easily and we were inside. I found myself wondering where John Schleicher had died. How ironic he'd been killed during one of his lesser crimes; a simple fencing operation. We went through the rear sitting room with its serene view of the now faded garden and cases of ceramics and other antiques, and entered the library with its high banks of shelves. All the books were carefully faced out toward the front edges. Cody climbed the ladder and placed the codex behind some tall volumes on a top shelf.

"How will we remember which ones it's behind? There must be thousands in here," I said as he slid the ladder back down the row.

"That's easy. It's a classy three-volume set of *Don Quixote*. Green leather with gold lettering on the title and ribs going down the back." Going out, Cody locked the back door and then the garden gate and we went back to Quebrada.

CHAPTER TWENTY
NINJAS

L uis Rosas and Yolo had experienced a humiliating delay on the road south of Querétaro, and Captain Gaspar was not complimentary when they reached him by cell phone. After a series of pointed comments on their mothers' employment history, he remarked that it would be up to them to see that it would not prove damaging to the Cause. Subcommandante Marcos was following this personally. After hanging up Gaspar arranged for a team from the Zapatista safe house in Querétaro to meet them at the roadside restaurant and deliver two different vehicles for them. One was a small Chevrolet that Rosas took for his own surveillance of Barbara's house, and the other was a van with a fruit company logo. Inside were four new tires. The Querétaro team remained behind to replace the tires on the Toyota and return it to the safe house.

Yolo and Rosas returned to San Miguel that afternoon to take up their positions and establish patterns of movement so they could determine their next move. They kept well out of sight.

On Wednesday morning a courier drove in from México City with Professor Sandoval's left hand. He turned it over to Yolo with instructions to leave it at the door of Paul Zacher's house to soften them up for the abduction that was being planned. They had

204

selected Maya as the victim, since she was out alone more than Barbara. Luis Rosas had been put off by the new security presence at Barbara's house but Yolo believed he was undetected at the Zacher house on Quebrada. The Ninjas had rented a small *casita* up on Callejon Atascadero, an address much frequented for short-term rentals by *gringos* and visitors from México City, which the locals called *chilangos*. The street had a diverse mix of inhabitants and the Ninjas' comings and goings would not be noticed. It was also inconvenient for cars, being extremely narrow and steep, and not navigable by vehicles as far down as their *casita*, so it kept the traffic away, an obvious benefit.

On Thursday morning Yolo was in position early about a block from the Zacher house down on Quebrada, but he could observe the entrance clearly. At about ten o'clock he saw the woman, whose name he did not know, emerge and pull away in the artist's white van. Zacher stood in the doorway and watched her go. After he and a much bigger man came out and got into a small Ford, Yolo moved into the traffic four cars behind them. He did not get a detailed look at the woman, but he could see she was wearing jeans and a close fitting white top. He noted that her hair came slightly below her shoulders. She turned right at the corner and then left on Correo, which turned into San-to Domingo after a few blocks and went up the hill into Atascadero. The van went through the arches and up into the rolling hills beyond. By this time the Ford had turned off.

The woman in the white van pulled into the parking lot of the Gigante Market. Just as Yolo was about to park nearby a Bimbo Bread truck cut him off, stopped briefly, blocking him in place, and then moved closer to the building. He had now lost sight of the woman as he pulled into a spot three rows over from her van. He jumped out and hurried inside.

A dozen or so small shops occupied the space before the entrance to the main market and Yolo scanned the interiors carefully without seeing her, and then went into Gigante. He picked up a cart at the entrance and began working through the aisles, taking a few items off the shelves for cover as he went. At the end of a row three or four over he caught sight of her and moved quickly up beside her. As she picked up a block of cheese with her right hand he grabbed her left arm firmly.

"What...?" She turned and saw the gun tucked in his belt.

"Just be very quiet. You are coming with me." He pulled her down the aisle, abandoning the carts. About half way down she grabbed a jar off the shelf as they passed and swung it at his face. He saw it coming but couldn't duck in time and it caught him on the top of the head. His vision narrowed for an instant as the jar shattered and splashed both of them with garbanzo beans, marinated in oil and vinegar. Dizzy, he lost his footing and they both went down in the slippery mess, arms and legs flying, but he kept his grip on her shoulder.

"I will shoot you right here," he said tensely through his teeth, as they struggled to their feet. People looked up from their carts as Yolo pushed her to the end of the aisle. Probably just another domineering husband. At the entrance they slowed to a walk. No one had followed them. At the fruit van he shoved her inside and fastened her arms behind her back with a pair of plastic handcuffs. Before he got into the driver's seat he swatted his tennis hat against the side of the van, scattering glass fragments over the pavement.

"Who are you?" she asked, as they squealed out of the parking lot, narrowly avoiding a truck full of bricks.

"Just a soldier."

"Where are we going?"

"You're going to stay with me until we get the codex. It won't be long."

"What is a codex?"

Yolo had a brief flash of alarm from this response, but recovered. "I think you know." His head was throbbing and he twisted the rear view mirror to look at it. There was broad red swelling at his hairline. "That wasn't necessary. Now we stink."

The woman was silent.

At the top of Callejon Atascadero he parked the van and followed her closely down the hill, shielding the handcuffs from view. Trash littered the steep concrete and he carefully avoided a spill of red paint that looked like it might be fresh. He unlocked a gate about a third of the way down and looked around as he pushed her through. No one was in sight. Just inside the door of the casita she turned and aimed a kick at his groin that he sidestepped and then shoved her down on a chair.

"That's enough," he said. "You will suffer for anything more."

"I need to wash this off. I can't stand it."

Yolo thought for a moment. The outside door was dead-bolted from the inside, and the key was in his pocket. The windows opened only in small sections within the steel frames, too small for anyone to wriggle through.

He knew from his earlier examination of the premises that the bathroom window was tiny. "You can take a shower," he said. "Then I'll take one. After that we can wash the clothes."

"What will I wear while the clothes are washing?"

Yolo went back into the bedroom and found extra sheets in the armoire. "How about this? You can wrap it around you." He handed one to her, then realized she was still handcuffed.

"Can I trust you if I take these off?"

She nodded. He released her and she took the sheet and went into the bathroom.

Yolo thought about his plan while she showered. He intended to wait until mid afternoon to generate anxiety, and then call Paul Zacher with details for the ransom. He felt good about things so far. The woman seemed more tractable now and the shower would probably relax her. He would cuff her to one of the bed rails while he showered. He didn't want her waiting for him outside the bathroom door with a cast-iron frying pan in her hand.

In a few minutes she emerged wearing the sheet and pulling a comb through her hair. Freshly scrubbed and free of the marinade she was attractive. Relaxed enough now to look at her more closely, he almost put his hand on her shoulder as she placed her clothes in the washer.

Yolo was not a violent man by nature; but he was dedicated to his cause and he believed that certain unpleasant things had to be done from time to time to keep things moving. After all, the Zapatistas needed to match the government in ruthlessness just to survive. He did not flinch from these things and he did not reflect much about them after they were done. Placing the severed hand at the Zacher house had not moved him. Surely it had belonged to a Neocolonialist oppressor. The courier had strongly cautioned him that if he removed the gold ring the message would be lost. Yolo was not tempted.

Most of his previous duties had been confined to guerrilla raids on government positions in and around Chiapas, and furnishing security for senior officers in the Zapatistas. He had never had his own prisoner before, and he found it uncomfortably exciting. Power over individuals had not figured much in his experience. He also sensed this was a test.

Although he was not a large man, Yolo was well muscled from working out and ate frugally. This last part was not difficult because rations could be irregular in the highlands of Chiapas. There was some foraging possible in the jungle, but the results were usually meager and Yolo did not care for snake meat. Lizards were occasionally OK. In the shower he soaped himself down and rinsed off, aware as always that water was scarce in many parts of México. When he came out of the bathroom and added his clothes to the others in the washer, he could see the woman still cuffed to the bed. He spun the dial, struggled for a moment with how to start it before he pushed it in, and walked toward her.

When he reached down to unlock the handcuffs she almost involuntarily touched his head at the edge of the bruise, now a darker red.

"Are you hungry?" he asked.

She nodded. "Anything but garbanzo beans." She managed a slight smile. "I'm sorry I hit you. It looks terrible." Yolo's hand went to his head.

In the kitchen he swallowed three aspirin and took some leftover rice and tortillas from the refrigerator. The woman followed him in and put the rice in the microwave. She wore the sheet like a toga, knotted over one shoulder so that her arms were free. The hem reached to the floor.

"Tell me about the codex," she said.

"You have not seen it?" This came as a surprise to him.

"No. I know nothing about it."

"It is an ancient manuscript of my people. I am Mayan from Chiapas, but the manuscript is from the Yucatán, where the people have not risen yet."

"But you think they will?"

"God willing."

"What does it contain?"

"I don't know, but the Subcomandante believes it will cause the others to pick up their rifles and join us. Perhaps the codex predicts this."

"And when they join you?"

"Then the government will have to bargain seriously with us because there will be two states in arms. We will no longer be between the sword and the wall. Maybe Quintana Roo and Campeche will join as well. But there is another thing too. I have been told there is no other Mayan codex in México. It is a question of who should own it—the descendants of those who made it, or the oppressors in México City."

"I think I no longer fear you," she said, after a pause.

"But I am strong." He gave her what he felt was a formidable grin.

"I can see that. But you fight for what you believe,

an ideal. Most Mexicans only fight for survival."

"Later I will make a call and I will exchange you for the codex. Then you will be free again. I wish you no evil. This is just something that must be done."

"Is that all? You will be done with me?"

He looked at her arm where the marks from his fingers were still visible. "I am sorry I hurt you." He reached out and touched her face. She didn't pull away. They moved into the bedroom and lay on his bed. Through the windows he could see the garden, parched and untended. He slowly untied the sheet at her shoulder and pulled it down to her waist. When he placed his hands over her breasts she pulled his face down to her mouth.

CHAPTER TWENTY-ONE

Even though I felt like we were under siege, I still had some business to do. Thursday afternoon I went down to Galería Uno to select paintings for an upcoming group show. I didn't have anything new to bring in, only three or four older things they hadn't seen; it was mainly a rehash of past offerings to clear their storage bins and I didn't expect a great deal from it. Ramon Rivera was more optimistic. I guess you have to be if you're an art dealer. After Maya had gone to do some shopping at Gigante in the morning she was headed back to the archive. Our paths didn't cross. Cody was up at Barbara's helping to circle the wagons. He said the situation there was getting increasingly tense as they waited for the Ninjas to make a move. I guess that was possible but I thought he really just wanted to see that the big nude of Barbara was hanging straight. He's a detail-oriented guy. It probably comes from all those years as a cop.

When I got back after four o'clock Maya hadn't returned yet, but I expected her for supper. At five I was diddling around in the studio, something that occasionally passes for productive activity, but I had to admit as I sat staring Maya's Tejuana costume that I was getting tense as well. I pressed it to my face; I was starting to get a bad feeling; maybe I should have gone with her to Gigante. On the other hand, although she resented being caught up in this, she also didn't care to be watched over too closely.

I heard Cody come back from Barbara's and go up to the guest room. I stuck my head in.

"Any action?"

"Nothing. Just a bunch of guys drawing wages. They're happy and Barbara isn't."

"What did she say?"

"She wondered why we couldn't do something to get this moving. She's sick of it. She's thinking of offering a bonus to anyone who can crack it open." He broke down his gun and started cleaning it. "You ought to do this too now and then. It picks up moisture from your armpit."

"There hasn't been much to break a sweat over, except Sandoval's hand."

"Even so. It's a humid spot. What have you been up to?"

"I've just been wandering around. I dropped some things off and set them up at the gallery, just to kill some time."

"That bad, huh?"

Just as we came downstairs Maya came in, dropped her purse in the kitchen, and set her laptop down in the dining room. While I was kissing her, the phone rang and she picked it up. There was a brief exchange and she handed it to me with one of those Mexican shrugs that implies that the world is incomprehensible. I've been here long enough to agree.

"*Bueno*," I said, the standard phone greeting.

"We have your woman," a man said in response, in Spanish. The quality of his voice was young and the accent was not local; possibly southern México. I looked at Maya. She shrugged again and her eyebrows went up. Her lips silently formed the word "Chiapas?"

"You have my woman?" I repeated. It sounded stupid even to me. I was missing something here; possibly more detective training would have helped. With Maya standing in front of me the only other person I could think of was Barbara, who was hardly my woman, despite her efforts, and I couldn't imagine that the Ninjas had broken through Reyes' men. Surely it was not Cindy, my old girlfriend from Cleveland. I hadn't seen her in seven years.

"If you wish to see her again," the voice continued with no awareness of my confusion, "we will need to have the codex. Do you have it with you now?"

"No," I said. They must know this. My mind was doing cartwheels. For some reason I checked my gun. I covered the receiver with my hand. "They're coming out," I said. That was clear; beyond that, I didn't get it.

"Play along," said Cody, leaning forward on the table.

"How do I know you have her?" I said.

"We picked her up this morning at the Gigante Market. Do you trust me, or do I need to send you another hand?" There was a pause where I didn't respond. This was the real deal.

"You've got my full attention now," I said.

"I will phone you at ten o'clock tomorrow morning to arrange delivery. You will have the codex ready by then." He hung up before I could respond.

"I'd better check your back again," I said to Maya as I put down the phone, "because I just heard they were holding you for ransom."

Cody was already on his cell phone dialing

Barbara. "Hi darlin'," he said. "Everything all right up there?" I guess danger brings people closer, because they didn't say darlin' in Peoria. "We just got a call they're holding Maya to trade for the codex, only she's standing here next to me. They'll call back at ten in the morning. I'll keep you in the loop." I thought I could sense the same degree of bewilderment on the other end of the line.

"Well," said Maya, gradually lowering herself at the table as if her knees hurt, "I guess that roasts the chicken."

"I haven't heard that one," I said. "Maybe it's 'our goose is cooked'?"

"I just made it up. I couldn't think of anything better."

"He's got the wrong woman. He must have plucked somebody out of the crowd, thinking it was you," said Cody.

"But he also knew you were there," I said, "which means he saw you leave. We've got to tighten security on this end."

Cody came around the side of the table and put his arms around her from behind and kissed the top of her head. "Jesus," he said. She pressed her hands over his. I just stared at her, thinking how close we had come. On the phone, I had only been processing information.

"There was a disturbance when I was at Gigante," she said. "I could hear it, and there was a crash like glass breaking and it sounded like some people fell down. From where I was I couldn't see any of it."

Cody and I sat down. We were in the bunker again. "This is the break," he said. He was calm now, in command. We had planned to draw them out, but now

215

that they had drawn us out, it didn't matter. We would move and retake control. "I think now it's time to show a gesture of good faith to the police. If they use the same tactics we used in Peoria, they'll want us to make the drop."

"Make the drop?" asked Maya. It was something she wanted to add to her idiom.

"Deliver the codex according to his instructions," said Cody.

"But what will we use for the codex?" I asked. "We can't use the real one because then the police will recover it, and we can't use our copy because it's black and white and obviously a photocopy; it would never pass."

Cody shook his head. "It doesn't matter. Give them a cookbook, if you have to, anything the right size. This guy is not going to stand there at the drop, wherever it is, and look at it, because he'll want to clear out as quickly as possible. He won't open it until he gets to his car at the earliest and probably not even then, and at that point the police can be in position to follow him. Just wrap it securely, so that it's not easily opened. Trust me, I've been around the block on these deals."

I could see that the Tejuana picture was not on the agenda for tomorrow. Cody reached Licenciado Rodriguez and told him what was happening. He agreed that I should make the drop, trying to give him enough time after the call so he could get his officers in place. We left it that we would call him back after we had our instructions. I thought it funny that he didn't suggest tapping our phone, but maybe that had already been taken care of. Probably long ago.

Friday morning we were up at six. We didn't

sleep much and we didn't do anything else either. Maya was padding around the kitchen barefoot in her Liga Méxicana *futbol* jersey. When she bent over the sink and saw me looking at her she flipped up the back of the shirt.

"Cute butt," I said, "but I'm too jittery to appreciate it. Now I'm going to wear the target for a while."

"Good time to clean that gun," said Cody, coming in and pulling up a stool at the counter. "Here's the kit."

He showed me how to disassemble the pistol and clean the chambers and the barrel. Afterward I spun the cylinder and reloaded it. I thought I made it look professional. Then I shuffled through our cookbooks, because some of them seemed about the right size, and found one called *The Encyclopedia of Herbs, Spices and Flavoring*. After I wrapped it in brown paper over several layers of newsprint, I taped all the edges thoroughly and slipped it into the tote bag while I waited for the phone to ring. I wondered how the hostage was doing, and whether she had any kind of clue what was going on. Probably not much more than we did. Possibly less. I hoped the Ninjas were treating her well. It occurred to me that we were playing with her life by substituting the cookbook for the codex, but on the other hand, there was no guarantee they would free her even with the real thing. Maybe I was rationalizing, but I couldn't have it falling into the hands of the police.

Maya was on her sixth cup of coffee and drumming her fingers on the counter. Cody was pacing. That was something he rarely did, he'd spent too much time on stakeout. At ten o'clock the phone did not ring.

It took five minutes more. They were playing with

us, or maybe their watch was off.

"Do you have the codex now?" asked the same voice.

"I will have it at noon."

"You will bring it to the northeast corner of the *jardín*. Do you know which one that is? There is a trash can at the corner next to the bench of the shoe-shine. Sit down and place it in the space between the can and the bench and then leave immediately. I will expect you at two o'clock. It this clear?"

"Yes."

"You will come alone."

"Of course."

"We will be watching you. Do not look around. If the codex is in order we will release your woman this afternoon." He hung up.

I immediately dialed Rodriguez and told him his crew could get into position at the *jardín* for a drop at two o'clock.

At one-thirty we left Quebrada and drove down to Galería Cruz to drop Maya off with Marisol. I didn't kid myself that Marisol would be any protection, but I wanted Maya away from our house and I didn't think the Ninjas would be following us today. Pablo Reyes had reported no sightings up in Los Balcones, and my best guess was that they were together getting ready for the drop. I left Cody on the corner to see Maya inside Marisol's house; he would walk the rest of the way to the *jardín* and approach from a different direction. He was wearing an old wind-breaker and a baseball hat; a retired person carrying a grocery bag stuffed with newspaper. I was doubtful about this as a disguise; it looked like camouflage on a rhinoceros.

I found a place to park a block away on Hidalgo and ambled slowly toward the *jardín*, doing a little window-shopping on the way; the casual *gringo* tourist, most likely lost. It was five minutes until two. My pulse was racing when I crossed San Francisco and climbed the steps to the northeast corner of the plaza. Halfway down on the same side and across the sidewalk I saw Rodriguez sitting on a bench reading a newspaper. He wore the blue jacket and cap of a street sweeper. The cap said *limpio*. It made me think of Delgado collecting garbage in Dolores Hidalgo. Rodriguez didn't look up. Further into the *jardín*, next to the bandstand, sat Cody reading a magazine with the grocery bag on the bench next to him. He was munching on something; it might have been peanuts. Three pigeons and a squirrel watched respectfully, but no one else did.

I sat on the bench next to the trash can and slid the tote bag into the space between as if I wanted to get it out of my way. I scratched my head for a minute, then got up and left the way I had come. Not an Oscar winning performance, but how could I embellish it? There was no room for dialog. My part was over and I didn't want to stick around and make the Ninjas nervous.

Back in the car, I swung by Marisol's to pick up Maya. Marisol wanted to give me coffee, but I had had enough already to float a small barge. I used her bathroom and we left. Cody arrived at Quebrada half an hour after us.

"He picked it up ten minutes after you left. He had been sitting on the southeast corner, so he could see you from the time you crossed the street. Not a big guy, rather dark complexion, good looking in a Mayan sort of way. He had on jeans and a khaki shirt. He could have been one of the guys who followed us on the Escobedo trip, but I didn't get that close a look at them. He didn't make any move to look inside the tote bag because he was watching you leave. He stayed on that corner by the trash can and waited until you were all the way down the street and had gotten into the artmobile and pulled out. Rodriguez had already moved out onto San Francisco, where he was poking around with a trash can over there. He waited until the Ninja had gone down San Francisco to Hidalgo and turned right, then he got on his phone to alert their cars. I couldn't see any more. I think this is going to be over fast. Their base has to be here in town somewhere."

Maya was fanning herself with a magazine, although it was not any warmer than usual. I pulled a deck of cards out of the drawer next to the silverware and she and I played gin rummy for a while. Cody was pacing again. Maya beat me every hand.

"Do you think they will let her go?" she said.

"If the police do their job they won't have a choice."

"I know how she feels," she said, shuffling the cards and then dealing. "She was shopping at Gigante and suddenly she had a target on her back."

My hand was lousy again.

We had been back nearly two hours when Rodriguez called. He said they had started with twelve cops out of uniform stationed in their own cars located all over town. I asked him why twelve and he said only that many owned cars. When the Ninja pulled out after his visit to the *jardín* one vehicle followed him for three blocks and then turned off, notifying the next car that he was coming into view, and so on, so that he never had the same car tailing him for more than a short distance. At the top of Callejon Atascadero the Ninja parked while the police vehicle went on past and parked around the corner. The police caught him out in the open as he walked down the hill and stopped to unlock the gate of the rental casita. They disarmed him and went in with a gun to his head. One of the cops placed the cookbook carefully in his car, wrapped in a blanket.

Inside they surprised the second Ninja with a woman named Elena Burgos, whose name they already knew from the purse she had abandoned at Gigante. He didn't have a chance to go for his gun. Oddly, Señorita Burgos rushed in distress to the side of the man they had captured out in the street, saying, "Yolo, Yolo...."

"And she wore a Yolo ribbon," said Cody with a grin.

"That's disgraceful," said Maya, digging her elbow into his ribs. "The poor woman! Who knows what she went through? I hope he didn't rape her. It could have been me."

"Sounds like the Stockholm syndrome in double time," I said. "Remember how Patricia Hearst became Tanya and started holding up banks with the SLA? The hostage joins the hostage-takers. It's legendary."

"I think it took months to bring her to that," said Maya. "I can't believe this Elena Burgos would turn so fast. She's Méxican."

I looked at her. "What would you have done?"

"I would have flirted with him for a while. I can be very charming, as you know. Maybe show him a little skin." She tossed her hair back and gave me her wide smile, the one with almost too many teeth and a perfect small dimple in each cheek.

"And then?"

"When he reached out to touch me I would have taken away his gun and shot him. Dead." Her smile did not change.

CHAPTER TWENTY-TWO

The voltage was running high at Casa Watt. All the lights, inside and out, were blazing as we drove up at eight o'clock. The Seguridad Reyes van had been moved out into the street and only one guard remained. Our guard was coming down too, but not totally. Cody was wearing an oversize shirt that had room for a .38, and his best khaki pants. I had left my gun at home. Maya made me wear a pair of black slacks and a bottle green silk shirt. I looked OK.

Barbara, of course, was terrific in a French blue silk dress that had the same V cut down to her waist back and front. The blaze of diamonds at her neck and swinging from her ears might have started the civil war in Sierra Leone. Maya, whose stock of clothes mainly consisted of three dresses, a couple of skirts and tops, and an aerosol can of spray-on jeans, had chosen to wear the same green number she had worn at the dinner with Jason Schwartz, with some of her heavy Méxican silver jewelry.

When I talked to Barbara after Rodriguez called she was practically hooting; as much as a carefully brought up girl from Montgomery, Alabama, with $40,000,000 can hoot. Which turned out to be more than I expected. She immediately decided to have a wind-up dinner party on Saturday to celebrate the end of the Ninjas and our return to normal life. She even considered for a moment inviting Licenciado Rodriguez, but I reminded her that we wouldn't be able to talk freely about the codex in his presence. She said that instead she would write him a nice thank you note. It was the only thing I had ever heard her say that sounded like it might have come from her mother.

A butler in a tuxedo met us at the door. I glanced in at the dining room as we passed. A handful of leaves had been removed from the vast mahogany table so it was now only about the length of a dining table in a middle size college dormitory. Intimacy on a grand scale.

On the sideboard in the great room two bottles of 1990 Dom Perignon awaited us. Alex Ross, the piano player who had worked Barbara's last party, right before Perry's death in February, was back with some quiet Bill Evans tunes as the butler poured the champagne. My glass was halfway to my lips when Cody began tapping on the side of his glass with a ballpoint pen. Ross paused in mid phrase and looked up.

"Before we get too rowdy in celebrating the end of this thing, I'd like to take a minute to remember Vincent Sandoval." We all joined him in standing. "He was a man who wanted only to advance the cause of Mayan scholarship, and it cost him his life. I respected him, I liked him personally, and I will miss him." He raised his glass. The butler stood frozen at the archway leading to the dining room.

We all drank a sip of champagne. "And I will always regret that we brought him into this," he finished. The eyes of both women were filled with tears. There was silence for a moment and then the piano resumed. I was thinking again about my role in bringing Sandoval into this disaster.

"And is it the end of this thing?" Barbara broke the silence. Her cheeks were slightly flushed as she again raised the glass to her lips.

As she spoke the last security guard passed through the dining room. I thought I heard him say, softly, "*Ojala*, God willing."

Barbara made a signal to Alex Ross and the music picked up the tempo a bit. I found myself wanting to lighten the mood. She came close to me and put her hand on my arm. "How do you know if you have that dress on right?" I said. "Isn't it the same both ways?"

"Don't painters know these things? The top is a little fuller in front, and the back is fuller below the waist. If that doesn't tell you, then you can always look at the label. But if you have to look at the label to get it right you wouldn't be wearing a dress like this."

"I see. Are you still liking the picture in that spot over the mantel?"

"Loving it. I've spent a lot of time up there since I've been under house arrest. It's become my room now. I am going to take out all of Perry's 'ancestor' portraits and brighten it up. Let's get together now that I can move about more freely and talk about what else you've got."

"What do you think about a Chinese robe picture? It would be a nice counterpoint to the nude."

"I like the idea. It could be casually sophisticated instead of inviting."

"I could see it with a carved fan in your hand, and your hair up. A bit of thigh from the slit up the side, but other than that, not much skin beyond your arms and face. The background would be dark, vague, undefined.

Sketchy against sharper definitions in your face and the robe, your hair. It could work. It would be good to have one of those carved wooden Chinese chairs, but I don't know where we'd find one here."

"Let me call Alvaro Zhou at the China Garden. He can probably lend me one. Are you ready for a margarita?"

She signaled the butler who made the rounds taking drinks orders. We moved out onto the terrace and looked down, leaning on the long wrought iron balustrade. In each section, floral metalwork bracketed a coat of arms in the center. I hadn't known Perry came nobility—I thought his family had left West Tennessee in the thirties. The sun was down, but the hills to the west were still edged with a reddish glow. The lights were lit in the garden and around the pool.

Barbara said to Cody, "I forgot to tell you. I solved my break-in problem." He leaned on the rail next to her and looked out toward the *jardín*. From that direction a string of firecrackers went off. No special occasion is required here, only a match or the end of a cigarette.

"Who was it?"

"That day I was going out in the afternoon. Gabriel, the gardener was coming to water and deadhead a few things. He takes care of the pool too. But what I didn't know was that his wife had gone into labor that afternoon and he called his cousin to take his place. Gabriel gave him the key and the security code, which he shouldn't have done. I would have understood if he had just not shown up."

"And how did you find out?" asked Maya.

"Three days later Gabriel came to the door. He handed me 5,000 pesos and a paper bag. In the bag was a pair of pink satin panties. He was deeply embarrassed and told me the whole thing. He said he would never trust his cousin again." She sipped her margarita.

"What did you say to Gabriel?" I asked, trying not to laugh.

"I thanked him profusely and presented him with the 5,000 pesos for his honesty. He didn't want to take it at first, but I said to think of it as a gift for his new baby. Then he lit up. He said now the baby has a *torta*, a sandwich. It must be a traditional thing here. After he left I threw the panties away. If only the other problem were so simple. Do you think they'll send more people after the codex?"

"I think it hinges on who *they* are," said Cody. "If it was only Jason Schwartz and the Ninjas, then they're wiped out now. I suppose we can stop calling them Ninjas; Rodriguez says they're called Rosas and Yolo. Paul thinks their motive is ideological and I'm inclined to agree. If that's true they're likely to be members of a larger group, and if they are, more will be coming."

"More coming. How many will they sacrifice?"

"Fanaticism is a stronger motive than greed. They might be prepared to go on with this for a while."

"But so are we," Barbara said.

"Of course," said Maya, nodding, probably seeing this running out until everyone in San Miguel was dead. She turned her face from Barbara's view and rolled her eyes at me.

Barbara took this as a vote of confidence from Maya, but she hadn't seen what I had, and I thought it sounded more like exasperation than affirmation in her voice.

"Cody, I have deep pockets. I'm determined to keep the codex and I'm not going to allow myself to be pushed. It's not my style. You probably know that already."

"Suppose you were up against a group like the Zapatistas?"

"The rebels in Chiapas?" she said.

"Yes," said Cody, hands on the rail. "We've been calling them Ninjas. I've been trying to think who might want the codex so badly and yet not want to cash in on it. What would the ideological reason be? According to Dr. Sandoval, the text shows the Mayans rising in revolt against the oppressors, and you know what the illustrations showed. Maybe that's why they want it, to use it to inspire resistance among those who haven't taken up arms yet. I'm speculating here. But if it is an ideological reason, what else could it be? Look at the murders. They have the hallmark of the true believer."

"Paul said the caller sounded southern, possibly Mayan."

"Yes, and when you also consider that the feds tried to make a case of national security involvement, it fits together. It's easy to dismiss that because you've heard what a joke it became during Watergate, but what if that's true this time? It certainly explains why the feds want the codex."

"But do you think the codex could really inspire revolt in the Yucatán?" I said. "That seems like a stretch to me. They must have better reasons."

"I'm not sure whether it would or wouldn't, but I've heard that the old ways continue in many parts of the

Yucatán. Not to the extent of ripping people's hearts out, of course. What matters to us is whether the Zapatistas think it might help spark an uprising. If they do, then it's them sitting across the table from us and playing the other hand."

Maya stepped over to the rail. "And their hand consists of four murders and a kidnapping so far. But I'm not unsympathetic to what they want; just to their means, since the last victim was mistaken for me. And poor Professor Sandoval. How could they justify that?"

Clearly there was no answer to this, beyond the fact that anyone can justify anything. The butler appeared from the French doors and said something softly to Barbara. She called us in for dinner.

The dining room was large enough to accommodate two dining groups, and for this gathering, Barbara had ordered a smaller round table set up in the corner of the room. The only chandelier, of course, was unused over the long refectory table, but all around us the picture lights were lit and there was a cluster of candles in the center of the table. For a small dinner party the feeling was right. There was a level of restraint I wasn't used to in Barbara. At a round table you can speak to anyone without turning.

The walls were rag rolled in a mottled persimmon, set off by eighteenth century Mexican colonial-style chairs with a brocade upholstery on the greenish side of teal. The table was a parchment shade in damask. The napkins matched the chairs. The butler brought a bottle of wine from the sideboard, where another was breathing as well, and filled our glasses.

"This is a 1982 Margaux," said Barbara. "It

should be just coming into its prime now. Perry had four cases of this brought down from Houston last year." She held her glass up to the light. "I invited you here tonight to say thank you for all you've done on the codex. I especially include you, Maya, because the abduction of that poor woman from Gigante reminded me of what kind of risk you've been taking too. I thank you all."

There was a murmur of surprise and thanks.

We started with a jicama salad with a spicy green salsa. The Margaux was a big wine and stood up well with it.

Cody sipped his wine reflectively. "I've heard it said that '82 was the year of the century in Bordeaux. Judging from this I can believe it."

"The 2000 vintage will be stunning as well," said Barbara, "once it's ready. We'll have to have this dinner again in twenty years and see."

"This is wonderful," said Maya. "I know we need to celebrate, but is this only the intermission between act one and act two?"

"It's probably not a one act play," I said. "But we do need a break."

"I'm keeping the single guard on duty in the house until we know. There are three of them in rotation, so they never sleep, but at least I do."

The butler brought in the next course; delicate servings of cheese quesadillas with candied walnuts and cilantro.

"Look at it this way," said Cody. "We won the first round. They're going to have to consider how much of their resources they want to devote to this, if they continue." He swirled the wine around in his glass as if he knew what he was doing.

"You mean there might be ten Ninjas next time?" asked Maya. I knew she could feel the target reforming on her back.

"Maybe it becomes too costly for them to come at us again. If it is the Zapatistas, they also have a war to fight against the government. Do they have resources to spare for this?" I was trying to sound hopeful. Maybe it was just the wine talking, and the margarita. And the champagne.

"Am I being too selfish here?" asked Barbara to the table at large. "Should I just give it up? Even though I don't even know where it is at this point?"

"I don't think so," said Maya, putting aside her apprehension. "I wouldn't want to be pushed either. The codex should end up with a collector or in a museum. It shouldn't be a pawn in political policy or military struggles. Anyway, they don't have any right to it. Professor Sandoval gave it to you and you accepted his terms. He's gone and you are the custodian now. The deal is made and the torch is passed, if you're brave enough to hold it. I'm not sure I would be."

Barbara said nothing, but looked at Maya as if it was the first time she'd had her clear support.

The butler returned and refilled our glasses from the second bottle of Margaux. When he brought large plates filled with marinated pork tenderloins and mashed potatoes with roasted garlic, Cody sighed contentedly. He probably didn't eat like this at home. The conversation drifted away from the codex and onto local politics, property taxes (absurdly low in México, Barbara paid just under $500 a year on her mansion), and whether the

231

new renovation of the *jardín* was justified in providing for handicapped visitors. It was kinder, but unhistorical.

"I never thought political correctness would come to México," I said. "It makes me sad." I realized I was not all that sad, but I was slightly tilted in my chair, maybe three or four degrees off true vertical.

After the main course we took a breather, and then the butler served coffee and Mexican brownies with ice cream. I began to hope Barbara was going to provide gurney service out to the artmobile.

When dessert was finished we moved back into the great room, and the butler followed with more wine. The piano player returned after taking a break while we ate. We were all feeling nicely mellow and I thought Maya seemed a little unsteady. She had spent so much time with a target on her back she needed to cut loose. Cody was all right; he had the capacity of any two of us. I was pleasantly limber. My elbows seemed ready to swing in all directions.

Maya was swirling the wine in her glass and observing it the way you're supposed to do at a tasting. Suddenly she brightened.

"I know. Let's dance!" She set down the wine on one of the three coffee tables and walked over to Cody and pulled him out of his chair. At the piano Alex Ross paused and looked at her with his eyebrows raised.

"Something slow," she said to him. Immediately he moved into *The Way You Look Tonight*, and Maya and Cody began to move across the floor. I was thinking how you could put thirty dancing couples in this room with space to spare when I felt Barbara move against my body with a shock.

232

"Put your arm around me," she said in my ear. It was more than a request. Her arm went around my neck and her cheek was pressing mine as we danced. I could feel her breasts against my chest. I don't know anything about perfume, but the subtle citrus blossom scent she was wearing caused important areas of my brain to dissolve. The first to go was the seat of common sense and caution. I found my fingers on the part of her back that was not covered by her dress. Her entire body conformed to mine and every part of it spoke to me in a language that was blunt, and required no fancy adverbs.

"This is *beyond* dangerous," I whispered. "Are you sure you want..." I started to say, but I could feel her smile against my cheek and I knew the answer.

A lot of people think that having nude models in an art studio is somehow titillating. The bare truth is that there is no more businesslike place in the universe. The whole process is framed by rules that prevent misunderstandings that might make the models uncomfortable. When Barbara posed nude for me these rules locked onto my head like radar. Whenever she approached the easel to see what I was doing, I always sat on my hands. I insisted that she always dress and undress behind a screen. I did this with every model, even Maya. Painting is all business to me.

Now as Barbara breathed into my ear, my resolve was shrinking and other things were growing in compensation. I was helpless without the studio between us. My right hand had rejected any input from the few parts of my brain still operating and was traveling freely over her back and shoulders, often inside her dress. I was praying that it stayed on her back and on the upper part of her body, but there was no way to guarantee it.

"I can feel your interest," she said in a voice that didn't go much past her lips, as she pulled away and looked into my eyes. The piano player started *As Time Goes By*. I felt like Humphrey Bogart in Casablanca, dancing with Ingrid Bergman. All I lacked was a white dinner jacket.

I glanced over at Maya. She was looking up at Cody and saying something funny, judging from the look on his face. Barbara was unexpectedly gripping my right thigh between both of hers. "Sweet Jesus," I said, "This is *such* a bad idea." But I didn't release her and she didn't release me.

In the course of painting her I had looked carefully at all of her, but never before from a distance of two inches. Now, as I looked at her skin and hair from less than that, I could see the extremely fine down blondes have below that wisp of hair in front of their ears. I surprised myself by taking part of her ear between my lips. Any sense of caution had left the building.

"I know exactly what you are thinking," she said, her breath warm and moist in my ear. "You are seeing yourself absolutely fucking my brains out until I scream."

A small insight, perhaps. A shot in the dark. But not without a tiny grain of truth.

"Delicately put," I said, as we moved across the floor. I think Ross was looking at us; I know he never looked at the keys.

"We should celebrate this victory again some time, just you and me," she went on. "Privately."

My right hand came up unasked and traced a line from her ear to the corner of her lips. I was trying to think how I could unobtrusively place my mouth on hers—what if I rotated just about twelve degrees to the left? Suddenly there was a tap on my shoulder. "Can I cut in?" asked Maya.

I guess timing is everything. Another twenty seconds and I would have had Barbara down on the sofa while I ripped her clothes off with my teeth.

Maya tucked herself into my body with a warm embrace and I realized she was too out of it to have noticed. But Cody's glance as he started to dance with Barbara told me I had not heard the end of it.

CHAPTER TWENTY-THREE

With the aid of more than a few aspirins I was able to walk upright in the morning, but not immediately. It took practice to get downstairs. Try doing one step at a time, I told myself. Rehearse the foot order; to operate best they alternate. Keep both hands on the railing. Normally I would welcome the bright sunlight, but this morning it seemed sharp and edgy, forcing its way under my eyelids like a sheet of cardboard. Eventually I was sitting in the kitchen with my third cup of coffee, appalled at my own behavior at Barbara's dinner. With a dash of guilty relief that I hadn't been caught, it was coming back to me bit by bit when Cody came in, dressed, and looking pretty fresh for an old cop. He poured himself a cup of coffee and sat down across from me at the counter. There was a grin on his face that I didn't like. It didn't take him long to get to the point.

"Fair amount of steam coming off you and Barbara last night." He sipped his coffee and stared out the window onto the garden, where the limes were in flower. They're almost always in flower. I don't think he could look at me.

"What gave it away?"

"Aside from the fact that most of the windows were fogged over, I think it must have been when

236

you had her ear in your mouth. You ought to be more careful with that. Those diamonds were big enough to block your airway. As a person trained in CPR, I'm not sure it would have been a good thing, thinking the kind of thoughts you were having about her, to wake up and find me giving you mouth to mouth resuscitation. It's lucky that Maya was celebrating so hard, because you've only got one guest room and right now I'm using it."

I had forgotten about the ear thing. I wondered what else I couldn't recall under my own power that I would soon be reminded of. "OK, I can see where that might have given you the wrong impression."

"Oh, I had the right impression. I'm a longtime student of human behavior. Near Ph.D. in psychology, remember?"

"I can't believe I did that. I completely let my guard down."

"I really don't get it either. You've spent all that time with her in the studio when she was naked, and nothing happened, right?"

"Nothing. I don't touch her in the studio. It would be wrong."

"It didn't look entirely proper last night."

"I was lucky that Maya cut in when she did be- cause if it had gone any further I'd have had Barbara down on the sofa while I peeled her clothes off with my teeth. That was the image I woke up with. Then I would have been moving the rollaway bed into the studio when we got home last night, or even sleeping in the garden. And Maya even knows what's going on. She told me a while ago that she sensed something in the air between me and Barbara. I agreed, but I said it all came from Barbara.

She's been trying to get me to sleep with her since even before Perry died."

"But you haven't."

"No. I've treated it like a game between us. It's been fun having her chase me like that and knowing I could handle whatever came up. But maybe I can't."

"You were handling her OK last night. I couldn't see your fingers most of the time because they were inside her dress."

"I don't think I dare touch her anymore. She had me vibrating."

Just then Maya appeared in the kitchen looking like she had slept in a haystack. She was still wearing a little makeup that had migrated outward from her eyes. Again she was wearing the *fútbol* jersey, only this time she didn't flip the back up.

"What warmth was that?" she asked in a foggy voice, squinting in the light as she pulled a cup out of the cabinet.

"Just the warmth of classic wines and good company," I said. "We're lucky to have friends like that." I was going to be lucky to have Maya if I didn't put the brakes on Barbara fast.

"There was plenty of that. Too much, maybe." I wasn't sure what she remembered, but I didn't want to pursue it. Her eyes were puffy and her hair was going in several directions. She looked like she might be ready either for an argument or a couple of aspirin. "How do I look?" she asked, wrinkling her nose at me.

"Like a million bucks. Do you remember that Barbara's coming at ten to look at still lifes?" I asked.

"No."

"Do you remember coming home?" asked Cody.

"No."

"I don't either," I said.

"I drove back," he said.

"You drank as much as we did," said Maya, defensively.

"Yes, but I have a bigger container."

I was deadheading some hibiscus back in the garden when Barbara arrived. The Seguridad Reyes man had driven her in his van. "I'll take her back," I told him and he returned to Casa Watt.

"You're looking remarkably intact," I said to her when we got up into the studio.

"It was a near miss."

"Too near. I don't want to think about it. I haven't thought about anything else this morning. Do you want to see some pictures?"

"You saw how it could be, didn't you?" Turning to me, she said this softly as we went upstairs.

I didn't answer, but I did see it. Artists have amazing visual powers, and I had retained this particular image with all its lush detail. I started pulling out some pictures from the racks. She looked to me like she was still agitated, but ready to move on to business. She focused immediately on one called *On Line*. It depicted a rack of spring dresses hung on a metal bar. The subject was less than startling but the color design was lush as the dresses moved in the wind with the sun passing through them.

"I'll definitely take that one," she said. "It can go in the pool house with that other one of yours with that pile of tennis hats. What was that called?"

"*Stacked.*"

Then she found another showing a pile of kitch-en utensils. "What do you think of art in the kitchen?"

"Art is a must in any room. We have one in our laundry room showing a pile of dirty clothes." I'll paint anything. "But what about the study? I thought you want-ed to liven it up?"

"I'm not seeing anything. Maybe those African masks, but I'm not sure. I'd have to see it in the room."

She took my hand as we stood there looking at it. I didn't resist because it was normal for her to be touching something, but then she pressed it to her mouth. I jerked it back.

"Jesus, Barbara, have some mercy. I can't touch you anymore. I'm sorry."

"I'm sorry too. I thought about you last night. You were doing terrible things to me. It was great."

"Don't. You're doing terrible things to me now."

"Would it be so bad to be with me?" She gave me her best look. "Would it really be so bad?" Like I hadn't asked myself that already about fifty times.

"In some ways it would be heaven. In others, I don't know. In any case, I'm not going to change the way things are. I'm going to be with Maya."

"We were so close last night."

"How far could that have gone? It was lucky she was right there in the room." We were whispering.

"And if she hadn't been?"

"I think you know. I was lost. We both saw it. Ev-erything would have changed."

"You would have done terrible things to me?"

"The worst."

She pressed her knees together. "You like thinking

about it, don't you?"

"Yes."

"I'll remember that."

"So will I. It'll remind me to keep my pants zipped."

Finally I packed up the African masks, the kitchen picture, and *On Line* and loaded them in the artmobile. She wrote me a check for $1800 for the last two, and I brought her back up the hill. Inside Casa Watt the Reyes man greeted us. There had been no activity.

Up in the study I pulled down a picture of a bearded St. Peter with a gnarled crook and put up the African masks. The subject altered the feeling of the room in the right direction, but the colors didn't work. "It's not right, is it?" she asked. She folded her arms over her chest and walked backward a few steps. Then she shook her head.

"No. What it tells me is that your idea of hanging more modern things in here is good, but that this particular picture is not right. The colors are too close to the wall paneling and it doesn't come off the wall. I'll take it back with me."

We stood looking at each other for a while.

"Is there really only one way?" I asked.

"To relate to men, you mean?"

"Yes; me in particular."

"I don't know. It just seems natural to go to bed with someone you care for. Don't you care for me?" She moved a few steps closer. "I think you do."

I could feel her breath on my face. "You know I do. But I'm searching for a different way to express it. I just can't give up Maya. Can't we be creative here?"

We came together and I gave her a fierce hug, pressing her against my body as if we would never see each other again. Then I picked up the mask picture and left without saying anything else. We had never even gotten to the kitchen picture.

It was not exactly friendship I was feeling, but it was probably as close as I could get without more practice. I took a circuitous way home, trying to sort out my thoughts. The situation felt like one where you are in love with someone, but she is already with someone else, so nothing can happen. Except here I was the one already committed to someone else and I was (more or less) preventing anything from happening with Barbara. But I was also hurting because I still wanted to have some part of her.

I could also see that this continuous dance toward the bedroom was having the effect of drawing us closer together, the way you would feel closer to anyone you had gone through an intense experience with. Like being in a shelter with someone during an air raid.

There was also what I think of as "studio intimacy," the process of reconstructing a person's body or face in paint where you have to process every detail. It might be some art school model, angular and boney, with flat breasts pointing at her toes and enough pubic hair to upholster a small hassock. Or you can end up feeling like you're actually inside the body of some paunchy old chairman of the board who would never speak to you on the street. This I had with Barbara in spades. I had been inside her in ways she never dreamed of, but not in the way she wanted. There had been times, with some portrait clients, where I had finally pulled back in distaste when the picture was finished, but not with her.

I found my way back to Quebrada eventually. I knew where I stood, and it was not a place of great comfort, and I didn't know where to step next.

When I went inside I could sense immediately that Cody and Maya were in the bunker again. Maya was dressed and her eye makeup was back in the right places, and Cody wore a serious look. They were sitting at the dining room table.

"Not more Ninjas, I hope?"

"Not yet. Rodriguez just called. A police van carrying Yolo and Rosas to a military interrogation was intercepted in México City this morning by the Zapatistas. They forced a smoke bomb through the air vent on the top of the van and put them all asleep. Then they jimmied the rear doors open and cut the chains on our boys and drove them off."

"So it is the Zapatistas?"

"Yes. The feds had gotten that much from them already, but that's all they got. It was the name, rank, and serial number thing."

"Do we know how they would have known the van was bringing Yolo and Rosas to the interrogation?"

"Exactly. The late Jason Schwartz's favorite inside source. The feds there need a good house cleaning."

"Well, there's one good thing. If they show up on our tail again the police can bust them immediately," I said. "We won't have to wait for them to make a move and we won't have to plead our case."

Maya turned to show me her back.

"Yes, it's there again," I said.

"I'm going to call Barbara and have her get the

full crew back," said Cody, and pulled out his cell phone.

"Back in the soup," said Maya. I felt I hadn't left.

"I was going to go home and clean the rotten food out of my refrigerator," said Cody after he hung up. "I guess it'll have to ferment a while longer."

"At least it was a nice party." I said. "A little like R & R. Slow dancing to good music with cute girls, and a lot of booze."

"But I suspect now we'll get shipped back to the front," Cody said.

CHAPTER TWENTY-FOUR

That night I dreamed of Barbara and it was more graphic than any dream I'd had in a long time. It picked up where the previous night left off and we were doing things friends shouldn't do to friends. Things painters shouldn't do to models. When I woke up I was pressing Maya against me and my right hand was between her legs. She didn't mind but it took me a while to go back to sleep.

The next day none of us wanted Maya to go to the archive. Things were just too tense. It was possible that the Ninjas might have headed back to Chiapas after their release, but none of us were betting on it. Naturally, there was not enough concentration available to drive the smallest paintbrush. Maya's Frida picture sat untouched and drying.

About two o'clock in the afternoon Licenciado Rodriguez came around. I thought he looked a little sheepish after his successful bust of the Ninjas had ended with the fumble in México City, but it was hardly his fault.

"Welcome to the hotspot," I said. "I regret what happened to the Zapatistas after all your efforts. Please have a seat."

"Thank you," he said, lowering his long frame into a leather chair in the great room. I say great room, but only because it's bigger than any room that led into it. "Sometimes things happen which we do not control as well as we would like."

"This happens among the *gringos* as well. Trust me."

"But we of the police are at present thinking that they may return here, even though the risk is much higher for them now. They seem to be focused on you and Señorita Sanchez, although, as you say, you do not possess the codex." He gave this a peculiar emphasis, as if to say that we both knew it wasn't exactly true. "I know you are armed, but all the same, additional protection might be of value. How do you feel about this? It is possible that we can make a trap for them."

"And we would be the bait?"

"Let us be frank with each other. You are already the bait, but you are lacking the trap. That part does not change." He shrugged. "You can see that."

I nodded. "I *was* alarmed by the kidnapping of Elena Burgos, since Maya was clearly the target. I think I would welcome any help you can give us, even as the bait."

"Excellent. I would like to station one of my men inside the house for a while, as you would say, around the clock."

Maya came into the living room at that point. I told her what was happening. She gave Rodriguez a big smile.

"I wonder if I could walk through the house again so that I can understand where best to place my security person?"

"I can take you through it," said Maya. She took him by the hand, which I could see surprised him, although it didn't surprise me. I knew her morale was improving now that we had some support. I went back upstairs and sat in front of the easel and noticed something I didn't like about her nose, but I didn't feel like mixing a batch of paint just then to fix a speck.

Cody was in the guest room reading a gun and ammo magazine he'd brought along and I stopped at the door. I'd never seen him hunt anything in San Miguel other than clues.

"Rodriguez wants to add security for us; a single man, in shifts. Do you see a problem?"

He looked up and moved his reading glasses down his nose. "Is he going to have a gun?"

"I'm sure."

"Then there's no problem."

I heard Maya and Rodriguez downstairs talking as they came through the *loggia* back toward the front of the house. Then the doorbell rang. In the way that something that changes your life snapshots your memory of the instant before it, the change in tone of their voices as they got closer to the door has stayed clearly with me to this day.

Cody dropped the magazine and launched himself off the bed, slipping past me toward the stairs, pulling out his gun as he went. I felt like the air around me was vibrating and changing color as I moved after him.

I heard Maya say, "It's a woman..." with a questioning tone in her voice, and then open the door. My gun was out too and I was right on Cody's heels when I heard the first shot as we came down the steps. Rodriguez, suddenly alarmed, had moved past Maya at the entry when one of the Ninjas appeared behind the woman and shot him as he was drawing his gun. Rodriguez collapsed backwards onto the stone tile.

Maya froze at one side. Cody yelled at the shooter, and as he turned toward us, shot him full in the chest and then again in the side as he whirled and went down. He did not move again. Maya had her hands on the sides of her head and was screaming something I couldn't understand. The woman had already run back out the door and was climbing into a blue van with some kind of lettering on the side. I saw her for only an instant but she looked something like Maya. Cody leveled his gun at the van but didn't fire as it squealed away from the curb.

"Three one eight, five four four nine, state of México license," he shouted as he knelt by Rodriguez. "Write it down and call an ambulance, now!"

Maya recovered enough to pull out her cell phone and dial the police. The Ninja looked like death. I knelt by his side and put my fingers on his pulse, but there was nothing. His eyes were open, but not focused. I sat down next to him, avoiding the pool of blood spreading from his chest and side. I held his hand for a moment, somehow feeling no animosity toward him. His gun was gone, I couldn't see where. He could have been our neighbor. This close, I recognized him from the roadside restaurant on the way to Escobedo, but I didn't know whether he was Yolo or Rosas.

Maya had moved away with the phone clenched between her chin and her shoulder, writing down something as she walked; I assumed it was the license number of the van. Cody knelt beside Rodriguez and was pressing his hands against the wound on his abdomen, trying to slow the blood flow. I dragged myself up beside them. Time was moving at a crawl and I saw in my mind's eye, oddly, the kind of plastic flower memorials that Méxicans like to leave at the scene of a fatal road accident. We could have two of them now, in our *zaguán*, one for the Ninja, and one for Ramon Xoc, whose body had been dumped here earlier in the year near the same spot, during out first case. I hoped we wouldn't need three.

"How is he" I said softly to Cody.

"Can't tell. He's gut shot, so that's bad, but not as bad as it could be. I think the shot missed the aorta."

Rodriguez's eyes were open but glazed and his expression vacant. He wasn't moving. Cody's arms were covered with blood up to his wrists. Suddenly we could hear the ambulance siren outside and Maya unlocked the door again after looking through the peephole to make sure it was them. Two patrolmen followed the ambulance men in. We backed away to let them work. Cody ducked into the powder room to wash his hands.

I went back to Maya; she stood with her hands over her mouth and a look of shock and horror on her face. She didn't look at the Ninja, only at Rodriguez.

"I think he'll make it," I said softly to her, rubbing her neck with one hand, but I really didn't know. The three shots were still ringing in my ears.

When they got Rodriguez on a stretcher he seemed to regain some degree of consciousness. His lips were moving and I could just make out the words, "Elena Burgos."

Cody stood on the sidewalk as they drove away, not looking like he had just killed someone. Maybe that came later. "I hope we see him again," he said. Maya took his hand and leaned against him. When

I slipped my arm around her waist she turned and buried her wet face in my shoulder. As we went back in a second ambulance was roaring down the street. We had forgotten to call one for the Ninja, the other crew had done it.

The ambulance crew briefly checked the man's body, made no attempt at resuscitation, and loaded him unceremoniously into the van. As it pulled out, a white Chrysler drove into the space in front of the house. A man I didn't know got out of the passenger side carrying a black satchel. It was too big to be a medical bag; it was probably forensics. From the driver's side emerged another man in a brown suit and a brown tie. We all knew him well.

He shook hands all around as he followed the forensics man inside.

"Licenciado Delgado! You're here? You're back?"

"Please, tell me first what happened here with Jesus Rodriguez."

Cody joined me inside and we brought him up to date. Maya was pacing back and forth behind us, avoiding the blood. The other officer who had come with Delgado took her by the elbow and gently moved her further inside, notebook in hand.

"But you are back with the Judicial Police" asked Cody.

"Since two weeks ago I have recovered my old position. It is by the grace of God, and also because my brother-in-law is deputy mayor. The police are like family."

"And you are recovered from your injuries?"

"Completely. I can work out now as before. But

tell me what happened here. I received a message about Jesus Rodriguez being shot in your house. This is from the Zapatistas? I was told about the escape in México City."

"It was definitely one of them," said Cody. "He was with the woman he kidnapped earlier, and a third person was in the van they escaped in."

We spent an hour with Delgado; he already knew why Rodriguez had come. Maya had finished with the other cop and gave him the license plate number of the van and he phoned it in immediately while the forensics man searched for spent bullets and whatever other clues cops need from a mess like that. We were all numb. The worst part of it was that Delgado apologetically took Cody's gun for testing. He said he could have it back to us the next day if it turned out that Cody hadn't shot Rodriguez.

"If you are finished with me I'd like to go up to the hospital," said Cody.

Delgado nodded. "He's at the new General."

I handed my gun to Cody. "You keep this for a while. You seem to get better use out of a gun than I do."

The clouds opened suddenly and the kind of downpour followed that often interrupts late afternoons in July. The water came in sheets, splashing high up on the passing cars on Quebrada as people ran for shelter, and the bowl of our garden fountain quickly overflowed the sides. Cody found an umbrella and handed me back the gun. "You'll need this more than I will. I'm just going up and sit with Rodriguez." He walked out with Delgado.

I knew nobody would be sitting with Rodriguez for a while, even assuming he got through surgery. Cody would be sitting in the waiting room thinking about the man he had killed. It was something he had to do alone. You couldn't talk it out because no matter how justified the shooting, the man was still dead. I wasn't sure exactly how it changed things, but the victim had been a soldier, not a murderer or drug lord.

Maya and I pulled out the buckets and silently scrubbed the entry clean. Nothing went away except the blood.

CHAPTER TWENTY-FIVE
CODY WILLIAMS

C ody Williams found himself still in a waiting room in the General Hospital at sunset. Licenciado Rodriguez had not emerged from the operating room. Cody didn't have the concentration to look at a magazine; instead he studied the room. The lower walls were done in a dusty shade of buff with robin's egg blue above and the seating was the same *equipale* style slat and leather design he had on his own small balcony. Hanging around with Paul had made him always notice colors now, and he was looking for distraction. Around him stood earthen pots with the same kind of big-leafed plants he might see in any serious garden in town. Through a long bank of windows he might also have seen the lights coming on from traffic on the Querétaro road, had he been looking. As it was, he noticed nothing more than his immediate surroundings.

But this evening Cody was also looking inward at darker vistas, toward a place where he had found himself several times before. He knew his quick action had prevented Rodriguez from taking another bullet; whether it also saved his life was yet to be seen. He also knew that the price of Rodriguez even getting to the hospital alive had been the death of the Ninja. From the staircase, twenty feet away, Cody had yelled at the man to get him to turn, which pulled his gun away from Rodriguez and Maya, and then he had shot twice to kill him. It was the only certainty available to him, and he had used it before. He had harbored no doubts about the accuracy of his aim at that distance, nor had he questioned the need for it. He had missed Maya by more than four feet; nothing to worry about.

Cody's eyes were closed. His breathing was even and unhurried. He sat hunched forward in the chair, his elbows on his knees and his chin in his hands.

In his mind he confronted the shadowy Ninja, who sat upright across from him and said nothing. Darkness covered the man's face like a shroud. He did not move. Cody's lips formed words of explanation, of justification. He was himself diminished by the Ninja's death. But further down within himself he was angry. There were times when it was possible to alter a high-risk situation to try to get some minimal control over it. This had not been one of those times. The action had already begun and there was only a single avenue of approach for Cody; down the steps with his gun ready, yelling to draw the Ninja's gun toward himself. Circumstance had dictated his action and taken away his ability to choose. So the Ninja had joined the trio of other men he had killed.

He cringed when he thought that it might have been Maya who died if the Ninja had gotten off a second bullet.

In college he had intended to become a clinical psychologist, but ended up walking away from the completion of his Ph.D. for reasons he still could not explain to himself. He had continued a family tradition by joining the police force, something he had sworn he would never do. It seemed to him that his early life had been a process of planning to take one fork in the road, and then, at the last minute, switching to the other.

The first time he killed a man had been more than thirty years before, when a group from the Peoria Police had joined Peoria County Deputies in a house-to-house search around the tiny town of Monica, Illinois for an escapee from Joliet Prison. He had just turned the corner into the kitchen of an abandoned farmhouse when the man opened up on him. The first shot grazed the top of Cody's left shoulder. The second went into the ceiling. Cody kept his gun level and got off two rounds as he fell back. Both hit the convict squarely in the chest.

No one had questioned the appropriateness of the shooting, since Cody himself had been hit first. But he'd rethought the scene a thousand times. It was probably the tenth house he had been in, and he was getting sloppy in his approach, no longer expecting to find the convict. His replay always began the same way, with his left hand coming up to push open the front door, the .38 caliber revolver gripped tightly in his right hand. He could feel again the chalky alligatored white surface of the door's weathered paint under his fingertips. As it swung open he saw the ragged hole in the hardwood floor, rotten from the leaking roof, and on his left, the staircase with light blue woodwork under the bare worn handrail. The newel post had been torn out—salvage for someone's restoration effort elsewhere, or maybe just firewood. He remembered thinking this, noticing it, as time inched toward fate at the rear of the house.

Stepping around the hole in the floor, he paused

and listened. From where he stood he could see into the living room, where a cushionless sofa stood pointlessly in the middle of the floor. There was no sound and he had no sense that he was not alone. The floor inevitably creaked as he advanced down the hallway. He reached a juncture where he could either turn right into the dining room or continue straight into the kitchen. He chose the kitchen and this was the point where the details of his memory dissolved in a rush of motion with no detail. He had simply no recollection of either shooting or being hit.

Cody was sitting on a rickety chair, bleeding over both the front and back of his uniform when his partner came running from the barn. This was where his recollection started up again. His partner checked Cody and the convict and ran back to the car to call it in. Cody sat motionless, staring at the man bleeding on the floor.

He knew the man was named Wilson Ames. He lay now flat on his back, eyes open, and an expression of surprise and pain on his face. One arm was thrown out almost at a right angle to his body, the other was partly under him. A trickle of blood ran from his open mouth, running down into the creases of his neck, but stopped before the pool he lay in. He was no older than Cody was himself; not more than his mid-twenties.

Cody shifted in the *equipale* hospital chair, and it creaked in protest.

In the thirty-four years since the death of Wilson Ames on the filthy kitchen floor of an abandoned farmhouse, Cody had seen him again many times. At first he was alone, then, a few years later, he was joined by a black man in his forties who was fleeing the scene of a gas station holdup when he tried to run through a road block set up by Cody and a different partner. Hitting a tree, he chose to shoot it out. He died in his 1970 Plymouth.

Cody didn't spend as much time rethinking that one; the situation had been forced on him. But still, when he saw Wilson Ames, the other one was there as well.

The third one gave him the most trouble; a sixteen-year-old kid driving down the street in a rough part of Peoria, just firing at the houses randomly. Was it PCP? Crack? Nothing he could deal with when the kid had a gun in his hand. Cody, by then Detective Williams, had spotted the situation while driving past on his way home. He called for backup, but he couldn't wait for help to arrive with a bullet going into a different house every ten seconds. He cut the kid off with his car and, jumping behind his open door, identified himself and yelled at him to drop the gun. Of course he didn't, staying in the car and turning his gun on Cody. The lower parts of his body were protected by the dashboard, and Cody's only option was to fire at the head and shoulders visible in the windshield. The kid took one in the face. The pair of dead men became a trio, and Cody began to see retirement on the horizon, still too far away to make out with perfect clarity, but part of it might not include remaining in Peoria.

When he turned fifty-three, he had his thirty years in and turned in his badge without regret. He left Peoria without his wife, and drifted down through México driven by an urge he didn't understand, but which he later identified as nothing more elaborate than escape. Donna's life was too settled and organized to accompany him. He stopped in San Miguel, thinking it was only for a time, then, sitting on a sunny bench in the *jardín*, decided to stay. The three dead men still joined him now and then, most often as he was trying to fall asleep. It was much like a round table discussion in a half dark room, except no one had anything more to say. He went over parts of it again and again, searching for other choices. Most of it still seemed inevitable, the simple power of circumstance, but not quite all of it.

He realized that these were almost the identical words he had used to console Maya, after she had killed Perry Watt earlier in the year.

"I don't know," she had said. "I don't think I made a choice. It didn't seem like it at the time."

"That's what I'm saying. You didn't choose what you did. You simply did it."

"So I shouldn't blame myself?" she said.

"You should do what you have to do to live with it, but you can't fault yourself for not choosing something different, because no choices were available."

"To not kill Perry was to let him kill all of us. Wasn't that a choice?"

"Not one you could have made. Anyway, if you hadn't killed him, I would have, one way or another. Count on it."

Maya faded from his mind, oddly, since often he privately used his highly sentimental image of her to exile the round table of the dead. So although they did not leave, there was no response either from the dark figure facing him; there never would be. Cody knew this would not be their last encounter.

The door to the operating room swung open and a man in scrubs came over to him. Cody opened his eyes. He realized he had been mumbling. It took him a moment to banish his thoughts.

"Jesús Rodriguez is stable. We have stitched him back together as well as we can, and I think he has a good chance to recover. You are part of his family?"

"Just a friend. I don't think he is from San Miguel, he may not have family here. Is it possible to see him?"

"Not yet. We'll let him rest for a few hours and see what happens. Perhaps in the morning. Why not go home and get some sleep? I must tell you, though, that if he recovers it will be a long time before he can come back to work."

A strong sense of optimism began to creep over Cody. After all, for a smallish kind of town in central México, San Miguel de Allende had excellent medical facilities manned by a highly professional group of doctors and nurses. The hospital was only four years old. Its design conveyed to Cody a sense of high technology united with cutting edge architecture and decor. The presence of the 8,000-member *gringo* community had something to do with this; many were retirees and the demand for first class health care was strong. Resources to pay for it were readily available. Occasionally a substantial bequest came to the hospital as well. These resources were now all focused on saving Licenciado Rodriguez.

Cody phoned Paul and Maya as he left the elevator on the way out. Wind and rain had come and gone and Cody had been oblivious. He realized as he crossed the lobby that it was now dark, although he'd been looking out the window for hours.

"It looks like he's going to make it," he said. "Came through the surgery fine, but he'll be out on leave for a while. Have you called Barbara? No? OK. I'll call her. It's hard to think of everything."

Now that Paul and Maya were about to get full time police protection, and one of the Ninjas was gone, Cody was going back home to clean his refrigerator. Sometimes there is consolation in small routines, if nothing else.

CHAPTER TWENTY-SIX

The rain lasted for two hours after we finished the cleanup and then it stopped as if someone had closed the tap. The clouds thinned and then parted, but didn't disappear. I knew our cistern was full again, as well as the garden tank where we piped our gray water. It was an odd renewal, full of death. I wondered how Rodriguez was doing, but it seemed like Cody would call if there was any news.

Later we went through the motions of eating dinner. Many things were still hanging in the air as I poured us each a stiff brandy afterward and we went up to the roof garden. The sun was edging downward over the hills. The air was cool from the rain and the deck was drying quickly. I wiped off the table and two chairs. As dusk settled in a three-quarter moon dodged in and out of the ragged clouds.

"They were coming for me," she said, looking off toward the Parroquia. "They chose me for the victim."

"Yes. But it would be good to let go of that, if you can."

"And that was the kidnapped woman from Gigante? The one you said must be having the Stockholm syndrome? I didn't think of that when I saw her at the door."

"Look's like she's got it. She was free and then she went back to him."

"Was he in the van, or was he the dead one?"

"I don't know. I saw them both on the road to Escobedo. But I don't know if it was Yolo who died or Rosas."

"I think it must be Rosas who died, because she went back to the van. If it had been Yolo she would have stayed with him."

"Is that what you would have done?"

"Yes."

"And what are you thinking now? I know you're still angry at the risk."

"Of course. But I am also thinking that all these things come from Barbara. Not only the things in the air between you two, but all the violence and death. Now Cody has killed another man; he probably thought he was finished with that. It isn't the codex itself; it's her wanting the codex, just like she wants you. I think she's like Perry. She's a collector. They were a good match."

"But I think there wasn't much love between them."

"Perhaps not, but they still had their reasons for being together."

She sipped her brandy and looked up at the way the evening breeze drove the clouds in scattered clusters across the sky. She lifted her heels up on the chair and drew her arms around her knees. I heard *mariachis*, dim and far away in the *jardín*. The tune was familiar but their optimism didn't reach us.

I put my hand over hers. "Is she evil? Is that what you see? Or is she just pursuing what she wants? Don't we all do that? You with your book yet to publish and me try-ing to push the limits of what I can do in painting?"

She looked at me calmly, as if she had thought this through and was miles past where I was.

"No one dies when we push. But we have now the two *federales*, John Schleicher, Professor Sandoval, Jason Schwartz, today the Ninja; that makes six, and possibly Jesús Rodriguez yet may die too."

"I can't argue it. I could say that Schwartz and Schleicher and the Ninja and possibly the *federales* were acting either from greed or politics, but you're right, they're all dead and perhaps the consequence is extreme. We signed on here only to facilitate what looked like a business transaction, just to help expertize the codex and help Barbara make the transfer. And now we're out of our depth in moral issues I don't think I can sort it out. What if the Ninjas represent a reasonable cause?"

"I do have some sympathy for them, but what about their methods? They would have kidnapped me to-day if they hadn't encountered Rodriguez. And then they shot him. Does a good cause justify anything?"

"Well, this is where it comes back to earth for me," I said. "The bottom line is that I now have two potential ways to lose you. One is Barbara, and the other is that you have become the key pawn in the codex game. If I didn't love you they wouldn't want you."

She said nothing for a moment.

"It's in your power to clear up one of them." She set her empty glass carefully down on the table.

"What do you mean?"

"Why not just sleep with her?" She looked up at me. "End the torture. Maybe that's where this is going, in the end. You talk about love, but I don't think you really know right now. Why not have a *gringa*, a *güera* (blonde)? All that blond hair, even here." She placed her palm between her legs. The evening was still warm despite the rain, but a chill went over me that was like passing through a January night back in the States. I couldn't say anything for a moment. It was not that I hadn't posed this question to myself, but to hear it from Maya was almost unbearable.

"Then you would leave," I said, after a moment.

"I wouldn't want to, but yes, I would certainly leave. You can see that."

"Yes. I can see it."

"But, still, you would have her, if only for a time. That's something. She is beautiful and she has more money than you would ever need in a lifetime. I'm sure she is skillful in bed, as you must have imagined many times." She said this without rancor, as if listing the reasons for doing something that was not of great interest to her, although she could see how it might attract others.

Her hand was still beneath mine and now I pressed it to my cheek. For once I could not read her face, but I didn't have to. Hearing her state the issue so baldly stripped away the element of bedroom farce that made Barbara so enticing. Coming through Maya's hand I could feel the immense connection we had nurtured over five years. I kissed her palm. She pulled her hand away from my face and came around the table toward me, then she placed her arms around my head and pulled it against her breast. I moved my hands up on her back under her shirt and pulled her down so she was sitting on my lap. We kissed for a long time.

I unhooked her bra and unbuttoned her shirt and pulled them off. Kneeling before her I pulled down her jeans as I nibbled her breasts. The clouds were still passing rapidly overhead and her face came in and out of the moonlight. Her expression was unreadable. I removed the cushion from the recliner and threw it down to the deck with the dry side up and pressed her down on it. Her legs came around me and she arched her back. Some time later as we lay there the clouds thickened and the rain returned, black and warm, and we didn't move. There seemed to be something still between us; I thought of Barbara's description of the sheet with an embroidered hole in it, but that's not what it was.

"I love you," I said. "Just you. There's nothing else out there that I need, and no one else could give me what you do. I hope you feel that too."

When we finally went downstairs Cody called to say Rodriquez was out of surgery and stable. It could have been true of all of us.

✠✠✠

The next morning Barbara had receded to a point far away on the horizon, not totally out of view, but nothing that required immediate attention. We were definitely feeling better and painting looked like a good distraction from mayhem so Maya slipped into the Tejuana costume, pinned her hair up as before, and we got to work. I had just a bit of the skirt surrounding her hands, and the hands themselves to do, then her hair and the background.

"It's good to be doing this again," she said. "It's better than shooting people or being shot at."

We hadn't spoken about the night before, but I sensed things were healing.

The picture ended just below her knees, and the costume was long, so I had no feet or bare knees to do, so the whole bottom edge was fabric. The phone rang a couple of times as I worked but I let the answering machine handle it.

We had just finished lunch when the doorbell rang. I made a sign to Maya not to move from the kitchen and I pulled out my gun and looked through the peephole. It was Diego Delgado again.

Maya came in from the kitchen in her Tejuana outfit and gave him a hug. I think at this point she would hug anyone on our side who had a gun. Naturally, he didn't resist.

"Have you seen Licenciado Rodriguez?" she asked.

"No, he is resting now. No one can see him, but he does not get any worse. So for now, we are hopeful."

"And the dead man? Who was he?"

"The Zapatista was named Luis Rosas. And," he said, "I have the gun of Señor Williams." He pulled it out of his jacket pocket. "Our tests have shown it was used only to kill Rosas. Please return it to him the next time you see him. We are thinking that he saved the life of Jesús Rodriguez."

"What about the additional police for security here then?" I asked. "This was what Licenciado Rodriguez was arranging yesterday. And Yolo is still loose."

"Loose?"

"He has his freedom."

"We will continue with the same plan. This is why I have come, to let you know that there will be a man arriving to stay with you in one hour or less."

"Thank you, Licenciado Delgado. Again, we're very happy to see you back on the job."

Maya moved toward him again. "And what about your family, how were they while you were gone?"

"You did not hear of this? Señora Watt visited my wife the day after my accident in the Jardín Botanico and gave her $10,000. She has been doing very well since then. Señora Watt also said she would take care of my family until I was released. She then paid my expenses at the hospital, the part that was not covered by insurance. She is now like family to us."

Maya looked at me with her eyebrows raised. "The *güera* did this?"

"She is a woman of great compassion. A credit to all *gringos*." There were tears in his eyes. "She has been like an angel to both of us."

CHAPTER TWENTY-SEVEN
NINJAS

For three days after the shooting of Licenciado Rodriguez, Yolo and Elena Burgos had waited and watched, planning their next move against Paul and Maya. On Thursday they loitered on the sidewalk by the small white Chevrolet on Quebrada. Yolo was wearing a blue coverall spotted with paint from covering the fruit company logo before they ditched the van, and Elena had on the same clothes she had been wearing the day of her abrupt departure from the Gigante market. They had taken on a special significance for her now and so she had washed them again, checking for spots of grease from the marinade, and put them on for the final chapter of the codex caper, as they thought of it. The clothes no longer smelled of vinegar.

If she had harbored any doubts before about joining the Zapatistas, the death of Luis Rosas had settled them. Elena had been a woman searching for something, and in the afternoon of her kidnapping from Gigante, she had found it in Yolo and his cause. While she was still vague on the details of the Zapatistas' problems, she found their power to inspire action irresistible.

Between Yolo and Elena waited a baby stroller containing a blanket stuffed with newspaper. They had watched the house long enough to learn the schedule of the police guards and they knew that at two o'clock the man inside would emerge and get into the waiting police pickup and drive away while his replacement went inside. An hour before, they had seen Paul Zacher load several pictures into his white van and drive off.

Elena looked at Yolo and touched his face. "He is painting masks, now. Did you see that last one as he put it in the van?"

Yolo shrugged; the only mask with meaning for him was the black ski mask he always carried, and he rarely had much to say before the start of a military action anyway.

At five minutes before two they crossed the street and without haste began making their way toward Paul and Maya's house. They stopped for a moment while Elena lovingly rearranged the blanket around the newspaper. She said a few words to Yolo, smiling and pointing at the stroller. The police pickup passed them and pulled over to the curb. The house door opened and the departing guard got in and drove off while the new guard stood for a moment surveying the street in both directions with his hand on his gun. Seeing nothing suspicious in the parked cars or even in the couple now approaching closely with a stroller, he turned to go inside. He had been told to watch for a woman, but not a couple with a small child, and he always did what he was told. It was as he placed his foot on the first step that he felt a gun in his back.

"Just continue going inside," said Yolo. "Keep your hands in front of you."

The three of them went through the door and

Elena closed it behind them. The stroller remained on the sidewalk with the bundle still inside.

Elena held her own gun on the guard and disarmed him while Yolo went farther into the house.

"Don't make a sound," she said.

There was a scream from the kitchen, as much in anger as fear, and something made of glass shattered on the floor. Maya emerged with Yolo's hand on one shoulder, pushing her along.

"Where is the big man?" he asked her.

"Gone back to his house. I knew you would come," said Maya. She was now fully as angry at Paul and Barbara for their stubborn pursuit of the codex as she was at Yolo and Elena for invading her house, but she was beyond the degree of outrage that required yelling. She said no more.

Yolo pulled a length of rope from his pocket and handcuffed the guard to the stair rail and then tied his feet together while Elena covered Maya.

"Where is the codex?" asked Yolo, when the guard was secure.

"It is not here and they didn't tell me where, just in case of this," Maya said.

"OK. Then you will come with us."

She couldn't help thinking that if she had been able to give up the codex she would probably be left at home now. She wouldn't have hesitated.

They left the guard on the stairs but took his gun and cartridge belt with them.

Yolo pushed Maya into the back seat of the Chevrolet and Elena climbed in after her. She cuffed Maya's hands behind her back. "You and I do look something alike," she said.

This was too much. "You could never look like me, not on your best day," said Maya, pleased to have the perfect vernacular phrase for this. Elena only smiled.

"You could have fooled me," said Yolo. "In fact, you did." He turned around and grinned from the front seat. "This is the last move today," he added. "When we get the codex you are free again, and then we are gone."

"Chiapas?" asked Maya.

"Of course. The only free state in México." The car pulled out, and at the corner turned toward Ancha de San Antonio, which as it left town became the Celaya road.

"And you?" said Maya to Elena. "Will you go to Chiapas as well?"

"Of course, I will be with Yolo."

"But he kidnapped you."

"The way I think of it now is that he *chose* me. I know it was fate."

"He chose you thinking you were *me*." She leaned into Elena's face. "He was trying to choose me. Can't you see that?" Maya was beginning to think Elena could rationalize anything. Apparently she wasn't that smart.

"True, it was a mistake at first. But then we realized as well that it was like fate. Perhaps like you were fated to be with Paul Zacher."

"I was never fated to be with Paul Zacher." She spit out the words. "I chose *him*. When I first saw him I could have ignored him." Maya had little respect for the traditional Mexican belief in fate, although she paid lip service to it occasionally. She had too long lived comfortably with the consequences of her own decisions to have any interest in the idea of some abstract principle having any influence on her life.

"It is the same," said Yolo over his shoulder. "The main thing is that a choice was fated to be made. Who makes it does not matter. Do you see this too?"

"Then was Luis Rosas fated to die?" asked Maya.

"Yes, most certainly," he said. "Perhaps we all are, who is to know? If the codex brings more people into the struggle for liberty from the Neo-liberal Colonialists, then some of them will die too. We are soldiers; that is all. History uses us. You must know this."

"And so his death has no special meaning?" asked Maya.

"None more than that. Have you no fated role?" asked Yolo.

"I am a historian. I never thought it was my fate, just something that always interested me."

"So you live for the past?"

"The past and the present. I like my life, except at times like this."

"We in the movement live for the present and the future," he said. "History is a lie told by the exploiters to justify their actions."

"In the past the Indians have joined with one side or the other. Early in the last century, they joined with Zapata. You take his name for your movement," Maya said. They passed Domino's Pizza with its string of delivery motorbikes lined up. Next to them, two burros with bags of soil were tethered to the wall.

"This time there is no side for us," said Yolo, looking back at the street. "We must make our own side because now we have the objectives of no one else. Then also there is no betrayal, as there always has been in the past."

"In some ways I can sympathize with the Zapatistas," said Maya. "The issue of land reform is real. But always in the case of revolution here it ends the same. New rider, but the same old horse."

"Then you see why I am here," said Elena, as if Maya had made her point.

"Perhaps, but I can't sympathize with the violence. Why did Professor Sandoval have to die?"

"Was he the man of the hand? I know nothing of this. We were told to deliver the hand to you so you would be frightened and cooperate. That is all," said Yolo. "It was a delivery like the pizzas."

Maya saw how easy it was to trivialize the victims of this struggle, but she said nothing. The last brightly painted buildings of San Miguel passed behind them as they edged the *glorieta* and headed up the hill out of town. Maya twisted her head around to look out the back window; no one followed them. She tried to think what Paul would do when he got home from Galería Uno. He would immediately see the guard on the stairs, then he would see the broken casserole on the kitchen floor. She knew he wouldn't panic; he never panicked. He'd call Cody and then set about trying to release the guard from the rope and handcuffs. Then they would come for her.

"Where are we going?" she asked.

"There is a farm here on the road to Santa Teresita, perhaps about eight kilometers farther. No one lives in the house now. We'll wait there for Paul Zacher to bring us the codex."

They drove on in silence for a while.

"Why are you called Yolo?"

"I took that name when I joined the movement.

273

My old name, the name of my family, was Fernandez, not a Mayan name. It was a name of old Spain given by the colonial masters."

"But Yolo is not a Mayan name either?"

"No. It is simply the name of my rebirth. I made it up." He shrugged. "When we take up the struggle, we invent ourselves."

"Then I should make up a name too," said Elena, playing with her gun, polishing a dull place on the barrel with her fingertip.

"What will you do in Chiapas?" Maya asked her. She was trying to plug this into her research on the Indian role in past revolts. Being a pale-skinned convert, Elena was not a good fit. Maya was not certain that Yolo was either. In the history books you never saw the individuals in the trenches except as statistics. No matter how rich the source materials, the average soldier remained faceless and anonymous. Yet Yolo had an odd cowlick off-center on the upper back of his head, and, when he turned, a wide grin punctuated by a gap in his upper teeth. She couldn't see him as a cypher. He looked more like a roofer, or someone with a vegetable stand in the Mercado Ramirez.

While Elena was thinking about her plans Maya turned back to Yolo. "What will you do with the codex?"

"It will be my honor to present it personally to Subcomandante Marcos. Then he will decide how best to use it. But whatever he decides, at least it will be in the hands of the people who made it, not those of the government, where it would become a symbol of their endless domination."

"And this will be in the jungle?"

"Yes. In the Chiapas highlands. More than that I can't say."

"The codex will not survive under those conditions. You will destroy your own history."

He shrugged. "It will serve our purpose. History has value if it can influence the present. Otherwise not."

"I will be called Magdalena," said Elena finally, as if making a breakthrough. "The fallen one. I have fallen for a cause and a man that I love." Her face was glowing.

"You're a romantic," said Maya. "I am not. I could not love someone who took my freedom."

"But you love Paul Zacher."

"I love him for what he is, not what he has made me. I was already what I am. He simply saw what I was."

"But he is only a painter; I haven't seen his work, but a painter can have no significance," said Yolo over his shoulder. "Unless he is like Castro Pacheco, and this I doubt."

"I don't know him."

"He made the murals in the city hall in Mérida. They depict the great struggle of the Mayan revolt in the Yucatán. What people call the Caste War."

"You've seen them?"

"Only in the book at the headquarters of the Subcomandante. But they are strong. They serve the Cause. They inspire revolt. And when we do finally go to Mérida, we will ride in triumph through the streets in jeeps, shooting our guns in the air. Then I will see them in person."

They passed a sign for Santa Teresita. "It is just up here," said Yolo. "There are a few animals and the fields are tended by the neighbor, but the house is empty. Soon we will call Paul Zacher. I think now he will cooperate. He is a smart man, isn't he?"

Unable to frame a response with the precise nuance she needed, Maya remained silent. She scanned the fields of corn as they entered a winding unpaved lane, then bumped over a narrow bridge that crossed a dry creek. Now that the worst had happened, she was no longer afraid. History had taught her that nothing is more frightening than the unknown. Yolo and Elena did not seem rabid in their radicalism, nor in their loopy confidence in the benevolent intrusions of fate.

"Now we are in the soup at last," she said quietly, thinking, "and now that I'm in it, it's not that hot or even very deep." Neither of the others answered. Perhaps they thought she was hungry.

The house at the end of the lane was small with a flat roof, overgrown with weeds edging the cracked white stucco. Of the two windows in front, one had several broken panes, and the door hung at an angle from the upper hinge. To the right, about thirty meters away, stood a shed with an attached corral. Two spotted horses watched them from behind the fence, switching their tails over their backs in the sun.

Yolo drove the Chevrolet down an overgrown lane to the paddock and parked it out of sight of the road. Elena kept a hand on Maya's cuffed wrists as they walked back up to the house. Yolo pulled the sagging door aside and guided Maya in ahead of him with one hand on her shoulder. The interior had a single room with a few pieces of furniture remaining from a previous tenant. There were two chairs and a rough table in one corner. Along the back wall, a counter with a stone sink stood under a window looking over the fields of corn, now taller than a man. Next to it was a back door of planks, still on its hinges. Yolo placed a gas lantern on the table.

"This will not take long," he said. "I think they will know we have won."

He pulled out his cell phone and dialed Paul Zacher's number. There was no answer. He left no message. "You two can sit," he said. "I will keep watch and perhaps soon he will return home."

"What then?" asked Maya. She was seated at the table with her wrists manacled before her now.

"When I collect the codex, if it is in order and not a cookbook again, I will release you at the same spot down the road, one hour later. Then we go back to Chiapas. It will be finished."

"Finished," said Maya. "No more targets," she muttered to herself. Like that would happen.

CHAPTER TWENTY-EIGHT

On my return from helping set up the show at Galería Uno, I paid no attention to the baby stroller on the sidewalk before my house, even though they weren't all that common in San Miguel. I'm not the sort that needs to pinch and kiss babies, and I haven't taken much interest in them since, well, probably since I was one myself, looking for companionship. I guess if I had been more focused I would have asked myself who abandons a baby on the sidewalk, since the stroller was clearly occupied. But it was nearly five and I was tired after making judgment after judgment of how and where pictures should hang for best effect. You couldn't really tell until they were up on the wall, and if they didn't work, then they came down. The gallery walls there are faced with a tan burlap material and it doesn't always flatter my work. Of course, the burlap makes it easy to hide the nail holes when you change the position of a picture.

In addition, Ramon Rivera represents some painters who I think should be more appropriately showing down on the fringes of Parque Juarez under Sunday morning umbrellas, not in a serious gallery. But Ramon is a businessman, and he knows what sells. This is not always true of me; I mainly know what I want to paint. If that overlaps with what sells, great. If it doesn't, then my home collection grows. Naturally over time, the home collection has come to reflect the less commercial side of my work. That would include Maya in the Tejuana outfit, still unfinished up in my studio. Maybe tomorrow I'd work on it again. After all, she would be posing dressed and it wouldn't matter if the police guard was hanging around.

I felt a rush of alarm when I inserted the key in my door and found it unlocked. This would require a serious talk with the guard. I didn't want any more near misses like the bungled Gigante kidnapping. Two steps inside the door, I knew this was not a near miss. I didn't bother to look around for Maya. The guard chained helplessly to the stair rail said everything.

I got a bolt cutter out of the toolbox in the studio and came back down to cut the chain off the handcuffs. "Tell me what happened, from the beginning."

He was contrite and deeply embarrassed but it didn't help me feel any better. While he called the station on the landline, I called Cody on my cell. "I'll be there right away," he said. "They'll be calling soon, so just hold tight, Paul." His voice was very clipped, as if he were holding back his anger. I knew well enough how deeply he was attached to Maya. He probably thought it was too deeply. It never bothered me, and she enjoyed it because he never got too close to her, unless she initiated it.

"You better stop and retrieve the codex," I said. "I don't think they're going to be fooled again."

It took Cody more than half an hour because of his detour to the Cuadrante house, and by that time Licenciado Delgado and a uniformed cop had arrived. The disgraced guard had left after telling them his story. Delgado was not pleasant and said some Spanish words to him I didn't recognize. Probably just police jargon, although it seemed to touch on something as well about the guard's mother and her unnatural sexual appetites, some of them involving animals. You had to wonder sometimes how they knew these things, but it's a close community. Word gets around.

That steely calm I feel when I'm desperate had come over me, and I sat down to wait. When he arrived Cody had little to say; I could see he was upset. His feelings toward Maya were much like those of a failed, but resigned, suitor; he didn't mind if I had her, but he'd be damned if anyone else was going to. Delgado talked to the neighbors, but no one had seen anything, so he decided to await developments. Cody and I sat calmly in the great room, but Delgado paced up and down.

"Tomás Leon of the federal police is in town on another case, but he will be joining us shortly." More firepower, I thought, no problem. "And this time do we really have the codex?"

"Yes," I said wearily. I wasn't going to explain it.

"When they call," said Delgado, "try to arrange the drop for after dark. It will be easier to get close to them, and it will give more time for Tomás Leon to arrive."

Just after 6:15 the phone rang.

"We have your woman. This time really."

"Is this Yolo?"

"Yes."

I tried to keep the image of Maya in chains from my mind. Just do business, I thought, bring this along. I suddenly felt that, even with more firepower than they had, our position was appallingly weak. Cody's hand was on my shoulder.

"I don't have the codex with me. I will need time to get it."

"We have little time."

"I know the codex is important to you. Maya is important to us as well. We can do business here."

"But she is not Mayan? Otherwise I think she would be with me."

"I'm sure she's considering it. I could have the codex by..." I saw Delgado raise both his hands with nine fingers showing. "Nine o'clock, really."

"That will work. On the road to Santa Teresita there is a sign for the town seven and a half kilometers from the beginning of the road, just as you leave San Miguel at the glorieta. Place the codex at the base of this sign at 9:30. We will have men with guns posted, so come alone and leave at once. Your woman's life will depend on this, and we will not be fooled again by cookbooks. Do you see this?"

"I understand. It will be the real codex." He hung up.

"Good job," said Cody, seizing my hand.

"I was just about to tell him what I would do to him if Maya was harmed."

"Bad thought. Why give him ideas? I think all he wants is to get out of here with the codex. He's had kind of a rough time himself, if you think about it."

We sat down in the bunker to sort things out.

"I can see this clearly now. Tomás Leon should be here within an hour," said Delgado, leaning forward with his elbows on the table. He had a greater airof sharing things with us than I'd ever seen before. "What I propose is that we come early. I think they have named a place for the drop close enough to walk to from where they are hiding, because they would not wish to have a car nearby with license plates that can be noticed. There are not many farms nearby, so we can probably determine which one they are using."

"And then?" I asked.

"We can't be sure how many people they have. It's Yolo and Elena for sure, because she was seen here by the security guard. Maybe more, maybe not," said Cody. "But remember that aside from Elena Burgos, we have never seen more than two of them here, and Rosas is dead."

"So it'll be Cody and I, you and the other officer, and Tomas Leon, if he gets here in time. That's five. That should be even or better. Surely they can't have more than five."

"I'm thinking now they don't have *any* more than they had before, because if they did they wouldn't be using Elena. She's untrained for these things," Cody said. "Trust me here."

"Leon will be here in time," said Delgado. "Let us try to be in place at the right farm by 8:30. It will be fully dark."

Normally I might be playing gin rummy with Maya as we waited. She was probably playing with Elena. I hoped Maya was letting her win, but somehow I doubted it. She'd want to beat them at something.

Just after seven, Tomás Leon was at the door. He looked unruffled, ready for anything. He had left his summer suit behind and wore black cotton slacks and a black outback kind of shirt with half a dozen pockets. On his left hip was a holstered gun held up by a cartridge belt.

"I'm glad to have you with us," I said to him at the door. He searched my face for a moment, then shook my hand.

"I'm happy to be here. Tonight we will end this, Señor." There was a level of certainty in his voice that I found reassuring.

He came in and greeted Delgado and the other cop. They exchanged a few words about Rodriguez. I was sweating and Cody was walking around a bit more than he usually did. I know he was thinking about Maya, about how if anything went wrong he'd blame himself. I was thinking that too. Leon was just cool, looking more at Delgado than at me. I wasn't totally sure what to make of him now that we were all on the same side, more or less. Most of the *federales* I've met down here, not that many, really, have a veiled look, but it's good to know who's backing you up. The main note of uncertainty was that Jason Schwarz had taken down two of them himself. To me, Schwartz had not looked that good.

The other cop wore the olive uniform of the local police, and Delgado, of course, was wearing his normal brown suit, which was dark enough to pass. Leon carried three black bulletproof vests in his left hand, the kind with Kevlar padding in front and several straps crossing behind. I half expected to see padding on the back too, but these must have been the budget versions. "I had only three of these," he said. I guess Cody and I were expendable—nothing new with that.

"We ought to go dark too," said Cody. "I've got something upstairs."

I went up to our bedroom to change too, and

the only black pants I had were dressy but I put them on anyway. The single dark shirt I had was my navy blue tee shirt that said STAFF. It would have to do. Better if it said FBI, but those were hard to come by. If we survived to get another case I'd have to take a hard look at my wardrobe. I stood for a moment in the studio and picked up the Tejuana outfit and held it to my face. "Let's just do business," I said to myself (and to Maya, wherever she was), and went back downstairs, thinking that, although I meant it from the heart, it still sounded like a mantra for the Kiwanis Club.

Coming down the steps I remembered Maya's questions to me about why I kept at this. In the present situation my reply seemed stubborn and insensitive. The very thing she feared most had happened, and I had allowed it. Not only was I going to have to explain this to her when it was over, but worse, it was time to explain this to myself.

Delgado got out a tin of something that looked like shoe polish. "Put this on your faces and the backs of your hands." We all sat there rubbing ourselves with black paste, and then Delgado went around and filled in any portions we had missed. "Don't put your fingers in your eyes," he said. "It burns, and only comes off with soap."

"Which also burns," I said.

"We look like a goddam minstrel show," said Cody. The Mexicans looked at each other and shrugged.

I rejected my shoulder holster because it would chafe over a tee shirt, and stuck the .38 in my belt.

At around eight we left. Delgado had found a nondescript unmarked car to use instead of his normal Judicial Police white Chrysler, and he and the cop and

Leon climbed in. It seemed like Delgado was the senior man in their group and Leon was along for backup, or perhaps to see that the national security angle was protected. I guess a major bust would do nothing but enhance Delgado's recovering reputation. Cody and I followed in the artmobile. We might well need the extra seating coming back for all the Ninja prisoners.

"Do you pray much?" asked Cody, as we drove down Ancha de San Antonio, heading out of town.

"Only that Barbara doesn't touch me again. The rest of it I can handle myself."

"Hasn't worked out that well, has it?"

"Not really. Maybe there is no higher power. Than yourself, I mean. If you can't make it happen on your own, then no one's going to help." I couldn't look at him. I didn't feel like laughing.

We all knew the Celaya road. There weren't that many ways to climb out of the San Miguel basin to the east and south. We followed Delgado up the hill past the glorieta, ignoring Los Frailes, a 1970s village next to the Malanquin, a private golf course and residential compound. Past the turnoff for Guanajuato we approached the general area of the town sign for Santa Teresita. Delgado's car slowed and I imagined they were scanning both sides of the road for farmhouse lights. There had been two or three within the first mile past the edge of San Miguel, but now I could see none. It was almost dark.

About a hundred yards past the town sign, a white reflector at the end of a lane caught our lights and we cruised past at a walk. Up the road a bit Delgado's car pulled over and the headlights went out. We moved in behind him. I slid the codex under my seat in case we lost the gunfight and needed a bargaining chip. Delgado came over to my window.

"We will all go in. Then, if it is the Zapatistas, we'll be ready."

Great. My first gunfight.

CHAPTER TWENTY-NINE

Twenty feet in from the main road, we slipped like Indians in black face into the tall corn beside the lane. It was about a foot taller than our heads, except for Cody's. He was hunched over. A little farther down was a narrow stream, and we had a whispered debate about whether to step briefly back into the lane to cross on a wooden bridge. In the end we waded through it, being unsure how far we were from the house. Back in the corn we followed the lane for at least a hundred feet as it turned, and then we could just make out the lines of a small house in the moonlight, and some distance off to the right, a shed with what might have been fencing on one side.

Delgado whispered back to us, "Go back and cross to the shed." When we came out of the corn I saw a dim light of triangular shape coming from the front of the house. As we approached the shed, we could make out the form of a man in the house near the doorway. His back was toward us.

"This could be it," said Delgado. "Paul, you and Cody and Hugo Peña go around to the back of the house. When you hear us make some noise to draw them out, go in through the back if you can, otherwise, if there's no way in, come back and go through the front. We'll wait for you to get in place."

This gave me no confidence; they hadn't scoped out the house. The three of us moved in a roundabout fashion toward the back of the house with drawn guns. As we came around past a back window, I saw three people inside. Maya was at a rough table wearing handcuffs. From the set of her mouth it was clear she was pissed off, but holding her tongue. It was not her best look, but they wouldn't have known that. Elena Burgos sat across from her, and a gun lay on the planks near her hands. I didn't see any cards. Yolo was facing in our direction, saying something to them. There were no others in view. The house was just one room.

We waited and suddenly through the night air a startled whinnying began. Yolo turned around, looked back at Maya and Elena, then pulled out his gun and headed out the front door. Elena rose from her chair and came to the door behind him, but didn't follow him out. Behind her back, Maya watched her, and then, as if an idea came to her, started looking around. We waited. I could barely see Cody and Peña, but I did notice the black shape of a door set in the white stucco of the rear wall.

When I thought I could make out the sounds of a scuffle near the shed I said, "Now!"

Cody threw himself against the door and we almost fell through it as Elena wheeled around, raised her gun, and then seeing three guns pointed at her, prudently dropped it on the floor. All the Ninja training in Chiapas couldn't have saved her. Hugo Peña recovered her gun and motioned her against the wall. "Silence," he said, "where is the key to the handcuffs?"

"Yolo has it. Do not kill him."

"It will not be necessary," said Leon, appearing at the front door, gesturing behind him. Yolo appeared in the light from the door, hands behind him. He had a defiant look. Suddenly he stepped backward and Delgado hit the ground hard as Yolo neatly swept his feet out from beneath him. He tried to run, but Delgado recovered quickly and seized one leg while Leon brought his pistol down on the base of Yolo's skull, and he flopped onto the ground. Elena cried out, but Peña forced his gun against her breastbone.

Maya ran over and pressed herself against me, still in handcuffs. She kissed my neck. It was over. I moved my hands softly over her back. "No more targets," I said. I discovered I was shaking too. I didn't know whether it was from fear or relief.

Peña and Cody went back down the lane and brought the cars up. Delgado carried the lantern out to the yard and he and Leon lifted the unconscious form of Yolo and put him in the sedan. Leon handed me the handcuff key. I unlocked Maya and she put the cuffs on Elena and gave the key to Delgado.

Leon was bending over Yolo in the back seat, then he turned to us. "He will awaken soon," he said. "Can I ride with you? Our car is full, I'm afraid."

"Of course," said Maya, rubbing her wrists, "But I will be driving. I need to be in charge of *something* for a while." I gave her the keys. I was not going to quibble with it. I had seen this side of her before; she was not easily led. If you wanted to handcuff her to the bed you had to ask her nicely, although you knew she liked it.

Delgado extinguished the lantern and then drove off with Peña and Yolo. I felt like my shoulders were slumping with relief as Leon got in next to Maya, and Cody and I slid into the second seat.

"Not a bad operation, after all," Cody said, pulling sliding the door shut. "No bloodshed; everybody walks away. A serious headache for Yolo, however. Some are happy, some not. A pretty clean deal, as far as these deals usually go."

We moved down the lane and out onto the highway. I wished my window could roll down because it had turned into such a lovely moonlit evening.

"How are you doing?" I asked Maya as she began to pick up speed.

"Better now. I knew you guys would come. Besides, they weren't that good. Their talk was just a lot of jargon about their cause, and the role of fate, and so on. Crushing the neo-liberal oppressors. I guess that's us. I never thought of us that way before."

"They didn't harm you?" Cody said.

"No. All the same, I'm glad this business is over."

"But there is yet one more piece of business, I fear, now that we are alone," said Leon as he pulled out his gun and pressed it to the side of Maya's head. "I cannot go back without the codex. First I must have all your guns." Maya kept driving and said nothing, but I thought I saw her head move away from the gun barrel a fraction of an inch and her jaw clench. "Señor Williams? Yours first, please."

"Of course," said Cody, cool as ice. "I thought you might have known Jason Schwartz before. It was probably a nasty surprise for you, though, when he killed those two *federales*." He reached slowly into his shoulder holster.

"This is true. Señor Schwartz was what you might call a loose cannon. We have this phrase too. But now I will have the pleasure of presenting the codex to Subcomandante Marcos myself. You cannot imagine what an honor that will be."

"And you killed Professor Sandoval," I said. A deep chill was settling over me. My jaw was tightening as I spoke.

"Yes, with the assistance of two friends of mine in the movement. My job with the government is over now, of course. But what a great time it was! Thirteen years with the colonialists. I knew every move they made, and, therefore, so did the Subcommandante." He accepted Cody's gun over the seat and placed it between his seat and the passenger door, out of reach of Maya. I was not surprised she wasn't being insubordinate at this point, yet I felt she would choose her moment.

"And now yours, Señor Zacher. Then next, we will have the codex." I had seen the mild menace in Leon before during his visits, but now his tone held a new dimension. I eased my gun out of its holster and was leaning forward to hand it to him when Maya suddenly slammed the brakes on hard, and the artmobile nearly stood on its nose. Whatever you want to say about these old Chevy vans, they did have good brakes, and Maya knew it. Leon was thrown forward into the dashboard and Cody and I flew into the backside of the front seats as my gun went off. The explosion was shattering in the closed van, followed immediately by a piercing ringing in my ears. The abrupt violence of it hung in the air like smoke. We were stopped on the highway and Leon did not move again. I could smell his blood flowing freely from his back and onto the seat below.

"You left your safety off," I thought Cody said as he leaned back on the seat, but I was nearly deaf.

"What?" yelled Maya. It was almost a scream. We would all be yelling for a while.

She looked over at Tomás Leon and briefly touched his shoulder and then withdrew her hand as if she had touched something foul.

"I hate this," she shouted at last, over the ringing in her own ears, as she pounded her fists on the steering wheel. "I hate this more than anything." Shaking her head, she started the artmobile again and moved off the road onto the narrow shoulder. I got out and opened the front door. Leon's face was pressed into the dashboard and I pulled him back against the seat. It looked like his nose was broken, not that it mattered; my fingers could locate no pulse in his neck. There was no blood on the black fabric surface of the vest but the Kevlar was oddly bulged outward over his heart. Blood pooled between his thighs from between the vest and his chest. When Cody came up beside me I moved aside and he looked in.

A moment later he removed his fingers from Leon's neck.

"He's gone. There's your bullet," he shouted, pointing at the peak in the vest. "It passed right through him and was stopped as it came out. These things work pretty well. But normally, you'd want to be facing the bullet. There's also a more expensive version that has a back to it."

CHAPTER THIRTY

I've gotten more skittish about using the word *over* now; it's not a dependable concept. I'm thinking of substituting "in remission," or perhaps "bottlenecked," in the future. There are other words like this that commonly appear in conversation, but don't fulfill their promise. 'Foolproof' is another one that comes to mind, although in the Zacher Agency, we've never had occasion to use it.

I had expected to get something worse than a slap on the wrist for killing a federal officer, especially by shooting him in the back at close range, but the authorities were more understanding when they discovered a record of numerous calls between Yolo and Tomás Leon on each of their cellphone records. Further examination of Leon's office files—the ones in his safe—showed extensive contacts with Chiapas. I can't say the feds were gracious enough to tell me this; Diego Delgado has his contacts in México City and was kind enough to let me understand why I wasn't in prison. He also remarked that the flag pin on our address on the police map would not be removed any time soon.

When the subject of the codex came up, we all denied any knowledge of it, except to say that Leon had been demanding it from us. Other than that, we told the story much as it happened. Naturally, as soon as we got back to town, Cody stashed the codex at—where else? Back at Cuadrante 13A. We left it there until Barbara needed it for the installation of her climate-controlled storage system.

In the end, I can't say I received any commendations from the government, but it would be accurate to suggest that their wrath was more than a trifle muted. They mainly didn't care for the *principle* of shooting *federales*. This particular instance, however, they could understand.

Unfortunately I couldn't save the passenger seat in the front of the artmobile. Leon's blood had seeped into the hole in the back and through the seams of the seat cushion and within a day the smell was about as strong as the ringing in my ears, which didn't seem to be going away either. I found a junkyard on the *libramiento* near the old bus station that had a replacement. The seat fabric was a different color, but it was as close as I could come. The difference would be my memento of the death of Tomas Leon, not that I wasn't able to remember it all by myself, especially every evening as I was trying to fall asleep.

Maya and I went around yelling a lot at each other for a few days, but in a happy kind of way. It was different from the times we had yelled at each other in the past. The walls of our house are thick, and Señora Ochoa next door doesn't hear that well either anymore. *Her* deafness is due to age, but in our case hopefully it will change.

We settled back into our routine, and I finished the Tejuana picture and retired the outfit to the prop drawer. Maya returned to hitting the archives again; claiming she had been feeling guilty about the time she lost during the kidnapping and while she was home but under guard. At least that's what she said. I suspect it had more to do with normalizing her life after a couple weeks of wearing a target. As for me, it was great to be able to move freely again through San Miguel unarmed. I still didn't know what I was going to paint next, but that was OK now. A little lounging about in the *loggia* reading Graham Greene and listening to some John Coltrane ballads seemed about right. Much better than stepping around dead bodies and severed hands.

In the middle of a glorious afternoon about a week after the death of Tomás Leon, I was just finishing Greene's *The Comedians*, when the doorbell rang. I wasn't expecting anybody, certainly not more Ninjas. But it was Cody.

"Out of rum punch?" I asked. "Come on in."

"I am never out of rum punch, but this afternoon I'd like a cold one, if you have one. And I know you do."

I got us both a Negra Modelo and we settled into the shade of the *loggia*.

"How are you feeling?" he asked, pulling at the beer.

"Good, and you don't have to shout; I can hear better now."

"Awfully sweet out here. I miss having my own garden. Just looking down on one from the third floor isn't quite the same, not that it isn't pretty." He paused for a while, looking over at the bamboo covering our back wall. At the fountain two grackles were fighting over one of the crusts we put out for birds. I knew there was something he wanted to talk about; but he wasn't in a hurry.

"I've been going over in my mind the events of that evening last week out on the road to Celaya," he said, after a while.

"Haven't we all." I slid *The Comedians* away from me on the table. Despite the title, it was not a funny book, nor, I suspected, was this conversation.

"I'm sure. Come to any conclusions?"

"Like what? You kill a man, even under those circumstances, what conclusion is there to reach?"

"You know what I think of? I say this as someone who's killed four people. Was there another way? Not merely to second guess myself, because that's always tempting to do, but to understand what I did. You know?" He leaned back in his chair, which squeaked in protest.

"I'm not sure I do." I didn't look at him.

"I didn't think of this at the time, it all went so fast. But then I began going over it the way a cop would go over it, piece by piece, with all the detail I could remember. Of course, when things are moving that fast you can't recover everything."

A chill was creeping up my legs and into my chest. It was not from the beer.

"When I handed Leon my gun," he went on, "naturally the safety was on and it was not cocked. I held it out to him butt first. That's only a safety precaution. It's what anyone would do who's used to handling weapons."

"Right."

"You see where I am going."

"Yes, I think I do." I took a long draw of the beer.

"Your safety was not on, although it should have been. The action was over, right?"

"It seemed like it, until he pulled his gun out."

"But it's not only that. Even being thrown into the back of his seat would not have caused your gun to fire, unless..."

"Unless?"

"Unless you had already cocked the gun, Paul. It's a revolver, the only kind of gun I use. You were already going to kill him. Your hand was down out of sight behind the seat because the gun was originally in your belt, and you were leaning forward. Leon couldn't see what you were doing, and he was trying to keep his eye on Maya as well. You were only a second or two away from shooting him in the back when Maya hit the brakes. She was trying to give us a chance to do something, but without being able to warn us what was coming, and that had no effect whatever on the outcome. Tomás Leon was already a dead man, even if she had only kept driving down the road back into town. That's all I wanted to say."

The two grackles decided to duke it out over the crust, and in the course of the fight, broke it in half. They each snapped up a piece and flew off. It was awfully quiet in the garden after they left.

"You were a good cop," I said, after a while, looking at the fountain.

"Still am. You don't lose it."

EPILOGUE

I picked up the phone. I wasn't surprised to hear Barbara's voice. "Paul, darlin'."

"Good morning."

"I'm going to have a party, an intimate one like before, for my unveiling."

"I would have thought you've been sufficiently unveiled already. Besides, I got a lot of flack for the level of intimacy at the last one."

"Tell me you didn't enjoy that. But I meant the unveiling of my new humidity and temperature controlled home for the codex. It's all finished. You have to see it. It's very scientific."

"No dancing?"

"Honey, that was Maya's idea, remember? But no, there will be no dancing. I'm not going to have Alex Ross here on the piano this time, just the dinner staff. You won't even have to bring your gun anymore, although it does make you seem, I don't know...a little dangerous. I liked that aspect of it."

I guess I had proven the danger part. It was lucky I hadn't shot Maya. I was even able to hear Barbara normally now because the ringing in my ears had finally stopped. It had been more than two weeks since the death of Tomás Leon.

"Does Saturday, the twenty-seventh work for you? I haven't called Cody yet."

"Saturday is fine. What can we bring? I think we're out of the '82 Margaux."

"Just bring yourselves. I've got more of the Margaux. Perry was always ready for a celebration."

Maya came into the kitchen in her nightshirt. Sitting down next to me at the island counter she peeled a mango and sliced it into bite size chunks before spooning plain yoghurt onto the orange flesh. I put my hand on her bare thigh as she sprinkled granola on the top.

"Barbara's having another party. That was her on the phone. It's on Saturday to celebrate the enshrinement of the codex."

Maya made a sour face. It wasn't from the yoghurt.

"No dancing," I said. "No music. Just hilarity and the warmth of good company."

"There was too much warmth before. I'll go if you promise to keep the heat down. If you feel like having your arms around anyone, let it be me, or even Cody." She slid her coffee cup toward me. "Could you fill this up for me?"

"Cody will be there, but no Reyes guards."

"They did a good job. She breezed right through it all without a scratch."

"Good luck follows her."

"Except with Perry."

"She came out all right. I don't think we'll ever see her begging down by the *jardín*."

On Saturday night we went back up the hill to

Casa Watt. I was feeling a little tentative after the fiasco of the last party, but I was armed with good intentions (and nothing else). The house was ablaze with light as usual. Maybe that's why it was called Casa Watt. Cody was driving.

"I hope I don't have to be designated driver again," he said. "Makes me feel out of the fun."

"You're always fun," said Maya as we walked up the steps. "Sometimes you're more fun than Paul. But I miss the Seguridad Reyes van in the drive. Do we have any guns at all tonight?"

"None," said Cody. "By the way, did you clean yours after you shot Leon?"

"Of course. That's just good manners." I said this briskly, but the tone of it was considerably lighter than I felt about Leon's death. There had been many wakeful nights over the past three weeks, especially after my garden conversation with Cody had made me confront the fact that I had been truly just a second away from shooting him in the back. I discovered that having a stiff brandy before I went to bed helped with the falling asleep part, but nothing helped deep in the night with staying asleep. I found myself pulling Maya closer against me, which often woke her up, but I know she understood. She herself was sleeping well now, and didn't ask me to inspect her back anymore.

There was nothing wrong with her back or the rest of her. She was oddly serene, as if for her the entire mess had fallen away. She seemed to not contemplate, as I endlessly did, what might have happened on the Celaya road if the jamming of the brake pedal had worked out differently. I reminded myself that she had killed Perry earlier this year, and had been able, with emotional support from Cody and me, to work through it to a point where it no longer bothered her. It was mainly now the occasional reference from Barbara that might set her off, but otherwise I could see no lingering problems.

Cody was dealing well with the death of Luis Rosas, it seemed, but Cody could be both hard and easy to read, and sometimes I didn't know if I was reading him at all. He had moved back home, of course, immediately after the death of Leon. The endless sleep-over had ended at last. I wondered if in the night sometimes his hulking frame could be glimpsed on his balcony, staring blankly down at the darkened garden.

I had done my share of this too; getting up at three or four in the morning and slipping out of bed when sleep wouldn't return, pulling on a sweater and heading downstairs, compulsively checking the lock on the front door as I went past. At times I would sit for an hour or more facing the unlit foliage just replaying that last night outside of Santa Teresita. But unlike Cody's silent confrontations with his own dead, I did not once face any shadowed figures during these hours; I was alone. They were times when I would have welcomed company.

The day after the kidnapping of Maya, Cody had given me the pep talk about how killing Leon had not been a choice; only the force of circumstance. This was before I recalled, with Cody's deft assistance, that I was going to kill him anyway. I hadn't been rushing forward to take responsibility, since I had convinced myself initially that I hadn't intended to pull the trigger. It's amazing how handy memory can be in helping to fictionalize events, especially if they were compressed into a few brief moments.

We stood before Barbara's massive mahogany door and I pressed the bell. When it opened Maya went in first and as we followed, Cody leaned over and whispered to me, "Keep your safety zipped tonight. You don't want to blow a hole in your relationship with Maya."

I could see I was headed for about ten years of crude safety jokes.

Barbara was triumphant; she hugged each of us closely and I recalled the way she had pressed herself against my thigh as we danced. She didn't repeat it, but that spot on my leg seemed to burn.

She was exquisite tonight, wearing slim cut silk ankle pants and a scooped tank top in the same cool red color. Her hair was up, held in place by a tortoise shell comb, revealing chandelier earrings sprinkled with small stones which matched her outfit. She wore no other jewelry. Her bare neck was inviting.

"Let's begin with champagne," she said. "The '90 Dom Perignon is gone but I have Cristal. I hope that's all right." She made a small gesture and the waiting butler brought out a tray with four glasses. We stood in the great room. As she had said, there was no piano player but the stereo played romantic Méxican songs in the background. I hoped that was as romantic as the evening would get.

"To the Sandoval Codex," she said, lifting her glass. "Home at last." I thought the champagne might be better than the Dom Perignon. "Come upstairs, let me show you the new system."

We followed her up.

"I know it's not quite right to call it that, since Vincent never had a chance to publish it, but I think it's a fitting memorial. If it ever quiets down enough to publish it, I'm going to make it a condition that it be called that," she continued.

"That could only be in a different México," Maya said.

In her bedroom, where I had been only once, after the staff intrusion, she stopped and faced the wall opposite the bed. Here the paneling was painted an ivory color and invisibly interrupted by two doors integrated into it.

"This is beautiful," said Maya. "The light must be glorious in the morning." I stared at the bed, a mahogany four-poster with canopy and huge pillows. The coverlet was a pale rose. Two huge mullioned windows came down to the floor with draperies that matched the rose on the bed.

"This is my dressing room." Barbara pulled one of the doors open and then touched the corner of a panel next to it and the other door concealed in the paneling opened by an unseen and soundless mechanism. Behind it was a steel door of bank vault quality, with a combination dial as big as my fist. She drew it open.

"This was part of Perry's dressing room, but I had them take some space out of it for the codex. Now there's access from the bathroom. I didn't want to get rid of it entirely, because—who knows?—some day I might find another man to marry."

"*Ojala*," said Maya. "I pray for it daily."

Barbara let this pass, perhaps taking it as good wishes from Maya. "Normally I keep the door locked, but I didn't want to fiddle with the combination tonight." Inside the walk-in safe, the codex was displayed in two double-sided frames under low lights, with space to move around them and see both sides. Atop each frame were controls and indicators for humidity and temperature. There was a small background hum from a power system out of sight.

"Professor Sandoval would be thrilled," said Cody.

It had a striking and unique presence, but all I could think about was how many people had died getting it here. "It's like having the Mona Lisa," I said, "but you can hardly show it to anyone."

"I know. It's strange having it. Even when I'm not looking at it I can feel it behind that steel door. And it's sad that it hasn't been published. Vincent thought it would make such an advance in the study of Mayan culture."

"It's just too hot right now," said Cody as we went back downstairs. "I can't think how you could announce you have it until the whole Zapatista thing is settled. And that's likely to take years. The best outcome for now is to have you sitting on it."

"It's like a nuclear waste dump. You've got to guard it carefully because it's so hot," I said.

"I'm not sure I like that analogy," Barbara said. "I don't know if any of you saw this, it's from one of the México City English language papers."

She placed a clipping on the dining table and we gathered around and read it.

San Miguel de Allende, GTO.
August 9

Sources within the San Miguel de Allende police department have revealed the existence of a bizarre plot to provoke rebellion among the Mayans of the Yucatán.

The scheme developed when a fraudulent Mayan codex surfaced in the hands of an American collector in this central bajio town of 75,000. The codex purported to be from the sixteenth century and predicted the armed rising of Mayans in the Yucatán, an area currently free of revolt. The collector, John Schleicher, while quietly offering the codex for sale in the American community of San Miguel, was subsequently murdered by the Zapatistas when information of it reached them. They ransacked his home and made off with the document. Two federal officers attempting to trace the codex were also murdered.

Professor Vincent Sandoval, of México City, the world-renowned expert on Mayan writings, was killed by Zapatistas after he examined the codex and determined it to be a crude forgery.

In the events that followed, a Zapatista courier was killed in an automobile wreck during a police chase while attempting to deliver the codex to Chiapas. It was subsequently returned by means unknown to San Miguel de Allende, where two women were kidnapped by Zapatistas in an attempt to force its release. In the gunfight that followed, more Zapatistas were killed and the codex was recovered. A federal officer named Tomas Leon also gave his life in the shootout.

Federal authorities, after having experts from the anthropological museum verify the fraudulent nature of this document, burned it Thursday in front of witnesses, but in an undisclosed location.

"Well," said Cody. "Now I finally know what was going on. Some times you can be right in the thick of something and the action is going down so fast you can't clearly make it out. I had that happen in Peoria too, but we didn't have a great newspaper like this to clear things up for us."

"I was very sad to learn the codex was destroyed," said Barbara, "and after all that effort and expense."

"And loss of life," said Maya. "At least the kidnapped women survived. I think that's the most important thing."

"Of course. And then it turns out the damned thing was a fake after all," I said. "Who knew?"

"At least it's over now," said Maya. "No more targets on our backs. Right? Right?"

Some of us nodded solemnly, but I didn't.

"So that's how they tie things off here," said Cody. "They create an official version."

"They had no Deep Throat to tell them the truth. I wonder what they really burned, if anything," I said.

"Probably they burned the photocopy you sent them," said Barbara.

"So the *federales* and the Ninjas won't be back?" Maya was still searching for certainty.

"Maybe," said Cody, "they'll figure the new owner will keep her head down and the codex will never be heard from again. That would be my guess, and my fervent hope. I don't need any more notches on my gun."

"Keeping my head down is not something I'm used to," Barbara said, "but I can learn."

Visit the author's website @
www.sanmiguelallendebooks.com